MISSING

Carole Hayman is well known as both an actress and a theatre director. She is a BA Honours graduate from Leeds University and a graduate from the Bristol Old Vic Theatre School. She has acted in and directed many plays for the Royal Court Theatre. She devised and co-wrote *The Refuge* for Channel 4, and *Ladies of Letters*, a co-written comic novel, has been adapted for *Woman's Hour* on Radio 4. She also wrote the BBC television drama series *Rides*. *Missing* is the first of the Warfleet novels and Carole is currently working on the second, *Greed, Crime, Sudden Death*, also to be published in Vista. She lives in London.

CAROLE HAYMAN

Missing

VISTA

First published in Great Britain 1996
by HarperCollins*Publishers*

This Vista edition published 1998
Vista is an imprint of the Cassell Group
Wellington House, 125 Strand, London WC2R 0BB

A catalogue record for this book is
available from the British Library.

ISBN 0 575 60384 4

Printed and bound in Great Britain by
Cox & Wyman Ltd, Reading, Berks

98 99   10 9 8 7 6 5 4 3 2 1

For Josh

1

A cold glittery night descended on Warfleet. The cloudless black sky hosted brilliant starbursts and a thin wind blew in off the sea, shaking the strings of red and green lights that served for Christmas decorations. The end of the pier was unusually illuminated. The Warfleet Players were holding their annual New Year's Eve dinner dance in the Quarterdeck saloon and, in contrast to the promenade, the hall was strung with bright white lights. They were Marsha Snelgrove's idea; she'd once seen them in trees in Central Park on a one-day coach tour of Manhattan. The sounds of the Stan Wainright quartet throbbed across the midnight-blue waves as they peaked and coldly curled round the rusted iron struts of the pier end. The stone-walled harbour bobbed with fishing boats, their bells tinkling as if in appreciation of the imminent celebration.

Back from the sea the little town clung to the steep streets as they climbed to become cliffs, now glistening white in clear moonbeams. Warfleet was an architectural patchwork, only recently reclaimed by conservationists. Now its Georgian townhouses had preservation orders slapped on them. They mingled eccentrically with fishermen's cottages, Edwardian terraces, Victorian arcades and a modern shopping precinct. Further out there were villas with orcharded gardens and an ugly council estate, avoided by anyone who was not obliged to live there.

Hovering over the town, towards the clifftop, were a couple of concrete gun emplacements. They still had a guarding aspect to the town, which was perhaps as well as, owing to the embracing cliffs, Warfleet had a cut-off air about it. Only the River Ripple joined it on one side to the flatter plains of the inland south,

1

though London, it was true, was only a couple of hours away. Beneath the town had once existed another life. A complex of smugglers' passages joined houses and alleyways to the sea. Some were now blocked by silt and pebbles. Others, it was known, were still open.

There was a tense air of expectation at ground level. Groups of sleeveless, excited youths were already out on the street. Lights blinked from every house as the town inhabitants readied themselves for a night of New Year Madness.

'Shut that bloody racket up, Warren!' Jean Peabody's head, haloed in Carmen rollers, shot round her bedroom door. 'I can't hear myself think!' Warren, immersed in his techno-world, barely registered her cry, but knowing its sentiments, casually extended one arm and turned a dial a fraction to the left. Loop Guru's wailing diminished minimally.

Jean Peabody sighed and returned to her dressing table, the powdery surface of which was covered with half-squeezed tubes of makeup and evil-looking hair equipment. She sat on a tuffet of a stool and began to pull the rollers out of her thin, vibrantly orange hair. She was going to a singles do at Crystals Nightclub. Belle, her friend from along the road, was calling for her in five minutes. Warren had insisted he was going out, so she'd had to get a babysitter for the other children. Hard on New Year's Eve – she'd had to pay double.

She pursed her lips to put on lipstick, but the shape they made perfectly reflected her state of mind. She was furious with Warren. At nineteen he was a worthless layabout with no prospects and no ambition. He didn't even pretend to look for jobs any longer and his track record with the police was disgraceful. It was those boys from the estate he hung about with . . . In her head Jean Peabody knew that she too lived on the estate, but in her heart she had always denied it. The one thing Warren was good about was the kids. And tonight he'd even let her down over them.

She heard Warren's door shut and called to him, 'When will you be back?'

'I'll be late,' said Warren as he shrugged on his denim jacket. He looked briefly at his bony face in the hall mirror and took a band out of his jacket pocket to pull his long blond hair back into a ponytail. 'I'll see you at breakfast.' That'll be the day, Jean Peabody thought but did not say; Warren never saw breakfast unless he came in with it.

Outside, Warren swung down the frosty street with his jacket flying open and only a black vest tee shirt beneath it. It was a sign of masculinity in Warfleet to wear few clothes in the cold. Warren despised wool. He was heading for the Admiral Nelson where he was meeting Carl and the others in the Public . . . who knew where they would adventure to later?

Caro Radcliffe too was applying lipstick. It was her fourth shade. So long was it since she'd worn it, she couldn't remember what was fashionable or what colour she looked best in. Jade would stare at her in sullen disbelief, she knew. She threw down Tandoori Red in despair and scrubbed her mouth with a tissue. She could hear Sebastian clearing his throat in the en suite bathroom. The sound, though historically familiar, was lately unaccustomed and it made her nervous. The door was ajar and in the mirror she could see a slice of Sebastian's back. His shoulders still reflected the early career of a rugby player, though as her eyes shifted down she could see a plump ridge at the top of the striped jockey shorts. She looked quickly away, embarrassed by her own indelicacy. It seemed too personal. Though Seb had been her husband for more than twenty years, he seemed to her now to be a stranger . . . or worse, an uneasy relative on a visit. She wondered how they would get through the evening.

Jade appeared at the door. Her hair was plaited into beaded dreadlocks and her skimpy top revealed almost all of her small pointed breasts. Caro suppressed her alarm. This was the way young women got themselves up now, she knew, criticism was useless. Jade said, 'Are you going to Jeremy's party?' Caro nodded firmly, preventing discussion, as if it were after all perfectly normal for a husband and wife, even if estranged, to go to a party

3

together. Jade raised an eyebrow and said, 'Well I'm going to the pub. Sarah and Mel are meeting me there. I'll probably be back before you.' She yawned slightly, to indicate that life in Warfleet was terminally dreary compared to the intellectual revelries of Oxford.

'All right, darling,' said Caro attempting to smile, 'don't bolt us out. I expect Daddy will want to stay on with old cronies.'

The cronies in question, as Jade knew, were Seb and Caro's oldest friends in Warfleet: Jeremy Taylor, his sister Antonia and his partner Darryl Willoughby. Caro turned back to the mirror and pretended to apply rouge. She could not bear to acknowledge her daughter's corrosive disapproval. She sensed rather than saw Jade move away and a few moments later heard the front door close and the crunch of gravel under Jade's Doc Martens.

Downstairs, in the gracious if shabby drawing room, Caro paced nervously as she waited for Sebastian. Jade was right. It would be awkward appearing in public with Seb, confronting the sharpest audience, old friends. Last year Seb had been absent for their New Year party, having run away to live with Wendy. Caro's eye flicked nervously to the letter, tucked behind the mantelpiece clock. She hadn't mentioned it to Seb. Had agonized over whether she should. Surely he would bring it up himself? It seemed ruthless, brutal, to thrust her knowledge upon him. Now she crossed to the fireplace and shoved the envelope corner further out of sight. In his own time, she was certain . . .

She walked about the room, noting that standards had dropped a little since Seb's departure. The stripped pine and clever bric-à-brac was carelessly undusted and the Indian rugs were grubby. One or two brass curtain rings were missing, causing the heavy William Morris curtains to sag here and there. Still, at least the drinks cabinet was full. To calm herself, Caro mixed a gin and tonic. She was clumsy with the bottle, spilling a little gin on her silk shirt. She rubbed a rough finger over the stain, annoyed but barely noticing. Her attention was focused on listening. She heard Sebastian coming downstairs and called, 'Seb . . . d'you want a drink?'

4

He came to the doorway and stood looking uncertainly at Caro. She glanced down at her drink but then up again at her husband as if trying to guess his mood. How long was it since they'd really communicated? Much longer than the time he'd spent away. Living with another woman. His face was still powerfully sexual with its full lips and heavily lashed deep dark eyes. His hair was wet from the shower, slicked back to show high temples with a few strands of grey. He'd worn it long in the sixties. She vividly remembered how a lock fell tantalizingly over one eye, urging one to reach out and brush it aside. He was, she thought as ever, very attractive. Yet at this moment, leaning on the door jamb, he seemed vulnerable, middle-aged. Like a ruined Pan, charming but defeated.

He said, 'I won't have a drink. I need fags. I'll walk to the off-licence and get some decent scotch to take to Jeremy's.'

'Wait a moment,' Caro said anxiously, 'I'll come with you.'

'No, no, you've just poured a drink. I'll see you there. Bring your car?' He laughed, with an effort she thought, and added, 'It's probably better if you drive anyway.'

Before Caro could say anything more he was out of the front door and she was left staring into her unwanted drink. The tears she had forbidden all week prickled sharply into her eyes. She shut them hard and clutched her glass. Its coldness seemed to numb her whole body.

'Not now, Jeremy,' said Darryl pushing his partner's hand away, 'people will be here any minute.' Jeremy forbore to say that few of their acquaintances would arrive before a party was swinging. Besides, he could hear his sister Toni banging about in the kitchen. No doubt Laurel Hopcraft would arrive shortly with her notorious home-made cheese straws. Laurel, it was true, was often first at a party. He turned away and sat on the edge of the bed to slip on his shoes. Darryl had just come out of the shower and had a damply attractive aura of toothpaste and Tuscany shower gel. 'Has Connor arrived?' demanded Darryl.

'Yes, yes, he's sorting out the wine glasses. Toni's making

mulled and there's champagne for midnight.' Darryl waved lightly as though these domestic details barely concerned him. His main problem clearly, as he stared into the cheval glass, was whether to wear the Comme des Garçons or the more rustic, rugged denim.

All bars of the Admiral Nelson were full to bursting. Warren stood, or rather lounged, one elbow on the bar, in a group with Carl, Travis and Lee, his estate buddies. The gang had stayed together since their truanting schooldays. They were drinking Red Stripe with steady conviction. Later they would go back to Carl's accommodating gaff and get stoned. The group was ringed by tables at which sat young women. They drank vodka and Bacardi and talked among themselves, keeping always a corner of attention on the boys. Pammy Snelgrove, a ripe, overfleshed young woman, hardly took her eyes off Warren. She giggled and flung her arms about, allowing her large chest in its constricting bodice to bounce about invitingly. Warren threw her the occasional perfunctory glance.

In the snug, Rumer Petulengro and her healing circle took up the main space. Later Rumer intended to perform a Druidical ceremony to usher in the New Year. It would take place on the beach and apprehension of the chill made the downing of several rounds of Famous Grouse essential. Jade and her friends passed on their way to the lounge bar, where the local DJ was spinning eighties records. Jade hadn't seen much of these friends, made at the Pony Club, since she'd gone to Oxford, but was now entertained by gossip of point-to-points and boyfriends with titles and money.

As they crossed the public bar, Warren looked up and saw them. His face tightened and he shifted his position, turning his body slightly away. His generous mouth took on an almost mean look. He caught Pammy's eye, then downing the remains of his pint, wiped his lips with the back of his hand and smiled suggestively at her.

* * *

The night hastened towards twelve. All over the little town in bars and houses, people with red faces and wide smiles celebrated the death of the old year with all its woes and looked forward, with foolish human optimism, to something better from the new one. As the clock began to strike they embraced friends and strangers, laughed and cried. Warren led the willing Pammy outside the Admiral Nelson to an alley. He pushed her up against the wall and bit into her neck, running his hands down her doughy body. As the last chime of the town hall clock died away he shoved four fingers into her, feeling her juices run to meet him. Pammy yelped and Warren thrust mechanically as she groaned and wriggled. After a moment he turned his head aside and laid his cheek on the cold brick. He gazed along the alley into the blue-black darkness, having a strong sense that something was missing.

New Year's Day did not bear out the promise of the night. A duvet of browny grey cloud lay heavily over the slumbering town. The streets were empty save for the odd tottering drunk. A lonely chip paper lay in the middle of the High Street, too tired it seemed to stir more than a corner in the windless morning. Only the fishermen were up early, casting solitary lines into the river. The Ripple was heavy with winter. Its current moved sludgily, bearing before it Coke tins, bottles, plastic bags; the debris of summer picnics. The overhanging, dead-looking trees occasionally discarded leaves and branches.

Below a willow a larger object was caught stubbornly on a protruding root. The muddy cattle, come down to drink, stepped delicately, avoiding it. Brown ripples broke over it and at last a stronger surge dislodged it and swept it midstream where the rain plopped dully on to the sodden cloth wrapped round it. Another eddy turned it over and a bluish white oval appeared at one end. The stream was moving faster here and tugged the dark shape onwards.

On the bank the silent fishermen sat shielded by large green umbrellas; occasionally a line would fly out from one and catch

7

at the water. The fishermen themselves did not emerge. They stared downwards, at the shallower swirls near the bank.

No one noticed the body.

2

Over four hundred middle-aged men disappear in Britain every year. Caro had heard this statistic before somewhere, but not until now had it had any bearing on her life.

The headline in the *Warfleet Chronicle*, 'Men Go Missing', had struck ice into her heart when she had seen it on the hall table. She had skim-read it for a word about her own missing man but there was nothing. Now, with a coffee and a cigarette . . . another habit of the last year . . . she read it again slowly.

Apparently some students at Stourbridge University, sociologists no doubt, had done a survey. There was nothing overtly alarming in the article, in fact it said reassuringly that the men often turned up . . . had sometimes faked suicide. Leaving their clothes, she supposed, neatly under a bush, with a note explaining their action. Their wives would be mortified if their Y-fronts weren't clean . . . and what did they do for a body?

Caro flicked over the page quickly to avoid the thought of a body. On the other side a man was advertising loft insulation. It crossed her mind that her own needed doing. There was a cartoon of a smiling artisan with a hammer. 'Why wasn't I born a carpenter,' Seb was always fond of saying . . . There, she was thinking in the past tense again and it had only been a week. Of course he wasn't dead. He'd just left as he'd returned. Suddenly and without warning. It had an awful and perfect symmetry.

'But Ma,' exclaimed Jade, when Caro showed her the article, 'these men might have been murdered.' She lingered breathily on the last word giving it its full thrilling flavour. She had recently appeared in *The Mystery of Edwin Drood*, the OUDS Christmas panto.

'Don't be ridiculous!' said Caro briskly, reclaiming the paper. 'Four hundred of them?'

'I can't imagine what it would feel like to have a member of your family *murdered*.' Jade was not yet ready to drop the horror aspect.

'Really, Jade, with your inventive powers?'

Jade glanced quickly at her mother – was she being sarcastic? Caro sat in profile. The familiar sardonic groove from nose to mouth gave nothing away. Jade noted, in passing, that her mother looked old. Her jawline was softening. Caro was twisting the strip of newspaper in her hands, still beautiful, Jade saw, though toughened and browned by country living, their backs scratched by gardening.

'Are you going to tell the police about Dad?' she asked in a small voice, suddenly humbled by what she recognized as her mother's genuine anxiety.

Caro looked up, laughing. 'Seb wouldn't be very pleased if a policeman traced him to his latest love nest.'

Jade's tender moment evaporated. Trust her mother to drag the drama down to a sordid domestic level. The implication of sexual activity, too, was unwelcome. A comical picture of her father, priapic bulge in jockey shorts, opening the door to a Keystone Kop, reared up in her mind. Urghh! It was typical of her mother to present her with an image like that at a time when they should be grieving. No wonder Daddy had left her.

'I think you should,' she said primly. 'Anything could have happened. It's not as though you still *knew* him.' She delivered this slap as though it were a matter of fact only. But pulling her mother's cigarettes towards her across the table and throwing a perfunctory glance for permission, she saw to her horror that tears were running down that same sad brown profile and dropping unchecked on the paper. 'Oh Ma!' said Jade, 'I'm sorry.' She ran round the table and pressed herself against Caro.

Caro's head thumped on to her daughter's bony, bead-covered breast and she gave herself up to shuddering weeping. The months of agony and despair followed by the week of fear since

10

Sebastian had 'disappeared' had eroded her reserves fatally. She felt like a chalky cliff in a storm, her foundations melting.

Jade held her awkwardly tight and murmured embarrassed soothing noises. Caro had a vision of her daughter as she must be with her lovers, half-woman, half-girl; child and unconfident mother.

'Don't worry, Ma,' Jade was cheering, 'I'll go and see the police. I'm sure he's okay . . .' there was just a hint of uncertainty in her voice, as though she wasn't, really, 'but we ought to report him missing.'

The day was Twelfth Night and Jade returned to the drawing room where she was superstitiously removing the Christmas decorations. It had been a strange holiday, she thought, as she lifted glass balls from the tree and placed them carefully in the tissue-lined box she had known since she was a child. Dad arriving on Christmas Eve without a word and departing on New Year's Eve the same way. What did it all mean? Jade loved her parents, but found their generation utterly mysterious. They never seemed to talk about anything. It was all subtext and guesswork. Jade's eyes at this point rested on the corner of the letter behind the mantelpiece clock. It had arrived at the start of the holidays. That time before the depression of Christmas had settled in, when it was still craft fairs and secret smuggling of presents and mince pies and holly gathering. Jade had found it in a pile of Christmas cards, still addressed to Mr and Mrs Radcliffe, had opened it mistaking it for one and, seeing it was a letter to her mother which began, 'You don't know me, but Wendy has told me all about you . . .' had read on and then quickly resealed the envelope and returned it to the pile.

It had sat, ignored, for another week, while Caro ordered a duck, made toddy for carol singers, invited people for Boxing Day drinks, almost as though things were normal. On the pretext of decorating the room, Jade finally forced her mother to sit and open the cards, watching her carefully as she got to the letter. Caro made no comment but she looked shocked and then confused and angry. Finally she put the paper back into its envelope and tucked it behind the chiming clock, as though it were no more important than a final demand.

Jade had seethed with dissatisfaction. Here was a potential melodrama and her mother was refusing her part in it. Now, with the New Year's Eve defection of her father, the letter had, to Jade, become crucial. She crossed, ostensibly to remove a festoon of artificial ivy from the mirror. As she raised her hand it fell on the letter; she plucked it out and, as swiftly as a criminal, took a pad from the desk and noted down the telephone number. She tore off the strip of paper and pocketing it returned the letter observantly to its post, removing only the ivy garnish. Her heart was beating fast, but if her mother wouldn't do anything, she must. This evening she would telephone Delia.

3

Delia was doing her Pilates exercises when the phone rang. Her back was straight and her neck was arched. It was acutely uncomfortable. 'Yes,' she said grittily into the receiver.

The voice on the other end was hesitant, nervous perhaps of Delia's brusque New York phone manner. 'It's Jade Radcliffe . . . I . . . I'm phoning because of your letter . . .'

It took Delia a moment to place the situation. Jade Radcliffe. Was this a writer whose novel she had rejected? Radcliffe . . . Oh yes, of course, Sebastian. 'Hi,' she said, more encouragingly, 'thanks for calling. I'd given up hope.'

'Sorry . . .' said Jade. 'Christmas and everything . . . a lot's happened.'

'Ummhmm.' Delia's interest was now fully engaged. 'Can we meet?'

'I could come to London,' offered Jade.

'No. No . . . I'll come down there.' Delia wanted to see Sebastian's home patch. Her curiosity about him was mild, but her sleuthing instincts, developed over years of chasing best-sellers, were unerring.

Jade mentioned none of this to Caro. The date was set, by Delia, for the following Friday, and Jade set out for it with some anxiety. She had tried, on and off, to picture the woman who owned the rather sharp American voice which had answered the phone and arranged the date in a brief and unsentimental manner. She'd had to consult her personal organizer before committing and said she'd drive down, having first excoriated the railway for its southern region service. She'd given nothing else away, but Jade

13

had since composed several scenes in which versions of Delia figured. She herself came out of them all rather well, being variously mature, sympathetic and sophisticated. The last was the most attractive.

She was mortified, therefore, to find that her chosen venue, the Bun and Oven, popular with Warfleet's street-cred set, had tonight been taken over. It was Rocking Fifties night in the pub. A band consisting of two lads and a drum machine was setting up, and soon guitar twangs and soft curses were heard from the stage area. The boys were done up as Teds, with winklepicker shoes and string ties. The clothes looked odd on them, giving their young bodies, below their chubby teenage faces, a lumpy, middle-aged outline.

A selection of people with bad teeth and ill-fitting jeans sat in the bar. Jade shuddered. It was all so . . . ugly. She lit a cigarette and watched as a youth with a quiff like an ice cream cone plonked a drink down in front of his girlfriend. She was clutching a white plastic handbag, no doubt to be danced around later, and her raw unstockinged ankles protruded from nasty market-bought denims; her feet looked like beef sausages squeezed into tight white high heels. She glanced up and caught Jade's stare. Jade looked away, embarrassed. Why on earth had she arranged to come here? This was far from sophisticated.

The band struck up with an Eddie Cochran number. Jade was horrified to see a man old enough to be her father split up two women and jive with both, twirling them at the end of each arm with grim enthusiasm. Nobody smiled. Several people chewed gum. If anyone asks me to dance I'll die, thought Jade. But she need not have worried. A great distance separated her from this peasant crowd. A distance they were aware of. She thought with nostalgia of her room at Magdalen. The solid stone walls, the latticed window, the familiar sounds of church chimes, clinking bottles, undergraduate laughter. The grace and glamour of it all. And above all the safety.

She was surprised by Delia, when she at last arrived. Whatever Jade had invented, it was never this small, slight, feminine-looking woman with smartly bobbed hair and immaculate low-impact makeup. Delia made straight for her table. Jade supposed she did rather stand out. She shook her rippling hair back and composed her face for a mature and sophisticated beginning.

Delia had driven straight from a television programme market. One of her authors was having a film made from his prize-winning novel, and they had been invited to a lunch by the production company. It had been an unpleasant experience. Gordon, her writer, had been cross that his programme seemed buried in the wall-to-wall product at the company's stand. The food in the overblown hotel was dreadful and Delia thought she had never seen so many men in flared trousers. The further visual assault of the pub was unkind of God, she felt. A swift glance around told her she was right to fear for her Volkswagen Golf parked neatly in a side street and a second that the thonged and beaded New Ager in the corner was the only contender for Jade.

'I don't suppose they have coffee?' she stated rather than asked as she took charge of the chair opposite Jade's, dropping her briefcase down beside her. 'God, what a day. What a bizarre place to end up in!'

Jade's chosen opening lines deserted her, she felt like calling for a prompt, but instead said lamely, 'Did you have a bad journey?'

'Sorry.' Delia extended a smooth hand with well-filed dark red nails. 'Rude of me, you must be Jade and I of course am Delia.'

'Of course,' repeated Jade, foolishly.

'It's good to meet you. As I said, I'd given up expecting an answer.'

'Well . . .' began Jade.

But Delia cut in, 'I wouldn't blame you, married to that bastard.'

'No,' said Jade, 'that's my mother.' Delia looked blank. 'I'm the bastard's daughter.'

Delia stared at her and gave a startlingly loud laugh for such a small, contained-looking person. The laugh did not match her checked Chanel suit, with its short but discreet skirt, nor her shiny pumps and even shinier helmet. It did, though, chime with the fingernails and wide red mouth. She crossed her legs, which were in excellent shape. She was, Jade thought, quite sexy.

'My letter must have been a shock. Out of the blue like that.' Delia now had a large gin and tonic in front of her and Jade a St Clement's. The laugh had eased the tension and suddenly the pub seemed picturesque, the music innocent and appealing. Jade quickly adopted Delia's amused, distancing view of the caperings on the floor. They shared a giggle at them. 'I thought best go straight to the point. Wendy's dead . . . and I must get in touch with Sebastian. There is a child, after all.'

That bit had not been in the letter.

Delia saw the alarm on Jade's face. 'You didn't know, of course?' she said. Jade shook her head and reached a tinkling arm for the St Clement's. 'Where is your father?' asked Delia, more gently.

'Don't know that either,' muttered Jade, still dealing with the shock tremors. 'He could be dead . . . or anything . . .'

'When did you last see him?' asked Delia, aware of the pictorial reverberations of her question.

Jade too gave a half-smile. 'New Year's Eve,' she said. 'They were going to a party. Dad said he was going out for cigarettes and that was the last we saw of him.'

'Didn't like the hosts?' queried Delia with another, but smaller, laugh.

Jade laughed too, but nervously. 'His oldest friends. Theirs. Used to be that is . . . It was all so peculiar. Him suddenly turning up, after all that time. Of course with Wendy dead . . .'

'He left Wendy months ago,' said Delia briskly. She thought but didn't say that he hadn't even known she was pregnant. 'So where was he before he came home? He didn't tell you?'

Jade shook her head. 'No. He didn't explain anything.'

Delia said, 'Well, maybe he had a third home. One none of us knew about.'

Later, as she undressed in the little seafront hotel, Delia analysed the bits of information rather as though they were chunks of a book her editorial skills could piece together. Sebastian had 'disappeared' from many women's lives, she suspected. She had little to go on, but Jade at least was helpful. The thin net curtains made ghostly movements in the slight draught from the window. Delia crossed to look out at the sea. She could just make out the chilly froth toing and froing on the pebbles. Above it, the black sky was cuttingly cold and starless. Delia thought, wherever he is I'll find him. It's an adventure. A crusade. Then, bringing herself back to earth, besides, I promised Wendy.

4

It was Caro's day for going to see her shrink. She had begun when Seb had first left, certain it was her fault, determined to rescue her marriage. Ingrid, as Caro thought of her – though her official name was Mrs Goldbloom – had attempted to persuade her otherwise, so far with no success.

'I must have done something wrong,' Caro would say desperately, balling her hands into fists and thrashing the air with them.

'Perhaps he was wrong for you?' Ingrid would suggest dryly, to which Caro would inevitably reply, 'No, no, it was me, I tried too hard to control him.' This would lead her on to her own fears of being controlled and thus to her mother. All inability to make grown-up relationships, it seemed, stemmed from that unequal partnership.

Caro felt a similar inequality in her relationship with Ingrid. She was distressed to find that despite her apparently authentic middle European accent, Ingrid was not Jewish. She had made a careful marriage. Caro felt cheated by this. She also found Ingrid – grey hair, grey eyes, grey skin, grey jumper – infinitely depressing. 'I think you are trying to tell me . . .' Ingrid always began and then went on to outline some idea Caro found entirely repellent.

She was constantly trying to end her analysis. 'It's too tiring,' she would say, 'coming up and down from the country, the fares are too expensive.' Ingrid would stare at her with pity and contempt. Of course, Caro didn't *see* her stare, her head was turned away as she lay on the couch, but she knew absolutely what the grey stare was saying.

Today she was early. As she turned the corner into her therapist's road, she saw another woman leaving. The woman looked

18

businesslike, she wore a fitted jacket and carried a briefcase, she walked along the road purposefully, then stopped and made a movement with her arm; Caro knew she was blowing her nose, then she saw the tissue, scrunched up now, put back into the pocket. She smiled dryly to herself, was that what these sessions were all about then? People arriving ready to go to work and leaving in tears an hour later to pick up their day, to pick up their pieces, to pick up their lives where they'd left off . . . fifty minutes on the dot . . . say it now or never?

She was reminded of a friend of hers in the seventies, who'd been very big in EST therapy. 'You have to cry for fifteen minutes a day,' she'd said. 'It's such relief, you've no idea. I mean actually being allowed to.'

Caro had often spent all fifty minutes of her sessions in tears, weeping inconsolably for something . . . for what? She didn't know, she had no words for it. All her life she had wept and wept, and when people said to her, irritated, 'Caro, what *is* the matter?' she'd only been able to shrug her shoulders and say she didn't know, she didn't know . . . which always brought on a fresh bout of weeping. She even found her therapist dryly clicking her teeth occasionally as yet again tears would well up and course down her face, ending up in pools in her ears, matting her hair, wetting the string on her glasses until it felt like a Cindy-chewed shoelace round her neck. Her thoughts were similarly chewed. Behind them, unshakeably, was the dull ache for the loss of Sebastian.

This was the first visit after the Christmas holidays. There was much to relate but Ingrid was not interested in a sequence of events, only in the 'feelings' about them.

'Well . . . I don't know,' said Caro, mopping herself from the revelations of Seb's unexpected return on Christmas Eve through to his equally unexpected disappearance a week later. 'He seemed uncomfortable, familiar yet unfamiliar . . . he hardly talked about anything.'

'I am interested,' said Ingrid relentlessly, 'in how *you* felt about it.'

19

'I was worried . . . puzzled . . . I suppose I assumed that he was back because Wendy was dead . . . though of course he didn't mention it . . .'

'Were you angry that he wouldn't talk to you?'

'Of course not. He looked ill . . . I was worried about him.'

She was lying, they both knew. She'd been in a rage all Christmas. How dare he just turn up like that, without even asking. Did he assume nothing had changed in his absence, that she would always be there? The awful thing was, she would be. Had been. Had not pressed him to explain his actions. Had not told him about the letter from this Delia person. Had acted as if everything was fine and he was just another place setting at the Christmas feast. Had cooked up a storm, been bright and entertaining. Even let him, silently, secretly, into her bed. They had made love, unsatisfactorily, but with craving. None of this did she admit to Ingrid, dwelling only on the fact that he had gone again, she didn't know where . . . and the overriding 'feeling' she had, was one of terror.

'Yet,' said Ingrid, colourlessly, rubbing her temple on the edge of Caro's vision, 'you haven't been to the police? Do you fear to find out?'

'Of course I do!' exploded Caro. 'I fear to find out anything. Everything. I always have.'

She remembered the first time she had 'found out' one of Seb's infidelities. It was nothing. A secretary. But the hurt had been overwhelming. She'd felt betrayed. Utterly abandoned. Yet even then she'd seen a certain ironic logic to it. Seb had, after all, been having an intense affair when she'd met him. He'd left that woman for her. Why should his behaviour now be different?

There had been many other dalliances over the years – PAs, script editors, that awful woman Briar who'd been his 'girl friday'. But Wendy was something different. He'd actually left to live with her. A real mid-life crisis. And Wendy was the first from the home patch. A dweller in Warfleet, their special place, family, previously out of bounds for entanglements.

The affair amazed as much as it grieved her. Wendy was a

20

librarian, for God's sake. You didn't have affairs with librarians! No wonder he'd spent so many hours 'researching'. Well, she'd got her comeuppance all right. Dead at the age of twenty-nine. The word dead brought on another bout of weeping. 'It *is* time,' said Ingrid, sighing gently.

Caro scrambled herself together and left with bits clutched about her. She walked down the street sobbing belligerently. She cried for loss. The loss of Sebastian, the loss of their life together. Whether he was dead or not made little difference, he had left her in spirit a long time ago. People stared at her, concerned or curious.

'My cat's just died,' she snapped at a man. He averted his eyes immediately.

When she got home, Jade was out. The place had the shivery feel of emptiness. This is how it had been for months with Seb gone and Jade at university. Soon it would be like this every day, with them both again having left her. At the Aga, Cindy woofed helpfully from her basket as Caro riddled the grate and heaved the fuel scuttle, but Cindy was so old now she hardly counted.

Caro opened the mail, not yet delivered when she'd left early that morning for London. Her heart sank when she saw a pale blue envelope. It was her mother's stationery. This would be about the threatened after-Christmas visit. Her mother's long weekends began on a Thursday and finished on a Tuesday, not necessarily the one following. Not even in her wildest love affairs . . . two since she'd met Seb . . . had Caro had such weekends.

To lift her spirits, Caro decided to go into town, walking the reluctant Cindy. The magic of the promenade, with its seagulls and tackle shops, never failed to cheer her. Today, however, she could see only poorly-dressed, cold-looking people and closing-down sales.

Ugly 'developments' had erupted all over Warfleet. Few knew what these excavations were to become, when the raw unhappy soil was patted back into place and the metal cages dismantled, but the inconvenience in the meantime was comprehensive. There

21

was a dogfight on the prom. The two owners slapped hopelessly at their charges shouting, 'Come away – leave it!' and 'Get out of there, bad boy!' Only the dogs were enjoying themselves. Displaying the only bit of impassioned life on the wintry promenade.

When it began to rain, hard sleety needles, Caro hurried back, thinking of slippers and crumpets . . . and Seb. How it had been when they had first found Warfleet. A happy period in their marriage. Caro, at least, had been happy. Seb had been filming nearby and she had come down to visit and found the little old-fashioned town enchanting. She'd fallen in love with its higgledy-piggledy streets and dramatically gothic skyline. They'd been thinking of a move out for some time, leaving it until Jade was ready for boarding school. Warfleet was perfect and Caro set about finding the house. The one she knew must exist. Kent peg and board and a climbing rose and a garden to grow her vegetables in. Four Trees had fallen into her hand and she had loved it instantly. In upper Warfleet, it had an acre of land looking down to the sea, as many bedrooms and bathrooms as one cleaning lady could cope with, and a comforting sense of solidity which even their volatile emotional life could not dent.

Caro had always felt at home here, never minding the absences of Jade at school and Seb in London, able to keep at bay the thoughts of what either of them might be doing; always busy, involved, the garden, the house, jams and pickles and vicarage fêtes . . . always happy. Until Wendy . . .

It had never occurred to her that someone who was a friend – well an acquaintance anyway, someone who'd been invited to her lovely home, made welcome as a member of the Reading Circle – could, in this way, betray her. She remembered well how Sebastian, coming down early one Friday, had first met Wendy, little insignificant Wendy, in the kitchen. She had dropped by on her bike to deliver to Caro a book just in, to be discussed next Thursday. Seb had ignored her, poured a whisky then made some crack about an actress's rump (he was at the time producing a film on D. H. Lawrence) which had caused Wendy to blush. Caro had been embarrassed for her, out of her depth with this urban banter,

22

and had made apologies for Seb's bullishness, saying he was, 'always like this on a Friday'. Wendy had pedalled away. Out of their lives, so Caro thought, and she had laughingly reprimanded Seb for frightening the horses. He had unrepentantly taken her to bed and fucked her ferociously and surprisingly. Only later did Caro bitterly surmise that he'd been turned on by Wendy's naïveté. Later, when it had all come out, she had gone to see Wendy. To beg her, really, to give it up. Remind her there was a child involved. Though of course Jade was by now a young woman. Wendy had taken fright and run away to join Sebastian in London. They had lived in his pied-à-terre, bought years ago for the weekdays.

Caro turned all this over and over in her head as she sat in front of the dying fire. Jade had still not returned and the crumpets had gone cold and sat wretchedly in their congealing butter. Caro was feeding one to Cindy when the phone rang. It was Antonia Taylor, her best friend, wanting her to go out for the evening. Caro said no, she was waiting for Jade to come in and besides she was tired and had ironing to finish.

Toni said, 'I know just what you're doing. It's no good sitting there moping. Now go and get your glad rags on, Jeremy's having a modern jazz night, and you and I are going.'

5

Delia had never seen Sebastian Radcliffe in the flesh. She had heard so much about the flesh, however, that she felt she was intimate with it. When she begged Wendy to tell her, for the umpteenth time, why she had disrupted her life by running off with a middle-aged married man, Wendy would sigh with pity, roll her eyes to the top of her head and embark on an ode to Sebastian's sexual skills. Delia wished for earmuffs at this point. The practices described sounded repulsive. Did anyone really want the cracks between their toes individually licked or their private parts tickled with a feather duster? Her wide red lips clamped together, while within them her small pointed teeth ground hard to prevent toads from escaping.

Jade, who had perhaps more actual acquaintance with Seb's body, described it to Sergeant Plummer. He laboriously filled in a form, taking care over detail.

'Plumpish, you say.'

'Sort of well-covered, really . . . you know, big, tall . . .'

'And good-looking?'

'Very.'

As they stood at the desk, a fair-haired young man came out of an inner room. He stared straight at Jade and she, used to being admired and unable to avoid looking for confirmation, recognized him instantly. It was Warren Peabody, one of her childhood tormentors. He and his gang had made her holidays from boarding school a misery. Warren had mucked out at the stables where her pony was kept. He'd been a dangerous presence in the stalls, where he lost no opportunity to sneer silently at the

24

young riders' middle-class privileges. Later he and his gang would follow Jade round the town, jeering and calling and mimicking her accent. When he left school he had gone to the bad. While she had gone to Oxford.

She looked quickly away, feeling herself still shamed by their mutual experience. She had time, however, to notice how beautiful he'd become. His face was that of a bony angel and the bold look he'd given her was from quicksilver hazel eyes.

Warren crossed to a frail-looking henna-haired woman who was standing like a quivering whippet by the desk. 'It's all right, Mum,' he said softly. 'It's not 'im.'

From the inner room came the sound of a drunken voice singing, 'I belong to Glasgow', as if in defiance of any acquaintanceship with Warfleet.

From the corner of her eye Jade watched Warren slip his hand under the woman's elbow and guide her to the door. He gave no further sign of recognition.

Sergeant Plummer was asking Jade if she had a photo. She fished about in her patchwork dufflebag and brought out an old holiday snap. Delia, craning for a glimpse, saw a face younger than she'd expected. Handsome and sensual with full lips and a dark stare. The whole attitude was one of ironic challenge. Interesting. She must get a copy.

The policeman stared at the photo as though judging the truth of Jade's description. Then with a sigh, which indicated disapproval – of Sebastian's good looks or of his lifestyle? wondered Delia – he stapled it to the SO5 and said, 'This'll go to Misper at the Yard. It'll be circulated.'

Jade said in a hushed voice, 'What if there's been foul play?'

The sergeant gave her an old-fashioned look. 'Do you have reason to suspect it, miss?'

'Well no . . .' admitted Jade, 'but . . .'

'If I were you,' said Sergeant Plummer, turning to a woman who'd come in to enquire about a missing dog, 'I'd go home and sit tight. Most of these chaps turn up eventually. He's probably gone on a bender.'

Delia felt the form was damned. It would be marked very low priority.

Jade's picture of the scene was far from satisfied. It was barely worth committing to memory. With a pout she turned from the desk and shrugged at Delia. Delia, too, had a sense of anticlimax. What had she been expecting? The humdrum Sergeant Plummer to produce a body? That, she felt, would have been morally fitting, as well as less time-consuming. Now she would have to search on without, it was clear, the help of a government agency.

When they came out it was sleeting. They ran to the car keeping their heads down.

'Where do you want to be dropped?' said Delia.

Jade looked up. 'I can't go home, I'm too upset,' she announced dramatically.

'Come back to the hotel,' invited Delia. 'A good stiff brandy'll see you right . . . Besides I need to talk to you.'

It was Antonia and Jeremy Taylor, the Radcliffes had been setting out to see on the evening of Seb's disappearance. Jeremy, famous for his hospitality, had been giving a New Year's Eve dinner party and no soirée chez Jeremy was complete without his sister Antonia. The pair were a bonded couple despite other partners in life, in Jeremy's case the languid Darryl Willoughby and in Antonia's a succession of young men, the most recent of whom was an ex of Jeremy's. Neither sibling seemed fazed by the incestuous implications of this – in fact they relished them.

Darryl was serving drinks, one eye on Connor, the partners' new employee in their antique shop and Darryl's most recent passionate fancy.

'Le tout Warfleet' as Toni called them, was there. It was always thus at Jeremy's occasions. The small jazz band playing in the corner of the open-plan sixteenth-century living room was the merest excuse for a gathering of the great and good of the town. 'Le tout Warfleet' was mostly gay, at least in the jazz appreciation sector. Several of the men sported nicotine-coloured tans suggestive of sunbed devotion, others had tattoos, or shirts open to show their torsos, against which gleamed heavy gold jewellery. Jeremy's own pudgy fingers were livid with rings. He waved them around like Christmas tree lights, as he chattered and giggled. The women, who were few, passed plates of food around. They knew their place, which was never seriously to disturb the men's absorption with each other.

Caro saw Laurel Hopcraft in deep conversation close by. She shifted to put another body between herself and the writer. When they had first arrived in Warfleet, Laurel had bombarded Seb with scripts and books she wanted to see on the programme. Seb had ignored them all, thrown them into a corner and forgotten them. Laurel had become darker and more bitter. Caro had avoided her since Seb had left.

Jeremy came fluttering up to her. 'Now my love ... How *are* you?' Dear Jeremy, she loved his innocent plump face, his belief that everything could be put right by kindness. 'No word?'

'No.' She grinned apologetically. 'Jade's decided he's committed suicide.'

An anxious look crossed Jeremy's face, but he didn't acknowledge the thought behind it, saying instead, 'Nonsense, Seb would never do such a thing, he's the world's greatest survivor.'

'Used to be,' agreed Caro, thinking of the vicious knocks Seb had sustained professionally.

'He seemed fine on Boxing Day.'

'But he wasn't himself when we were alone, he was almost like a stranger.'

Jeremy forbore to say that it was over a year since they'd lived together. He pondered aloud, 'Nervous breakdown?'

Caro slowly nodded. 'He certainly seemed disorientated. Capable of anything.'

She had told no one, except Ingrid, who like a priest could say nothing, about the letter. The secret hung on her heavy, like the gold jewellery on the men. Should she have forced Seb to talk about the death of his lover? Had he been calling out for help with his grief, help she hadn't offered? Perhaps he'd gone to seek it elsewhere. It would all be her fault as usual.

'Your father doesn't even know Wendy's dead.' Delia rolled the last of her brandy round in the hand-warmed glass and tipped it between her pointed teeth, throwing back her head extravagantly.

'But . . . I don't understand . . .' said Jade, confused by her third drink as much as by the information. 'Why did he come home, then?'

'Who knows . . . maybe he just had nowhere to go for Christmas.'

Jade shook her head as though to clear it; her heavy locks swung round her face and her earrings and necklaces chattered. 'So when you wrote the letter . . .'

'I had no idea if he was with you, but I assumed you would know at least something . . . after all, you were . . . family.' Delia said the word as though the feel of it in her mouth was slightly distasteful.

'And all that time he had another one.' Jade's eyes were moist.

'Yes, little Harry.' Delia paused. 'He's now my ward. I'm his warden. Or whatever you call it.'

Jade stared at her, the brandies having removed all constraint. It certainly seemed unlikely. This smart, executive woman, so much her own person, so little to do with bothersome things like babies, so . . . careless was not quite it. Casual, then, sceptical, in her appraisal of the events around her. How could she be a mother?

'I've no intention of pretending to be his mother,' Delia, as though prescient, was saying. 'I've no qualifications for that. I shall install him down here with a nanny.'

'Down here?' Jade's brandy-infected eyes opened wide.

'Why not? Wendy left me her house. My flat in town is tiny.' Jade could picture the tight apartment, designer sterile, passion-proof, lacking all softness. 'Besides aren't children supposed to be better in the country?'

* * *

28

Caro was dancing to a Steely Dan number, 'This is my Haitian divorce'; it had been one of Seb's favourites. How suitable, she now thought, made ironic by two whiskies. Caro had been more into Californian music, she still occasionally played an old album. Jade called it, with contempt, 'Mum's cock rock'. Toni was dancing with her, but had weaved away, in a spectacular solo performance. Toni was an artiste and was in everything flamboyant.

Caro envied her friend this spirit. They'd first met at the Seafarer's Centre. A craft fair was being held and Toni was much in demand for portrait sketching. Young Jade had been fascinated and had insisted that Caro have one done for her birthday. It still hung on the bedroom wall. Caro thought it revolting.

During the sittings, though, Toni had become a friend. She had been Caro's touchstone for Warfleet, drawing her into the town's charmed circle. Caro had been grateful at first, with Seb and Jade away so much. She had been flattered to be invited to the parties and musical events. She herself had started the Book Reading Circle. Seb had been amused by it all, but kept at a distance. He found the town's attempts at artistic élitism absurd. Laurel Hopcraft apparently agreed with him. She would engage him for hours on the subject at parties. She never came to the Book Circle readings.

Caro saw that Laurel had forced Connor on to the floor. Darryl kept throwing wild glances at them. How did Jeremy manage, Caro wondered, to keep going in his relationship? Darryl was perpetually unfaithful, in mind if not in body, but Jeremy seemed, generously, never to notice.

She had tried, after the first, not to notice. But Seb's indiscretions had become more and more visible. It was almost as if he were forcing her to pay attention. His behaviour over Wendy had been outrageous.

'Poor Wendy,' Delia was saying. 'She had such a short time of it.'

'Maybe it was enough,' said Jade, thinking of Romeo and Juliet. 'How did you know her?'

29

'I came over on a postgraduate grant to do my PhD. I answered an ad in the union news for a flat share. It was Wendy. She looked after me. Mothered me, really.' Delia laughed briefly. 'I never ate properly even then. We were like a married couple by the end.'

Delia looked away, surprisingly upset by the telling of the tale. She had been lonely at first in England, having left a powerful network at Rutger's and an even more powerful family in New York. She'd needed to escape . . . especially from her mother . . . but in Wendy she had indeed found a surrogate. They had stayed bonded though their lives had gone very differently. Delia's early marriage, partly contracted she could now admit so that she could stay in the country, had turned out badly. Wendy had nursed her through the crack-up. She in turn had nursed Wendy in her last months. The experience had been both irritating and horribly moving. Delia prided herself on her tight control – she ran her small empire with a prison ship accuracy, intimidating even to herself sometimes – but Wendy's death had penetrated all her defences. She said in a low voice, 'I'll never know why she chose to bury herself back down here, she was really bright and funny.'

This was not Jade's picture of Wendy whom she knew only as a wispy unsmiling presence in the library. She did recall Wendy's having given her Noël Coward's plays to read when she had first become theatrical.

'I'd better go,' said Jade. 'Ma'll be worried.'

'You'll tell her you've met me, won't you? As for the rest, it's up to you . . . but I'd be grateful for any leads you could give me.'

Jade nodded. Delia, she could see, was determined. 'How long are you staying?' she asked, wondering if she had space to procrastinate.

'Another day,' said Delia, her mind's eye blinking over the pile of manuscripts sitting in her office. 'I'm going to see the house and . . . set about finding a minder.'

Jade thought how strange it would be to have a half-brother living on the other side of town. She felt a great curiosity to see

30

him. 'When will you bring the baby down? I'm going back to Oxford on Tuesday.'

'Can't you stay a little longer?' Delia was thrown at the prospect of losing her only ally.

'Hilary's started,' said Jade, 'I'm only still here because ... I didn't want to leave Ma.'

Delia nodded, and lit a cigarette, thinking. 'Perhaps you could introduce us, before you go?'

'Okay,' agreed Jade, 'if I can bring her round.'

'I'm sorry,' said Delia, sounding it for the first time, 'if my turning up has upset you?'

'I don't mind,' said Jade, 'it's all good material.'

6

Caro's hangover the next morning was staggering. As she took, very slowly, a tea bag from the caddy and, with great care to move nothing but her wrist, poured boiling water on to it, she thought that part of her sick despair was because this morning her mother was coming.

Jade had been in bed when she returned, parking the car diagonally on the lawn, she now saw, and creeping upstairs to lean over the bathroom sink considering whether to vomit. She remembered furious words from Toni to Laurel Hopcraft and what amounted to a fight between Darryl and Jeremy, blundered into by herself on her way upstairs to the lavatory. She'd been astonished, never before having seen Jeremy give way to marital tension. There had been some undercurrent at the party which she couldn't understand. A kind of paranoia.

She heard Jade coming downstairs and called, 'I'm going to meet Granny at the station.'

'Want me to come?' asked Jade without lustre.

'No, you could perhaps have some elevenses ready.'

Caro looked at her daughter. It was like surveying the ghost of herself as she had been twenty years previously. Today Jade's costume consisted of a cheesecloth top over a tie-dyed Indian skirt and below that belled Tibetan slippers. Did Jade, she wondered, wear knickers? She, Caro, certainly never used to. She stopped herself from asking her daughter this intrusively intimate question.

'Mummy?' Caro knew Jade wanted something when she used this word, abandoned in her teens as 'suburban'. 'Can we talk later?'

'Of course,' said Caro. 'Let me just settle Granny.'

She drove slowly to the station, wary of the double vision and praying the large number of pills she had swallowed would blunt feeling before her mother's arrival. Caro had never 'turned to' her mother, as women, including the Queen, were supposed to. Her mother had always played the child and she the adult. One of the reasons she had married Sebastian after an absurdly quick court-ship was because he had seemed a grown-up.

When Caro, fresh out of the UEA, had entered television as a researcher, Cynthia had been unimpressed. When, however, she had landed a job on a top new arts programme masterminded by the brilliant young Sebastian Radcliffe, Cynthia had come round a little. On meeting Sebastian she had been charmed and when Caro told her they were engaged, she could hardly believe her daughter's good fortune. She had adored Sebastian, flirted with him quite openly. Caro felt for once she had fulfilled her mother's expectations.

Jade had made coffee and passable scones and Caro, who had had a tiresome journey with Cynthia, was grateful. Cynthia had wanted to know, as she put it, 'everything'. Caro told her, as usual, as little as possible, knowing, as she did, that all blame would be laid at her door. She had parried the probes as best she could with her head still thundering.

'I've reported Dad missing,' said Jade, as soon as Cynthia had been taken upstairs where she would set about rearranging the furniture.

'What?'

'I went to the police yesterday.' Caro was speechless. 'Do you mind?'

'Of course . . . not.' Caro's voice sounded breathless. It was real suddenly. She turned away for another blast of black coffee. And to hide the fear in her eyes. After a moment filled with the chink of crockery she said, 'It was brave of you to go alone.'

'Actually I wasn't alone. Delia Henderson was with me.' Caro turned so quickly she almost dropped the coffee. 'I read the letter,'

33

blurted Jade. 'It was by mistake . . . at first, then I thought, when Dad went off again, someone had got to deal with it.' Jade's tone had now become quite self-possessed, defiant almost. Caro felt like a small child told off for bad behaviour, a feeling not unlike the one she'd had in the car with Cynthia. A slow resentment rose up in her.

'Before you say anything . . .' Jade held up a hand '. . . that's not the worst. Ma . . . there's a baby.'

Caro sat heavily in the wickerwork kitchen chair. Jade's voice came from a long way away. 'So you see . . . we're all in the same boat really.'

Wendy's house was on the edge of a small council estate, though it was not itself council property. Delia had let herself in with Wendy's keys, smelling at once the whiff of gas mixed with damp peculiar to unused properties. A quick tour had shown her a tidily furnished two up two down, with a modern kitchen and bathroom. From the bedroom window the small garden was winter bare, but apart from needing a prune still looked trim and well cared for.

Delia nodded, satisfied; it wasn't exactly a palace, but it would be fine until she could pin Sebastian down financially. Wendy, of course, had had no such thought in mind when she begged Delia to find Harry's father. 'He would want to know,' she had insisted, her voice still powerful in her used-up frame. 'He always wanted a son. Promise me you'll tell him!'

Delia, who would normally have found such a request absurdly sentimental, was moved by her. She still could not fully grasp that Wendy, finding herself pregnant after Sebastian had walked out on her, had chosen not to tell him. I'd have been on the blower toot sweet, she thought, remembering occasions when she had been. Even more mystifying was that though Wendy had known she was dying, she had made no attempt to contact Sebastian. Some kind of pride, Delia supposed. Wendy had refused any attempt on Delia's part to call him, demanding he be told only 'afterwards'.

34

Delia felt acute irritation as she opened drawers in Wendy's bedroom. There were her underclothes, clean and modest. Not at all the garments of an adulteress. How, oh how, had Wendy got into this? She was, she recognized, a little jealous. She didn't think she'd ever felt the feelings Wendy had expressed. Her relationships were on the cool side. Her most recent lover, a younger man, had left because, he said, she didn't notice him. 'It makes no difference whether I'm in the room or not,' he'd said plaintively. Delia had to admit, it didn't.

There was a corner shop Delia went into for cigarettes. Adverts for services offered or desired were stuck in a wire grille on the door. Perhaps she should put a card in for a nanny? The woman in front of her looked familiar. She was small and thin with red hair, and when she turned with her newspaper and carton of milk, Delia remembered the woman from the police station. She followed her out and saw her disappear into the alleyways of the estate. She wondered about her story.

Caro worked two evenings a weeks at a local veterinary surgery. When Jade telephoned Delia that afternoon, as planned, she said Caro had agreed to meet her after work. Delia was to go to the surgery.

At seven-ten Caro came out of the vet's inner sanctuary, looking rather flushed. She had been helping Miss Troubridge, the vet, wrestle with a particularly difficult poodle.

'I'm a receptionist, really,' she said to the space above Delia's head, as she stripped her slightly bloody white coat. 'But here it's everyone for themselves.' She had no doubt she was talking to Delia as, apart from her, the surgery was empty. The recession had bitten deeply into pet owners' pockets.

Delia swung a black-stockinged leg as she leafed through a copy of *Family Circle* circa 1985. 'No worry,' she said benevolently.

In fact there was, as Delia made clear as soon as they were seated in the Admiral Nelson with their gin and tonics.

She had every sympathy . . . but limited time for this project . . . Understood how Caro must feel . . . but after all . . . a baby . . . Didn't want to make things worse . . . but any lead, etc, etc . . .

Caro, still battling with the residue of her hangover, let the gin slip down before saying she would put Delia in touch with Briar, Seb's ex-assistant. 'If anyone knows where he is, she does. She's always known everything.' Considerably more than his wife had, she thought wryly.

'Wendy you see, had nothing to do with Mr Radcliffe's public life; she knew very little about it.'

I'll bet, thought Caro; he wouldn't have wanted to be seen out with that little turnip. Kept her indoors for cooking and fucking. 'What did she die of?' she asked politely.

Delia looked suitably glum. 'Leukaemia. The galloping sort, she refused to be treated when she was pregnant.'

Caro couldn't help seeing the pale, wasted Wendy kissing her child goodbye. She shook her head to dislodge the image and muttered conventionally that no matter how she herself had felt, it was indeed terrible.

'We'll be moving down here next week,' said Delia. 'I'll commute to London.'

'Really? You'll find it very quiet . . . after the life you're used to.' Caro thought, she'll be bored rigid in a fortnight. Delia's pointed teeth snapped together making a nut-cracking sound. 'People make wrong assumptions about people like me. You enjoyed it after all . . . you and Sebastian.'

They left the pub shortly afterwards. Delia bleeped her Volkswagen from a hundred yards and it answered back merrily. Caro declined a lift, saying she was on her bike. She stood with her arm lifted in a salute long after Delia had departed.

7

A week later Delia and Harry were established in Wendy's cottage. Delia had hired a Norland Nanny to 'tide her over', but even as senior editor, her pay at the small publishing company was not enough to afford it. Wendy had left nothing and then there was the cost of a baby and extra for all the travelling . . .

Jade had left a list of helpful phone numbers and suggestions before returning to Oxford. But after three days, during which Harry had cried incessantly and the Norland Nanny had made it perfectly clear that a poky terraced house in which she had to share a room with her charge was considerably less than she was used to, Delia was close to despair. She had to find someone local.

Money was on Caro's mind also. Her anxiety was polarized by a call from Noelle, Sebastian's agent, demanding to know whether Seb would be fulfilling his commitment on the television programme.

'There's been a lot of talk in the business, darling. I mean, has he lost his marbles or what?'

Caro pulled distractedly at some fronds of hair, then stopped, remembering it was coming out in handfuls. 'It's no good asking me,' she said desperately. 'I don't know where he is or what he's doing.'

There was a short, speaking silence on the other end of the phone, as though such incompetence was beyond the parameters of Noelle's comprehension.

'I'm trying to run a business here,' she said at last. 'You know I adore the little shit, but a contract's a contract, Seb knows that.

His leave's up, he should have been back in the office Monday.'

Leave, thought Caro, I didn't know he'd had any. 'Doesn't Briar know anything?' she asked.

Noelle made a sound that might have been a spit. 'Woman's a fool. Stupid fat girl who gets drunk at parties.'

From this Caro surmised that Noelle had got nothing from Sebastian's ex-assistant.

'Well,' Noelle growled, 'he's supposed to be at this do in the South of France next week. If he doesn't turn up to that, he can forget it.' The phone was smacked down, leaving Caro's ear still ringing.

So Sebastian was in trouble at work, she pondered, measuring out her mother's hot chocolate. This was certainly a departure. No matter what personal stress had occurred in the past, Seb had never let it interfere with his work schedule. Perhaps he had, as Noelle suggested, really lost his marbles. If the pay cheques stopped, what would she do? Throughout their estrangement the banker's orders had gone unmolested. Whatever Seb's other arrangements he had always paid the mortgage and the house-keeping. It was what had given Caro hope. He was keeping his foot in the door, so that it must remain open.

She sat stirring her coffee and staring out of the kitchen window at the mild, almost spring-like day. What *would* she do? The helping out job at the vet's, taken for interest's sake only, would hardly keep this place going. Her pay there barely covered what she gave the gardener, which reminded her, she wanted him to set her tubs this week, it was almost too late for daffodils.

Of course she had once been an ace researcher. Had she not married Sebastian, she would by now have been a . . . a what? Producer's assistant, she supposed, like stupid fat girl Briar, who'd snapped up the job when she had left it.

She took the hot chocolate upstairs – Cynthia was not an early riser – then telephoned Toni for support. They hadn't spoken for a few days.

'What's all this about Seb's bastard being in town?' Toni was never one to skirt around an issue.

'My God,' said Caro, 'does everybody know?'

'Jeremy bumped into Laurel, who knows this Delia woman from publishing. You know what Warfleet's like for gossip.' Caro did. 'You've got to wash your hands of this. Get a job. You're perfectly capable.'

'Oh Toni, don't you start. I've had my mother on about it.'

'How long's the old bag staying?'

'Hush,' whispered Caro, 'she might be on the extension.' They giggled like naughty schoolgirls. 'She's going tomorrow. I'll take her up to town when I go for my appointment.'

'Discuss it with Ingrid, why don't you,' laughed Toni. The idea hadn't occurred to Caro. Analysts weren't for discussing practicalities, Ingrid would want to examine her 'feelings'. 'Come round tomorrow evening,' said Toni expansively. 'I'll cook. Jeremy might drop by after his town-twinning meeting.'

Cooking and keeping house were not things with which Delia had any dealings. In town she was usually out to lunch and had M & S packaged dinners. This week had exercised her culinary repertoire to the full. The only feeding the Norland Nanny did was with a bottle, and she expected her meals on the table. After scouring the local papers without success and trying all the leads Jade had left for her, Delia was reduced to putting a notice in the corner shop grille: 'Wanted, childminder, 7 days a week. Good rates. Apply immediately to Honeysuckle Cottage.'

She was attempting next morning to check the proofs of what she now perceived to be a really dreary novel, when there was a light knock on the front door. After waiting a moment for the nanny to open it, which she did not, Delia made an exasperated sound and went to the window. Through it she saw a young man, his fair hair caught back in a ponytail, shifting casually on the doorstep.

'I've come about your notice,' he said when she opened the door, 'childminding.' Delia shook her head at once explaining awkwardly that Harry was only a baby. 'So what?' said the youth laconically. 'I've looked after all my kid brothers.'

39

Delia could think of no unprejudiced post-feminist answer to this so she invited him inside, thinking dimly that he might undertake at least some heavier household duties.

Half an hour later she had agreed that he should be childminder, while his mother came in to clean. He would do the cooking. 'I've 'ad more practice, see. She was always working.'

'Right,' said Delia, in the tone of one relieved, if uncertain. 'And you can start next week?'

'Any time,' shrugged the youth. 'Me Mum too, we're both out of work at the moment.'

'I'll pay five pounds an hour,' said Delia – the nanny cost her twenty. 'And what's your name?'

For the first time the young man looked her straight in the eyes: his, she noticed, were a deep dancing hazel. He grinned, showing crooked white teeth and his bony face became quite beautiful.

He said, 'It's Warren Peabody.'

8

'For Christ's sake get angry!' Toni's bared teeth looked like a tiger's, her face in close-up as she yelled at Caro was large and threatening. 'God knows what good bloody Ingrid's doing you!'

Caro was alarmed: Toni's facility with public anger had always embarrassed her. 'But . . . I'm not angry . . .' she said clinging to the drink Toni had just given her.

'Don't make me laugh. Don't give me any more of that turn the other cheek Christian crap. You're fucking furious!' Toni had artistic licence with language.

She was certainly furious, crashing about the room, blundering into furniture and spilling drink and cigarette ash. After a moment she sat. Caro looked at her anxiously.

'Don't look at me as if I was going to beat you. I'm not your mother . . . or your husband.'

'Neither of them beat me,' said Caro stiffly.

Toni laughed, showing the back of her throat. 'Not literally perhaps. But they certainly had you running.'

Ingrid had said something similar that morning. Caro had denied it. All the way up in the car her mother had been at her most infuriating. 'But I don't understand, Carolyn. How could you have not asked him what he was doing, surely you must have *talked* to him?' It was ironic coming from her mother, to whom Caro had never 'talked' in her life. In the Johnston home, every thought and feeling had been tailored to present the picture of a happy family life. Caro had always known her thoughts and feelings were bad and that she wasn't allowed to have them. Ingrid, and now Toni, were now trying to prise them out of her. God knows what damage she might do if they succeeded.

She knocked her drink back and said nothing. Toni had calmed down and surveyed her gently. 'Look, Caro. All I mean is, stop taking all the blame. You've got your own future to think about. Why not encourage this Delia woman to do the footwork? It's no skin off your nose. At least if she finds Seb you can do him for maintenance.'

'We both can,' said Caro grimly.

The doorbell chimed and Toni rose saying it would be Jeremy. Caro refilled her glass thinking how wonderful it must be for Toni, living the life of a free spirit in the certain knowledge that there would always be Jeremy to come back to.

His face as he came into the room was lacking its usual cheery expression, however. It looked dull and puffy and his eyes were pink. Had he, wondered Caro, been weeping? Not the result, surely, of a planning meeting?

Toni came in carrying the local paper which had just been delivered. She scanned the headlines quickly. 'Nothing about any bodies,' she laughed. 'Besides, Seb would go for something more glamorous. The Clifton Suspension Bridge at least.' Caro shuddered and gulped her drink. Jeremy was silent but kept his back turned. His shoulders looked slightly saggy.

The evening improved after a couple more drinks. Jeremy rallied. He entertained them with a wicked account of the Twin Town Committee. The vicar's wife, Fenella Pepper, had wanted a reception at the vicarage. Laurel Hopcraft had drawled that that was absurd, this was a secular event to advance trade, besides the Belgian burghers were of a different religion. Scott Harvey-Dickson, the local MP, a great mover and shaker, had suggested a pageant with a medieval theme to it. Glyn Madoc, a journalist with the local press, had reminded him that the French were still smarting over the loss of Agincourt and Marsha Snelgrove had complained about the smoking.

Their petty squabbles and spiteful remarks seemed, in his telling, hilarious. Caro had laughed without the slightest twinge of

42

guilt. She was, she realized with a little shock, quite out of love with Warfleet, with its small-town small-mindedness.

When, however, she lay in bed later, with the light and the radio on, a deep depression descended. If only she were more like Toni, able to express her feelings. Instead they were locked away like so many dirty habits, eating away at her confidence. Toni was right, of course, she must get a job. And she could help Delia. If only it didn't seem so profoundly . . . disloyal. She reviewed her morning session with Ingrid at which she had tried to discuss these very feelings. It had left her as confused as ever.

Something about this morning was prodding the back of her mind though . . . She'd arrived, early as usual, tetchy from negotiating the city's terminally sick infrastructure and, having parked, approached Ingrid's office. A little cat came out to greet her: she hadn't seen her for months and thinking her dead had cried on Ingrid's couch about it. 'Office,' she mused to herself as she walked. Interesting that that was the word she chose. Office, a place of business, a place where business was transacted, unfinished business. An engagement between two people for money. How much unfinished business did Ingrid have to deal with? How many other people's?

She saw as usual the previous client leave, rubbing a runny nose with a balled-up hanky. Today she wasn't looking as businesslike as usual. Business again. She was wearing a rather loud jumper and some ill-fitting trousers that made her bottom look large. 'Well, she must have left home at about six to get to her appointment on time,' thought Caro dryly. She was glad that she herself didn't have to go to anybody's office after her meeting. She could go home. She could make herself a strong cup of coffee. She could have a croissant, perhaps a bath with some lavender drops . . . She could cosset herself.

So what was it exactly that was jarring in this picture? The shape of the woman's bottom came into focus. The straining trousers struggling to contain the blubbery overweight body. And then the hair colour . . . the walk . . . of course! She knew that

43

back view. Had seen it stomping round her own garden following Sebastian with a clipboard. It was the blowsy Briar, Sebastian's ex-assistant. Caro turned over, gritting her teeth. Suddenly she found she could be angry.

9

First thing next morning Caro telephoned Delia. A man's voice answered and said Delia was in town for the day but would be back in Warfleet later. Caro replaced the phone, feeling rather more curious than before about Delia's private life.

Delia had gone to London to see Briar. She'd delegated her junior in the office to track her down and make an appointment, by lying and cheating if necessary. Zo, an ambitious young woman, had used her media moles to get Briar's home address. Since Briar had refused a meeting on grounds of ill-health, Delia intended to doorstep her.

She had second thoughts as she parked in the fashionable Fulham street – residents only, but she'd put the fine down to expenses – and saw the house shuttered and silent. She rang the doorbell, which played a brief tune but produced no further action, and then knocked hard at the lion's head knocker. There was a heavy shuffling in the passage and then the sound of bolts and a chain and the door opened enough to show a sliver of body.

'Briar Turner?' said Delia, in the manner of a policewoman.

'She's out,' said a blurred voice, and then, 'Are you selling something?'

Delia pushed at the door. She was sure she was talking to Briar. 'Hi, Delia Henderson, my assistant rang you. I'm sorry to come unannounced but I'm just up in town for the day and it's kind of urgent.' The door opened a little wider and Delia could now make out in the hall a shapeless figure in a furry dressing gown

45

which covered a grubby-looking nightie. 'Briar,' she said with certainty.

The figure said, 'I'm not well. I've got the 'flu. Can't talk to anybody.'

Delia said, 'It's about Sebastian Radcliffe.'

There was a silence and then the figure sighed and said, 'Okay, I suppose you'd better come in.'

Briar's sitting room was a post-modernist nightmare. Delia searched for a comfortable seat while Briar was making coffee. Piles of videos lay about and on the walls were framed awards for the programmes that Briar had made with Sebastian. She came in carrying a tray and switched on a living flame gas fire.

'Been off all week,' she said shortly.

Briar's illnesses, which were frequent, were under discussion with her analyst. Ingrid maintained they reflected her 'feelings'. Had Delia known this, she would have judged them to be at an all-time low at the moment. As it was, she was wondering if Briar was ill or an alcoholic. She smelt slightly of whisky and had all the appearance of a person under water, grappling to come to the surface.

After they had drunk their coffee, Delia leaving time for Briar to get a grip, she began to explain her mission. Briar was silent until Delia got to Wendy's death and Harry. Then she let out something between a howl and a gurgle. Delia waited politely but when it was clear Briar had sunk back into her twilight zone, she continued urgently, 'So you see, I really have to find him.'

'Good luck!' said Briar with a snorting laugh. 'He seems to have women everywhere. All I know is the shit's hit the fan at the office.'

'Do you know where he was living all those months before Christmas?'

'With me,' said Briar angrily.

When Delia got back to Warfleet she was tired and not pleased to see Harry still kicking on the fur rug in front of the fire.

46

"E's 'ad 'is bath,' said Warren, coming in with a bottle of formula. 'I was just gonna give 'im 'is bedtime feed.'

It was on the tip of Delia's tongue to tell him to do it in the bedroom. She wanted to kick off her shoes, watch the news on the telly, stretch out with a drink on the same fur rug on which Harry kicked so merrily.

She swallowed the words, knowing that a look of hurt would replace one of doting affection currently on Warren's face.

"E's a good little chap,' he nodded, taking Harry on to his knee and cradling him professionally. Harry's lips closed round the teat and he made loud sucking noises. A slight thrill went through Delia's body. Her nipples stiffened. How odd, she thought, perhaps it was revulsion. This had certainly characterized all previous dealings with babies, mostly her sister's children. And she had an aversion to seeing women breastfeed in public. How could they draw attention to their cow-like status she wondered, affronted on behalf of all women.

To deflect further baby talk she asked Warren if there had been any messages.

'Yes. One,' he said. 'A Mrs Radcliffe. She asked if you would phone her.'

Interesting, thought Delia; their last encounter hadn't prepared her to think Caro intended to be helpful.

She telephoned Caro who said she was busy tonight but could they perhaps meet tomorrow?

'I'm in conference all day,' said Delia, 'a colleague coming from London. How about the evening?'

'Come round,' said Caro. 'I'll expect you for a drink about seven.'

Really, thought Delia, replacing the phone, in Warfleet people's lives revolved around drinking.

Caro was meeting Toni for a drink this evening. They were going to draw up a list of jobs that she could apply for. The morning's grim resolution had not evaporated. They met as usual in the Admiral Nelson, the comfy old-fashioned pub, well patronized, in the lounge bar at least, by 'le tout Warfleet'. Caro bypassed several acquaintances who were attending Rumer Petulengro's Healing Circle, a weekly event held in the snug, and settled herself in a corner.

She was surprised to see Toni, beer bottle in hand, approaching from the snug. As she sat, looking slightly troubled, Caro said, 'What on earth were you doing in there? You haven't gone all mystical on me?'

'Oh, I'll try anything.' Toni laughed. 'They're attempting to contact lost spirits. I thought it might be interesting.'

Caro thought it morbid but didn't say so. The subtext of her relationship with Toni was that Toni did the criticizing.

She fetched out her list and began to go hesitantly through it. 'I thought . . . well it's just an idea . . . but I . . . I'm good with plants . . . What about market gardening?'

Toni sighed heavily. 'What about your brain? I mean have you considered the people you'd be working with? The best conversations would certainly be with the greenery.'

Caro's heart sank. She was apprehensive of Toni in this mood. She could easily demolish the list and destroy Caro's delicate confidence.

'Something literary,' said Toni definitely, 'you're always reading.'

'Yes . . . but . . .' began Caro.

'The librarian's job's going free.' Toni laughed rather cruelly.

Caro fell silent. She was not in the mood for black jokes. She'd racked her brains all day to come up with jobs for which she felt fitted. It had appalled her to find out how short the list was. She needed support from Toni.

Toni saw her expression and said in a kinder tone, 'I'm not much good at this tonight. To be honest, my heart's not in it.'

'Is something wrong?' Caro asked immediately.

'Yep.' Toni looked away. 'But I'm not sure what. I'm worried about Jeremy.'

'Is he ill?' said Caro, thinking of Jeremy's shaky look last time she had seen him.

'There's something he's not telling me.' Toni shook her head. 'I've never known it before. He always tells me everything.'

'What about Darryl?' asked Caro. 'Is he causing trouble?' Her mind went back to the struggle on the stairs – Darryl had been pushing Jeremy.

'He's bound to be involved,' said Toni glumly. 'He's nothing but trouble.'

This wasn't the first time Caro had heard Toni express negative feelings about her brother's long-term lover. She'd always assumed there was a certain amount of jealousy.

'Is it another affair d'you think?' She saw again Toni shouting at Laurel Hopcraft, and the sultry Connor standing by with lowered eyelids.

'Something worse I think . . . They've weathered so many . . .'

Just now Caro couldn't imagine anything worse. Except perhaps death. She pushed away the thought that if Seb had been dead, she could at least have mourned properly.

The Healing Circle was drifting out of the snug now. Caro searched their faces for signs of spiritual awakening. But Rumer, whose real name was Janet and whose day job was running a wig boutique in Stourbridge, headed straight for the bar and ordered a double whisky. 'She's certainly in touch with the other sort of spirit,' Caro murmured.

'What?' Toni took in the crowd.

'Rumer . . . contact with the dead must take it out of you.'

Toni said darkly, 'Not as much as contact with the living.'

10

The drinks trolley, a wedding gift from her mother, looked well stocked, thought Caro. She wanted to appear the perfect hostess at what could be a difficult meeting. She altered the position of a bowl of cashew nuts and then pulled nervously at her hair in front of the mirror. She'd spoken to Jade earlier in the day, who'd said she was coming home for the weekend and would give her a henna treatment.

The doorbell rang at exactly seven. Goodness, thought Caro, she must be formidable in business. In twenty-five years she'd never known Seb be on time for a meeting.

When she opened the door she was startled to see Delia had someone with her. 'This is my colleague, Zo Acland,' said Delia, clacking into the hall on London pumps. 'I hope you don't mind her coming along – she knows the story so far.'

Zo, who was wearing Doc Martens, a ring through her nose, and an ash-blond punk haircut, demanded a beer and stood in front of the fire drinking it from the bottle. Delia sat neatly with her long lycra-clad legs together and held a gin and tonic. Caro poured herself a large scotch and hovered with the cashews.

All three were nervous. Caro said, 'I called you because I've decided to give you all the help I can. There's an address book . . .' she produced it '. . . and his agent says next week he may be at Cannes.'

'Umhumm,' said Delia. 'I talked to Briar: his company are banking on it.'

'You talked to Briar?' said Caro quickly. 'What else did she say?'

'Plenty,' said Delia. 'I'm not sure you want to hear it.'

'She's bloody angry,' contributed Zo, out of nowhere. Caro looked at her properly for the first time. These boy-girls made her nervous. She wasn't sure how to behave with them. Several of Jade's friends had been through their androgynous phase, but this was the first time she'd had an adult version in the house. Zo looked very at home, standing in front of the fireplace.

'I'd like to know,' said Caro firmly, somehow encouraged by Zo's sturdiness.

Zo said, 'I tracked her down, and Dee went to her house.'

'She was not pleased,' said Delia. 'She pretended to be ill until she realized I meant business.'

'Typical,' said Caro. 'She was always letting Sebastian down with mysterious bugs and diseases.'

'This time it appears that he let her down,' said Delia. 'She was at home getting over an abortion.'

Caro's mouth fell open. 'You mean . . . his?' She could barely whisper.

Delia nodded. 'He left Wendy to live with Briar. He left Briar when she became pregnant. And . . .'

'Came home to live with mother,' said Zo grinning. 'I hope you've had your tubes tied.'

Caro was too shocked to find the joke either witty or offensive. 'Did he *know*?' she asked.

'This time, yes,' said Delia grimly. 'He tried to persuade her to have an abortion. She wanted the baby. After many dreadful scenes he walked out, leaving her, really, no option.'

Caro shook her head. All the pictures of Sebastian she had for many years denied, came into vision.

'All men are prats,' said Zo. 'It started with Adam.'

'One other thing,' said Delia. 'Did you know Sebastian's programme was in trouble?' Caro shook her head dumbly. 'Falling ratings, rows with executives. Briar is acting producer at the moment, but she says it started when the company was taken over.'

Caro could only stare. She'd been out of that world for so long. Had no idea of the state of the television industry.

51

'TV sickos,' said Zo, as though this was enough explanation. 'No wonder he went AWOL.'

It occurred to Caro in a blinding moment that Sebastian was one of the men she'd read about. *Wanted* them to believe he'd committed suicide. She shook the terrible thought away. Surely not even he could be that deceitful?

'Awful shock,' said Zo. 'Have another drink.' She took the glass from Caro's limp hand and gave her a generous double.

'What are you going to do next?' Caro managed, after the liquid had scalded her oesophagus.

'Leave for the South of France next week,' said Delia, as though there were no question. 'He may turn up. It's worth a try. I wondered, do you have any recent photos?'

Caro went to the desk drawer and took out an album. She flicked through the pages, avoiding looking at the pictures until she came to some taken two summers ago before Seb had left with Wendy. The sight of him sitting in the garden with his battered straw, bought on their honeymoon, pulled down almost to his smiling eyes, caused her a sharp pain in the heart. She gave the snap quickly to Delia.

Zo had picked up the album and was studying the photos. 'You were a hippy,' she said. Caro looked up sensing disapproval, but Zo said, 'You looked wonderful.' Caro felt ridiculously flattered. She crossed and peered over Zo's shoulder. 'This your daughter?' asked Zo pointing to a picture of Jade aged six, all gappy teeth and pigtails.

'Yes,' said Caro, 'she's rather a beauty now.'

'Not surprised,' said Zo, looking into her eyes. 'You are beautiful.'

Caro felt a small shock pass between them. She turned away, knowing she was blushing. She was bewildered. Deep in her womb an erotic chord was twanging.

'Is she your only child?' Zo was saying.

'Yes,' said Caro, 'I wanted more but Seb didn't . . .'

'Oh, that reminds me . . .' Delia pocketed the photo and made to go. 'There's another little problem . . .' The two women looked at her. 'Harry,' she said. 'There's no one to have him while I'm in France. His childminder takes care of him during the day, but I can't leave him in charge at night-time.'

There was a silence. Delia and Zo exchanged a look. Then Caro said bleakly, 'I'll have him.'

11

On Saturday morning, getting out of a taxi from the station, Jade was astonished to see Warren Peabody pushing a pram down her parents' drive. He stopped at the gate and gave her a brief nod. Her mouth dropped open but no sound came out of it. "'S Harry,' said Warren cheerfully, pointing into the pram. Jade, despite herself, followed his finger and saw a tuft of gingerish hair and a fat wet fist under a blue honeycomb blanket. She could detect no family resemblance.

'I mind him.' Warren became expansive. But Jade, fearing what he might say next, pushed past him. Warren put his hand on her suede thonged sleeve and said, 'Want t'come for a walk with us?'

Jade looked at him fully for the first time. His long-lashed eyes looked green today. A day of mild dampness and weak winter sunshine. 'No . . . no . . . I don't think so,' she almost stammered. The memory of other walks stood between them.

'Come on,' said Warren, 'you wanna get to know him.'

Jade jerked her glance away feeling herself hot around the collar – did he *know* then? How rude of him to admit it. She looked back, ready to meet his sneer with haughtiness, but Warren was smiling. His face looked vulnerable and friendly . . . and very attractive.

'Okay,' she muttered. 'I'll just tell Mum.'

'She's havin' a rest,' said Warren. 'Harry kept her up all night.' Then, seeing Jade's eyebrows rise, he continued, "E's been stayin' with her.'

Jade felt as though there was nothing more to say. Her life was taking a turn more bizarre than any play she had been in. She pulled her jacket together and dumping her dufflebag behind the hedge followed Warren as he turned the pram to take the lane down to the river.

Twenty minutes later they sat side by side smoking and staring at the muddy swirls of water as they tossed dead leaves downstream. And dead bodies, thought Jade, imagining herself as Ophelia. Warren flicked his stub accurately into the centre of a whirling pool and they watched as it was sucked under. Warren's other hand rested on the pram handle, which he butted gently to and fro, rocking the sleeping Harry.

Warren had explained the situation to Jade, managing more considerately this time to let her know that whereas no one had told him the relationship in so many words, there were no secrets in Warfleet. Jade was wondering how the scene would end. She felt she had little control over it.

Eventually Warren said, 'My Dad went missing.'

'Recently?' asked Jade politely.

'Six years ago. Went down the pub. Never came back. Me Mum's still looking for 'im.'

'Are you?' asked Jade, with moderate curiosity. It was all too obvious what had happened to Warren's Dad.

Warren shook his head. His long blond hair swung close to Jade's face, it had a clean, washed smell. It reminded her of childhood shampoos – Silvikrin, she remembered.

'Me Mum pesters the p'lice. They let us know when they've hauled in a suspect. Poor sods. 'S never 'im. Me Mum won't accept it.'

Jade nodded. That's how Caro would be, she was sure, though she would pretend otherwise.

'It's seven year before you can declare them dead. You know, to get married again.'

Jade could not imagine Caro doing that. Though she supposed she was, for her age, quite attractive.

'What are you studying . . . at Oxford isn't it?'

'I'm reading Greats,' said Jade in a superior tone, suited to the subject.

55

'Reading,' stressed Warren, aware that he'd been corrected. 'Sounds nice. Better than car mechanics.'

Jade had noticed the hand that rocked the cradle had grubby nails on the end of long, finely formed fingers. The back had one or two scars on it.

Harry woke up and began to whimper. Warren took him from the pram and dandled him with ease, laughing and nodding into his sleepy face. Jade felt a sharp jealousy. Warren wasn't related to him.

'Want a go?' Warren was saying. He put the now smiling baby into Jade's arms, but continued teasing and tickling and occasionally pretending to bite the chuckling Harry.

Jade held her half-brother awkwardly, frightened her bangled wrists would hurt him. Harry clutched at her hair, catching a strand or two and pulling.

'Here, let me,' said Warren. He gently took the baby's fist and unwound the lock, but instead of letting it go, kept it between his finger and thumb and pulled Jade's head round to him. Their mouths met and opened like flowers. Jade gasped as their tongues locked and a shocking thrill shot through her body. She opened her eyes wide and gazed straight into Warren's, gold and flecked now and dangerous-looking.

Caro woke with a jump from a dark and dreaming sleep. She was falling . . . falling . . . and bump! landing, her eyes snapping open and her heart pounding. What had she been dreaming about? Sebastian had been in it she was sure, and strangely Zo, who'd seemed a saviour, a sort of gallant knight riding to her rescue. She must discuss the dream with Ingrid.

That reminded her that she must also tell Ingrid about the current situation. How would she explain . . . justify . . . having Sebastian's love child in the house? Would she say that, as usual, she felt responsible? Clearly some failure of her own had driven Seb to this action and now she must step in and take care of the result.

In truth she had hardly seen Harry. Warren arrived early in the morning and departed after putting the baby to bed. He seemed to love the little chap and Harry was easy to love, being the gurgling, chuckling type of baby, fascinated by his own moving parts and seemingly always contented. He had woken only once, last night, and cried, and Caro had gone into his room and joggled his cot. She was surprised at how unmaternal she felt. For years after Jade had been born she'd wanted another baby. Yet, though Harry had whimpered pathetically all night, she could not bring herself to cuddle him.

Glancing out of the bedroom window as she pulled on her jumper, she was shocked by the sight of Warren pushing the pram up the drive with Jade beside him, also guiding the handle. They were like a young married couple, she thought. Jade in this light looked so like her, and in the pram was Sebastian's baby. Clearing her throat, she turned from the window and began brisk displacement activity.

Downstairs, as they crossed the threshold, Jade and Warren reverted to their more normal personas. It was as though the last hour had taken place in some enchanted forest. Jade was putting on the kettle when Caro, controlled now, came into the kitchen and welcomed her.

Warren said, 'I've gotta go in t' town. Harry needs things, so I'll put 'im in his cot for a bit – 's that all right, Mrs Radcliffe?'

Jade turned her back, relieved and disappointed. She felt again the sharp ecstasy of the kiss, Warren's hair sweeping her neck, his hand slipping inside her coat, the long fingers finding her nipple. She threw tea bags into the pot, ashamed and angry. How could she? A peasant! What on earth would Delia think, or worse, her peers at Oxford? She pushed aside the thought that no kiss among the dreaming spires had aroused her as had this one.

Not until the back door closed did she turn with the tea and smile for the first time at Caro. They sat with their cups at the scored kitchen table, hearing the blackbird cucking busily as she foraged in the garden, alert for another sound, that of a wakeful baby. They sat in separate consuming thought. As it happened, sexual. Caro had returned to her dream and the image of Zo, disturbing and attractive. She recalled the firmness of Zo's hand as she had shaken hers goodbye. Her grin, which parted over straight white teeth with a disarming gap in the centre. Jade was wondering what it would be like to sleep with Warren. Her thighs tingled at the prospect. She longed to wrap them round his long slender back and grip him into her. Her hand fell on a teaspoon and both women started. They exchanged a guilty look. Each saw enough in the other's eyes to turn away, embarrassed.

12

The weather was unnecessarily chilly in the South of France. Delia opened the door of the small apartment she had taken in Juan-les-Pins and pulled her coat together against the icy wind. She was cross that she had to stay so far out, which meant the added expense of hiring a car. Briar had a suite at the Carlton Hotel, but had not invited her to share it.

As she walked down the Croisette towards the Festival Centre, Delia hunted the passing faces for signs of Sebastian. The people were for the most part florid and unstylish. Salesmen, she supposed. The women looked overweight and bleary or frighteningly anorexic. God knows what they did.

The Festival Centre was a gloomy neon tomb. Rather like being in the vaults of a world bank, Delia imagined. It had a fetid, uncreative atmosphere. People in suits scurried about, hailing each other as though they'd met by desperate chance in the desert. The same people had probably faxed each other not three days previously.

Delia felt out of her depth. This market had none of the illicit fun of the Book Fair at Frankfurt, though the programmes advertised seemed to be mostly about sex. No wit was apparent. She saw Briar across a busy gangway, waggling her finger at a group of suits and laughing immoderately. Delia's red lips pursed in scorn. Nevertheless she headed towards her only hope, intercepted several times by people who claimed to know her.

Briar said, 'Oh, so you made it? No one's seen Sebastian, but there's a cocktail party given by RTV tonight – he'll be there if he's anywhere.' She turned away, claimed by a large-nosed man with yellow teeth whose whisky-tinged breath Delia experienced from several feet away.

At a loss, Delia wandered round the stall. It was plastered with shots from soaps and sitcoms, as well as several photographs of Seb's programme – celebrity artists who'd appeared on it, the award-winning films on writers and musicians. There was one shot of Seb meeting the Queen, surely not an aficionado of his programme? Delia studied his face, still handsome though slightly ruined-looking, the overlong hair, untidily pushed back, the dark eyes hiding secrets. Yes, he was sexy, she admitted. Would she see this face across a room smelling of power and aftershave, full of otherwise uninteresting people?

To pass the day she went to the market, where she haggled over some artichokes and wandered about the old part of the town, peering into churches, cursing the cobbles and ending up in a couturier street where she was shocked at the prices. Everywhere she stared at the men as she passed. Several stared back suggestively, but if they thought her bold look an invitation they were too busy to take her up on it.

She was not going to go all the way back to Juan-les-Pins to change, so, after renewing her lipstick in the Festival Centre's lavatories, where one woman was crying and another being sick, she sauntered into the vestibule of the Grand Hotel and up the stairs to the party. The balconied room she entered was indeed crammed with people. Waiters were circulating with trays of champagne and finger food. So much, thought Delia, for all these claims in the press of budget cutting. Presumably that was for programmes only.

Briar, when she at last located her, was holding forth to a mixed group of men about her newly-acquired producer status. 'It's a doddle,' she proclaimed. 'Half the job is being nice to people . . .'

And the other half, thought Delia, is drinking. It crossed her mind that Briar would be exactly the sort of producer of whom so many of her clients complained. Interfering, bossy, condescending and amateur. The kind who believed they could always improve on a writer's work since the writer didn't mean what they'd written in the first place. How on earth could Sebastian have tolerated such an excess of vulgarity and ignorance? His sexual taste must be diverse indeed. Briar could hardly be more different from the fastidious Wendy.

Briar focused on her long enough to introduce her to someone called Phil and someone called Dave. She'd counselled Delia earlier to sell a couple of projects to RTV. 'Only ones with development cash, bunch of tight-fisted arseholes.'

The implication, Delia felt, was that whatever the project she chose to pitch, her body would have to go with it.

After half an hour Delia was at desperation point. There was no sign of Sebastian and though she asked repeatedly, no one seemed to have seen him. She found Briar flat on her back in the powder room, and told her she was leaving.

Briar mumbled, 'Bye S'mantha . . .' and slumped back, her eyes rolling to the top of her head and her mouth falling open. Delia wondered if she should force a shoe horn between her teeth in case of epilepsy, but could not bear the idea of touching the slobbering face and in the end left her there, resolving to tell Phil and Dave on her way out that their quarry was in need of a fork-lift.

A young man was standing at the top of the stairs as she exited. He held out his hand and said, 'You're Delia Henderson, aren't you?' Delia agreed that she was, though the young man's face was unfamiliar. He was saying, 'Sean McCaffety . . . I came to see you a few months ago . . . I wanted you to publish my novel . . .'

A faint memory stirred in Delia, but so many young men – and women – came, wanting her to buy their novels; maybe Zo had dealt with this one.

'You turned it down,' said Sean.

'Oh, I'm sorry.' Delia was curt: after a day like today this was the last encounter she needed.

'It's okay,' smiled Sean. 'It was a good thing really, I sold it to an American publisher.'

Delia's eyebrows shot up: had she missed something?

61

'They're crazy about Ireland,' grinned Sean. He was charming when he grinned, very Irish suddenly.

'Good. Great.' Delia tried to sound enthusiastic.

'Yes, and now some producer wants to make a film of it.'

'You're a very lucky young man,' said Delia judgementally. 'Most writers wait a lifetime for that.'

'I know.' Sean became humble. 'Of course we haven't got the money yet. I'm supposed to be talking to people here about it.'

Phil passed them on the stairs at this moment brandishing a jeroboam of champagne. 'Going on to Celine's,' he blew in Delia's face. 'Wanna come . . . ?' He flung his arm around her waist and tottered, nearly pulling her over.

Sean jumped forward and steadied her as she struggled out of Phil's sloppy grasp.

'Later perhaps.' She smiled tightly, aware that when sober this man was powerful and might hold a grudge. 'You go ahead.'

Phil staggered away and Delia turned to Sean. His longish red hair flopped into his blue eyes, which held an expression of concern. His face was eager, ready for any emotion she dictated. He was so like every other young man she'd been involved with. After a while they merged into one – she wished they could have a generic name, an easy one to remember.

'Shall we leave?' she said with the faintest smile. 'Where are you staying?'

'On someone's floor,' admitted Sean. 'It's not very comfortable.'

'I have a place in Juan-les-Pins.' She fished for her car key and held it out. 'You can drive me.'

13

Sunday mornings in Warfleet were usually quiet affairs. The air would have a weekend feel to it, an occasional church bell or clock would calmly chime, a seagull or two would fly overhead disturbing the peace with their crying, in summer there'd be the sound of lawn mowers. This morning, Harry had begun to scream at seven-thirty. Jade and Caro had taken turns to rock and soothe him, Jade picking him up and throwing him over her shoulder as she had seen Warren do, but nothing stopped the noise for long and eventually Jade said she would put him in his pram and push him round to Warren's. Her motives were mixed. One, she genuinely wished to stop Harry crying and Caro being cross. Two, she wanted to see where Warren lived. Three, she wanted to see Warren. It was officially his day off, but she didn't feel that mattered.

Caro drank her coffee slowly and gratefully. It was her third cup, but the first she had tasted. She planned to put in some bulbs and then perhaps to see Toni. She was startled by a ring at the doorbell as she hunted for her gardening gloves in the understairs cupboard. Annoyed that her moment of peace was to be interrupted, she went to the door, smoothing her yet uncombed hair . . . now a vibrant aubergine . . . and pulling at her lumpy sweater, which was strictly for gardening occasions. On the doorstep stood Zo.

Zo was wearing full motorbike leathers and indeed a shining Honda stood propped in the drive. She smiled her gap-toothed smile and said, 'Hope you don't mind. Felt bad about you being lumbered like that. Came to see how you're managing.'

'Oh.' Caro was acutely aware that she was looking like Wurzel Gummidge. She could not quite drag her eyes away from Zo's zips and chains. Her boyish figure was well suited to the tight leathers: she had no hips at all.

Zo put a buckled boot on the threshold. 'Can I come in?'

'Yes . . . yes . . . of course,' said Caro, feeling stunned. 'I was just going to do some gardening.'

'I won't stay long,' Zo assured her. 'My parents live a few miles away, I'm often down at the weekend.'

Caro could not imagine Zo having parents. She stepped aside and let her in, her mind fleeing to the fridge . . . Would Zo be expecting lunch? She was striding ahead to the kitchen where she sat in the wicker chair by the Aga, fondled Cindy and picked up a Sunday paper. She seemed perfectly contented.

Jade hovered on the edge of the council estate which contained Warren. Cherry Tree Walk was where he lived, an unlikely address in this bleak, breeze-block ghetto. Harry was sleeping now, lulled by the pram's motion and Jade had lost confidence. She was unused to the role of courtier and felt herself very inelegant. Nevertheless she pushed Harry down the treeless street until she came to number thirty-nine, the Peabodys' castle, a sad-looking pebble-dashed semi.

The woman who'd been in the police station came to the door. Behind her was noise and the smell of Sunday lunch, and a cat shot out of the door between them.

'Mrs Peabody?' asked Jade uncertainly.

The woman looked suspicious. 'Yes?' she answered, taking in Jade's accent and mode of dress, both highly irregular in this neighbourhood.

'Is Warren in?' blurted Jade, feeling like a teenage love-victim.

"E's watching telly,' said Mrs Peabody, as though this ended the enquiry.

'Could you tell him . . . Do you mind . . . Jade Radcliffe . . . Harry's been very upset . . . I . . . *we* . . . were worried about him.'

Mrs Peabody turned her head, still guarding the door, and shouted, 'Warren!'

There was no reply and after a further unwelcoming stare, Mrs Peabody said, 'You'd better come in.'

Between them they heaved the pram into the hall. Mrs Peabody scurried back to the steaming kitchen, pointing to the living room door and warning, ''E don' like to be disturbed when it's "East-Enders".'

Jade pushed open the door and saw a room of cheerful squalor. Warren was sprawled on a sofa of mustard-coloured uncut moquette, staring at a massive television screen below which squatted an equally monstrous video. He put out an arm to pick up a half-full beer bottle from the floor and saw Jade standing frozen by the door.

'Hello,' he said looking startled and, after a moment, pleased. 'How long have you been there?' He uncoiled his long body from the sofa and seeming perfectly at ease, unshaven, with dishevelled Sunday hair, came towards her.

'I'm sorry,' stammered Jade, '. . . to disturb you . . . Harry was . . .'

''E's teething,' said Warren. 'Fractious is 'e?'

They went into the hall and bent over the pram, where the cherubically snoozing Harry was the picture of peace.

'He was . . .' insisted Jade, now openly embarrassed. 'Mum asked me to . . .'

''S okay,' grinned Warren. 'Fancy a drink? We'll go down the pub and leave 'im.'

He slung on his leather jacket and pushed open the kitchen door. Several children of various ages sat at the kitchen table, a Nintendo game was passing between them, the radio was on and Mrs Peabody was clattering things at the oven.

'Won't be long, Mum, 'alf an hour,' said Warren.

Mrs Peabody followed them to the door, as if she couldn't believe it.

After coffee, Caro gave her guest a tour of the house while listening to Zo's monologue about herself, her career and ambitions. She certainly had those, thought Caro enviously, as she displayed nooks and beams and the size of the airing cupboard. Rather as though tempting a prospective lodger, she had reason to think later.

Though essentially a country girl, Zo had early opted for an international life, moving to London after A-levels – 'University wasn't an option,' she waved dismissively, 'too tame. I wanted to be where life was' – and doing various jobs including bartending and working for a courier company (hence the bike) before landing a proper job as an editor's secretary. 'My Dad, I've got to admit. He's in publishing . . . kids' books . . . he twisted an arm for me . . .'

She found she liked it, the world of words, she took more and more of her editor's work home with her and was soon assisting in commissioning decisions. She graduated to selling short stories and from there, in a sideways move, became junior editor in Delia's firm with a special brief to search out new young female writers. 'Post-modernism's dead,' she opined airily, as Caro led the way through the conservatory to the garden. 'Stories are what people want now. It's always the same in a recession.' Caro admired her grip on world affairs, as she pointed out the indoor vine, and what would soon become a bank of tulips.

The day was another of those false spring ones. There were even some gnats dervishing over the vegetable patch. Zo brushed them away unseeingly.

'What will you do, now?' she was asking, 'I suppose you need to work . . . can't be much in Warfleet.' Caro agreed that there was not. Zo said, 'I could put some stuff your way . . . reading. We always need intelligent readers.' Caro felt, again, absurdly flattered. 'Do you ever come up to town?'

'Yes,' said Caro, the grey shadow of Ingrid hovering, 'at least once a week.'

'Good,' said Zo, leading the way back to the conservatory. 'That's settled then.' She grinned, to make the statement seem less bossy. 'I'm used to taking people's decisions for them.'

She stood aside to let Caro pass before her through the french windows. Caro was thrown by the courtly gesture from another woman and stumbled slightly on the step. Zo's hand shot out to catch her and for a moment their bodies were very close. Caro felt the same sharp sexual pain as before and looking into Zo's eyes saw that she felt it too. Zo bent her head, she was the taller, and kissed Caro firmly on the mouth. They stood, rigid with the electricity between them, for a long time, their mouths moving on each other's. Zo's hand touched Caro's breast. But barely had she found the hardening nipple when a voice called.

'Hello . . . anybody home?' And through the garden gate came Toni. The three regarded each other, astonished.

The pub which Warren frequented was on the edge of the estate and was, this Sunday afternoon, empty. A laser machine ping-ponged in the background and the TV was on, showing the ubiquitous 'EastEnders'. Jade felt flattered that Warren didn't watch it. Instead he watched her as they sat, silent, with their halves of bitter.

Jade avoided looking back. His stare seemed too knowing. Nor could she think of anything to say. Every topic she would normally have introduced seemed out of place, pretentious even. After a while she did look at Warren and in a moment was smiling as he winked at her. His eyes, the colour of Sunday-morning sherry today, were remarkable, she thought, quite apart from the devastating effect a look from them could have on her.

'Wanna play?' said Warren, indicating the fruit machine. He sauntered over to it and dropped in a coin. In seconds, it seemed, the machine coughed back a huge gobbet of money. Jade was impressed and drew closer, entering into the anticipation and then the delight of winning. After half an hour Warren's pockets were full. He casually dropped a few coins into a Barnardo's box on the bar and then said, 'Shall we go? Dinner will be ready.'

Did that mean she was invited, wondered Jade? How odd that would be, wonderful research though . . .

Outside, her excited face glowed in the cool air. Warren laughed and took her hand and swung her along as though he and she were sweethearts.

14

Why were French croissants such a disappointment, wondered Delia, as she pushed aside the remains of a rubbery breakfast. Sean was still asleep, his young body exhausted from the effortful night. At first he had been shy, almost unwilling, but Delia had wrapped her experienced thighs round him and hung on until it was finished. There had been some gratification for her and, judging by his cries, much for him, though Delia suspected he was awed more by her power than by her body.

She was waiting for him to wake so she could quiz him further. Last night as they had shared a post-coital Gitane he had started again about his book and told her the name of the man who wanted to film it. It was Sebastian Radcliffe.

'I met him in LA,' he explained. 'The publisher sent me over to talk to some of his contacts.'

Delia's whole body had gone stiff. Seeing her nipples stand out, Sean had taken it as a sign of returning sexual urges and anxiously started to fondle them. She'd pushed his hand away, barely noticing, and said, 'Sebastian is in LA?'

'He was,' said Sean, 'three weeks ago.'

He'd stroked her flank, still certain she was aroused. And indeed she was. The excitement of the chase did have a sexual aspect to it. This unexpected break in the dreariness of the last few days was absolutely thrilling. Looking over Sean's head, she'd caught him to her and ground her hips up into him. He'd fallen gratefully on top of her and, shortly afterwards, asleep, leaving Delia gazing wide-eyed and wide-mouthed into the darkness.

Now she wanted hard facts. Telephone numbers. She considered rifling Sean's briefcase, a battered writerly affair with international flight labels on it – it would be quicker than having to make conversation. But hardly had the thought formed when Sean stirred and groaned and sat up, his red hair fluffy in the morning.

She took him a cup of coffee and dismissively stroked his head, wondering how quickly she could introduce her subject.

Sean said, 'What time is it in LA?'

He's reading my mind, thought Delia, startled.

'I promised I'd ring Sebastian.'

The phone sat on the bedside table by Delia. 'I'll do it,' she said quickly, 'give me the number.' Her heart was pounding as she pressed the buttons. In a moment she would hear Sebastian's voice. Her mouth was sticky with expectation.

A series of astral buzzes was overtaken by an alien ringing tone, then the disappointing click of an Ansafone. A treacly Californian voice assured the listener that BJ Kane and Sebastian Radcliffe were unavailable right now, but to leave a name and they'd call back. It ended with the instruction to have a nice day, in this woman's voice strangely suggestive.

'Ansafone,' said Delia, feeling desperately cheated, 'who's BJ Kane?'

Sean took the phone and left a message with Delia's phone number, asking Seb to call him there later. It crossed Delia's mind that it was impertinent of him to expect to stay, but she dismissed the thought – she needed him.

'Did you arrange to meet again?' she said in as idle a tone as she could manage. To deflect any hint of keenness, she ran her hand down Sean's white, freckly chest and caressed his belly button. Sean lay back and closed his eyes, his face growing pinker as Delia's hand travelled.

'Yes,' he breathed. 'I'm going back to LA when the festival ends . . . Ah . . . that's . . . Oh . . . I'm supposed to take an offer with me.'

Delia paused for a moment. 'I'll help you,' she said. 'I have handy contacts here. You'll need me to do the deal.' She laughed. 'You'd better give me your bloody novel.'

69

Sean opened his blue eyes and gazed at her with a mixture of wariness and hope. 'Really,' he gasped, as she went to work again.

'Mmmm,' said Delia raising her head. 'I might even come with you to LA. We can tie all our interests together . . .'

Encouraged by this awesome proposal, Sean gained confidence. He turned Delia over and raising her hips, thrust into her quite roughly. Delia, her face buried in the pillow, let out a muffled scream. Her pointed teeth clenched down on the foam-packed pillow. It was like being fucked by proxy.

A couple of days later, Delia sat in Charles de Gaulle airport lounge, irritably flicking through a copy of the *Bookseller*. She was irritated because the connecting flight to Los Angeles was delayed and because Sean was already tiresome. Young men have such monumental egos, she thought, as she paused at an article about a female agent who'd once been a friend (she hadn't weathered well judging by the photo; publishing was hard on women). For one thing Sean wanted to screw all the time, while she was sore and bored with it, for another he talked about his 'work' all the time, as though there were something to it. Their conspiracy had produced one good thing, which was a potential deal with RTV's Phil; development money for the film, on a brief synopsis Delia had constructed.

She'd speed-read the novel, picking out salient scenes and characters, packaged it up with a couple of Hollywood names, promised English publication by her company, produced, as the coup de grâce, the magic of Sebastian Radcliffe.

'Thought he'd done a bunk,' said Phil. 'Everyone's talking about it.'

'Not at all,' said Delia, 'he's in LA. We talked to him yesterday . . .' She crossed her fingers behind her back at this point. 'He's talking to some big names.' She refilled Phil's glass from the champagne Quill and Pen Books was providing, and made sure he got a good whiff of Trésor. I should be making more money, she'd thought that night, as Sean groaned and writhed inside her. I've been agent, producer, editor, sleuth. I should be running a company.

Sean was crossing the concourse with two cups of disappointing French coffee. He'd tried several times to contact Sebastian, but each time had encountered the voice of BJ telling him they were out, mentioning swimming, tennis, riding, running. Their lives were a whirl of sporting activity.

Now, Sean said, 'I tried again. No go. They've gone to a beach party.'

Delia said tartly, 'I wonder he has any time for film-making.'

Sean shrugged and said, 'It's all schmoozing. You can make a deal over a barbecued sausage.'

Delia glanced at him, appalled. He took the death of grace for granted. It was all about money for Thatcher's generation.

On the plane she considered her tactics while Sean, in headphones, watched a movie starring computers and hardware. Not the kind presumably he would make – his book was a mixture of Irish whimsy and political intrigue – yet he seemed completely engrossed in it.

They would check into a hotel, a cheap one, as Sean seemed to take it for granted she would be paying, and then she'd send him to make contact. Her name would have to be kept out of it – she couldn't be sure Wendy hadn't mentioned her – but Seb would be invited to the hotel for a meeting. She'd have to think up an excuse to get Sean out of the way, then when Sebastian entered the room, she'd be there to confront him. At this point she stopped. She had no vision of how the scene continued.

She shrugged and tossed back her martini . . . an American one, so not disappointing . . . and prepared to sleep the rest of the flight. Perhaps in a dream it would come to her.

15

Once or twice a year Jeremy had a wine tasting. They were high-profile occasions. Le tout Warfleet would reel out into the after-noon light and go home to bed, slightly squiffy and with a sense of accomplishment. It wasn't everyone who could distinguish between an exceptional Nardique and a vin ordinaire, and who had the bank balance to pay for it. Caro had been now and then, though after three glasses, she was lost, and had no idea what she was buying. Of course now, she couldn't afford it . . .

None the less, it was a tasting Toni had come round to tell her about on Sunday morning. There had been some confusion in the garden. Zo had withdrawn with an almost pantomimic bow, Caro had gestured towards Toni and croaked a greeting. Toni had laughed wildly and come forward talking about daffodils. Apparently they were out in the churchyard. Caro and she had devoted the next twenty minutes to pretending nothing had happened. Zo had stood by the Aga, coffee in hand, smiling and saying nothing.

Tonight, as Caro put on her makeup for the event, she was aware that Toni, on her own, would demand an explanation. And what would it be, she wondered?

Toni had stayed and stayed and eventually Zo had said she was expected at her parents for lunch and had straddled her bike and departed. Watching the tensed neat figure, at one with the machine as it zoomed up the drive, Caro had felt a great lurch of desire. She wanted to put out her arms and call Zo back to them. She wanted their breasts to touch, their tongues to entwine, their hands to . . . her hand, now holding a mascara wand, trembled. 'Stop! Stop!' she told herself. 'This is getting dangerous.'

72

The phone rang as she struggled into her only decent pair of court shoes. 'Fuck-me pumps', Toni, who'd abandoned formal dress for leggings and trainers some time ago, called them. There would be no one there this evening, thought Caro, as she hobbled to the phone, to benefit from the suggestion.

It was Zo on the phone. Caro's heart almost stopped when she heard her voice, she had to thump herself hard in the rib-cage.

'Are you okay?' asked Zo, hearing Caro's cough. There was concern in her tone – genuine, Caro was certain.

'Fine,' she spluttered, 'hair in my mouth.' Then casually, 'I'm getting ready to go out, actually.'

'I won't keep you,' said Zo. 'I've had a fax from Delia.' Caro's heart was now beating bewilderingly fast. Delia? What on earth was she to do with it? Zo was saying, 'She's gone to LA. She's got a lead on Seb. It means she'll be away longer.'

'Good grief,' exclaimed Caro, 'I wasn't expecting this.'

'I know,' said Zo, 'I'm awfully sorry. I've got a hell of a week with Delia away, but if there's anything I can help with . . . ?'

Caro, confused, said, 'I don't know . . . I'll have to think . . .'

'Are you up in town this week?' asked Zo. 'At least I could give you dinner.'

Ingrid followed by Zo? What a thought! 'Yes,' said Caro, 'tomorrow.'

She put down the phone and gave way to panic, stumbling round the bedroom picking up clothes and discarding them, rifling her jewellery box, scattering perfume bottles. At last she almost fell on to the bed, holding her heart for the pain in it.

Downstairs Warren was babysitting. He'd got a video and a packet of crisps from the supper Caro had left him. When she came down, walking carefully with high heels and shock, he said, 'You look a bit pale. Shall I ring for a cab?'

Caro nodded. She said in a shaky tone, 'Warren, could you move in? It looks as though Harry's staying indefinitely.'

* * *

73

Later, in the cab, she wondered what Jade would say. She'd mentioned coming home again this weekend, on the grounds that Caro needed moral support. Caro had been surprised and touched. Usually visits during term time were limited to birthdays. She tried to remember what Jade had said when she'd arrived back late with Harry. Something about being asked to stay for lunch and having played computer games with the children. Perhaps it would be all right then? She shrank from her daughter's disapproval, but her need for Warren was greater.

Jeremy's house beamed with light as the cab approached it. The weather had turned again and the night air was biting cold, the ground flinty beneath Caro's stilettos. Marsha Snelgrove, glass in hand, flung open the door to her, smiled with unusual friendliness and ushered her through to the main room, where a circle of people in various stages of intoxication sat with flushed, thoughtful faces.

The guru they eyed was holding up a crystal glass filled with a clear ruby liquid. It twinkled fierily in the flickering light from Jeremy's low-slung candelabra, holding out promise of secret nights of passion. Several people nodded, rolling it round their mouths, seduced by its jewelled smoothness.

Laurel Hopcraft shook her head. 'Too rich for me. Instant migraine.' She leaned back, feeling her temples as though the curse was already descending. Scott Harvey-Dickson nodded vehemently: 'Lovely cellar wine.' Glyn Madoc shouted jovially that it wouldn't last long in his cellar! Rumer Petulengro appeared to be consulting her Tarot cards. Fenella Pepper had passed out in the corner.

Jeremy, all mellowness, came forward to greet Caro. He gave her a hug, saying, 'Welcome my dear. You remember Gerard don't you?' The wine merchant looked up and nodded, his dark gypsyish face flashing a quick smile to Caro. There was something knowing in his look, she felt. He, like Jeremy and Darryl, was 'of the other persuasion'. Embarrassed, she looked away, as a glass of wine was put into her hand. 'You must catch up my dear,' Jeremy was saying. 'I'm just going to see to the nibbles.'

Caro sank into the atmosphere. Shortly, Toni came out of the kitchen with a plate of cheese squares. She winked at Caro and jerked her head towards the stairs. Caro pretended not to catch her meaning. The wine bottles came and went, the chat got louder. Large cheques changed hands. People congratulated each other. Toni caught Caro on her way to the loo and hissed that they must talk later. Caro nodded, now too drunk to care. The combination of Gerard's absurd accent and charming smile with the flavours of his mysterious treasures, wove a magic they were all caught up in.

Suddenly voices were raised and there was the sound of a slap, then a loud crash came from the kitchen. Le tout Warfleet sat in dazed silence staring at the kitchen door. It was flung back and through it hurtled Darryl as though shot from a gun. He spun slightly, regaining his balance and then, ignoring the wine tasters, bolted for the stairs which he thundered up, muttering furiously. The listeners heard, '. . . fucking bastard . . . fuck you . . . teach you to fucking meddle . . .' Darryl disappeared and from overhead came thumping footsteps and the sound of drawers being wrenched open.

In the room below there was not a murmur. The unnatural silence was broken by the sound of sobbing from the kitchen. Toni leapt up and ran to the door, Caro followed more slowly. By the fan-assisted oven stood Jeremy with a rolling pin in his hand. Tears ran down his plump cheeks. At his feet was a smashed plate of vol-au-vents. He held up his arms and said between seizures, 'I hit him . . . I couldn't help it.'

Laurel Hopcraft came to the door. 'Can I do anything . . . ?' she asked, her beady black eyes drinking up the scene, as though from another wine bottle. Toni rushed to shield Jeremy, who went limp and dropped the rolling pin. Caro shored up his other side and together they led him from the room, nudging Laurel into the wall as they struggled past her.

In the sitting room the buzz of conjecture stopped at once on Jeremy's appearance. But before Toni and Caro could get him to the stairs, Darryl swept down them, suitcase in hand, and announced to the company that he was leaving. Jeremy broke free and stumbled towards him, but Darryl pushed him away and seconds later the front door slammed leaving Jeremy tottering against it. 'He's drunk,' he wept, 'the silly sod. He doesn't know what he's doing.'

Jeremy's bedroom, which was absolutely Jeremy's though he had shared it for nearly twenty years with Darryl, was a royal delight, all swags and drapes with a chaise longue and an angelically carved fourposter. On it Jeremy lay, moaning softly. Toni had given him an eye pack and two aspirins and taken off his shoes. Now she waited anxiously for him to drop off.

The group had gone, adjourning with Gerard and his bottles to Marsha Snelgrove's. In the kitchen, Connor was cleaning up, but apart from that it was quiet. Toni put her finger to her lips and gestured to Caro, who was perched uncomfortably on a Queen Anne loveseat. The drama had made her quite sober. She followed Toni into the hall and they sat at the top of the stairs sharing a cigarette.

Toni said, 'Jeremy slapped Darryl, Darryl went for Jeremy's throat, Jeremy dropped the vol-au-vents when he grabbed the rolling pin.'

'But what were they rowing about?' asked Caro, still stunned by the turn of events.

Toni shrugged. 'Jeremy wouldn't say. Kept repeating that Darryl was drunk . . .'

They fell silent, both thinking their own thoughts. Caro's were that Darryl was frequently drunk and had not, to her knowledge, hit Jeremy before. She slid her glance to Toni, wondering if she was thinking the same. Her friend looked sad and every bit her age suddenly. Caro was struck by the down-side of being a free spirit. What happened when you got old and tired and couldn't attract any more? There was no familiar fireside face to run home to, no relationship to pick up like a comfy piece of knitting. No wonder Toni was so dependent on Jeremy.

Toni stubbed out the fag and groaned comically.

'Relationships,' she said. 'God save me from ever having another one.'

Caro looked away and said nothing. This was not the moment to take Toni into her confidence.

16

Caro obsessed for an hour over her costume. She had nothing, *nothing* that could possibly double for Ingrid and Zo. And if she changed, where would she do that? Not at Ingrid's office, certainly, where the lavatory was so pristine, one was almost afraid to pee in it. Besides, what would she change into? She rifled the closet again for any garment with a zip or chain. She was not, as Jade would put it, 'street-cred'.

Jade! Now she must have something. She ran into Jade's bedroom, recently refurbished by her daughter in the style of a hippy knocking shop. She threw things out of the cupboards and drawers . . . latticed trousers . . . thonged vests . . . incomprehensible bits of material with see-through gussets. At last she settled for a short black leather skirt, now discarded by Jade as 'non-ecological', and a bomber jacket decorated with jewelled studs. God knows what Ingrid would make of it.

In the car she switched on to Classic FM. She needed a calming tonic. She thought, as always on this journey, of what she would say . . . admit . . . to Ingrid. She felt guilty, like a Catholic going to confession. Butch up, she told herself, you don't pay sixty quid a session to be treated like a child. But in a way, of course, she did. And how would she explain these new and devastating feelings? Could she even discuss them?

It turned out that she could. She felt a surge of interest from Ingrid. They'd never really talked about sex before. Of course, Caro didn't exactly mention sex. Ingrid pressed her to be more explicit.

'Well,' said Caro, shielding her crotch, horribly exposed, she feared, by the leather miniskirt, 'I get a sort of pain . . . here.'

78

'You mean you desire penetration?' asked Ingrid, sitting forward in her chair.

'Yes. No. I don't know.' Caro felt herself blushing. 'I mean what with? Fingers?'

Ingrid rubbed her temple and said, 'Are you asking me how lesbians make love?'

Caro was aware of her rocking slightly. 'I'm saying . . .' she took a breath '. . . I wouldn't know what to do . . . but whatever it is . . . I want it.'

There was a pause then Ingrid said, sighing, 'I think the rest will follow.'

Caro felt seasick as she walked down the street afterwards. The ground kept slipping away beneath her feet. She remembered acid trips from her youth. And the paranoia that accompanied them. It was a relief to have admitted how she felt, but also very ground-shaking.

It was a couple of hours before she was to meet Zo. She had thought she'd have tea. But suddenly her uncertain feet took her in the direction of Sebastian's office.

It was years since she had entered this plate-glass programme emporium. The commissionaire was different, as was the liftman – of course, the company had changed hands. When she had worked here it had been Len, who'd seemed to be part of the fabric. He too had come from Warfleet way, Sebastian had often travelled by train with him.

As the lift rose to the fourth floor, think-tank of the arts, Caro studied herself in its new sepia-tinted mirror. No doubt as the programme executives got older, they needed the mirrors to be kinder. She didn't look bad, she thought. The Biba-ish hair, the pale face with Jade's black kohl eyelids, the provocative costume revealing good legs – she could pass, in this light, for her younger self. She gave a nervous giggle.

She made for Sebastian's office, with its goldfish bowl walls and pink furniture, like a homing pigeon. She stopped short in the doorway. Sitting behind Seb's smoked-glass desk was fat girl

79

Briar. In one hand she held a telephone, in the other a sandwich. She was speaking and eating at the same time, occasionally spitting into the receiver. Caro went through every emotion from shock to anger. By the time Briar noticed her, stopping mid-bite, she'd settled for an icy resentment.

'What are you doing here?' said Briar, banging down the phone.

'I could say the same to you,' replied Caro, trying to lighten the accusation with a casual laugh. The laugh was a failure.

Briar said, 'I've taken over.'

Caro said quickly, 'While Sebastian's away.'

Briar shrugged. 'Not my decision.'

A cold feeling gripped Caro's insides. They'd ousted him, that was it. In a few weeks, after years of service. God this was a callous business. Her thoughts went back to the liftman.

'New controller,' said Briar, stuffing the remains of the sandwich into her mouth. 'New ideas. Different approach. Need somebody younger.'

Caro almost laughed in her face. Technically she was younger of course. But without Seb's style or wit, without his intellectual vigour. She took in now that not only the incumbent but the surroundings had changed. There were some hi-tech chairs in place of Seb's comfy suede sofas, the art on the walls was of black and white nudes, to Caro's eyes pornographic.

Briar said warily, 'I've told Delia all I know.'

'Yes,' said Caro, 'I was just . . .' she wasn't sure what she was doing, in fact, and finished lamely, 'passing.'

'If you've come to have a go at me you can forget it.' Briar bared her teeth nastily. 'Seb's brought it all on himself. I've got nothing to feel sorry for.'

It flashed through Caro's mind that Ingrid should be proud of at least one of her clients. Briar was nothing if not confrontational. She realized she hadn't seen her leaving in tears that morning. How would Briar fit Ingrid's sessions into her new executive schedule? Perhaps now she had got one, she wouldn't need to bother.

'I haven't come for that,' she said. 'Actually it was more . . . nostalgia.'

'A killer,' snapped Briar. 'Get rid of it.'

A man appeared in the doorway. Briar leapt to her feet. 'Jed,' she breathed, 'did you want me?' The man hovered, as if undecided. 'This is Jed Rosenbaum,' Briar stuttered, 'our new controller. This is Mrs Radcliffe . . . Sebastian's wife . . . she was just . . . passing.'

Caro focused on the man. He was youngish and ugly, with heavy brows and eyes that shifted away from contact. He looked familiar . . . but from where she wasn't sure. She said, 'How do you do.' He nodded perfunctorily and passed on, perhaps afraid, like Briar, that she might challenge him.

Briar had subsided over the desk, like a Michelin man with a puncture. At this level of anxiety, thought Caro, she'd soon be returning to therapy. 'Goodbye Briar,' she said. 'I wish you everything you'd wish Sebastian.' She walked briskly away, astounded by her cheek. As she entered the lift she remembered where she'd seen the controller before. In her day he'd been the tea boy.

17

Caro found herself laughing as she neared Zo's place of work, a distinguished-looking Regency house in a terrace off Mayfair. Thank goodness all publishers hadn't been moved to Wapping. Quill and Pen Books announced itself, in its façade at least, as an establishment of old-world courtesy. She said as much to Zo, who came bounding downstairs two at a time, carrying a great pile of manuscripts.

'Don't you believe it.' Zo grinned. 'We're owned by a multi-national. But we're their posh little imprint.' Caro shook her head, disappointed, but cheered up when she saw Zo take champagne out of the hospitality fridge. 'Some things,' said Zo, 'I insist on.' They clinked glasses and for the first time looked properly at each other. Caro's heart fluttered as Zo's dark eyes registered approval. 'You look fab,' she laughed, 'and just right. We've got tickets for a rock concert.'

Caro had not been to a rock concert since she was Jade's age. As they approached the venue among crowds of fans, she became very anxious. She was too old and, with these young women in their Doc Martens and slashed jeans, wrongly dressed. Zo said, 'I've got a spliff. Would you like some?' They ducked into an alleyway and Zo lit up. Dutch courage, thought Caro taking the joint in trembly fingers. She looked round, fearing discovery, then took a long toke, another thing she hadn't done since she was Jade's age.

Her head swam and the feeling of seasickness returned. She leaned against the wall, aware of Zo's closeness. She could feel her warm breath in the night air. 'Okay?' asked the laughing eyes.

She looked into them, giggling stupidly. Zo took her arm and led her to the entrance.

'I'm starving,' said Caro, enjoying herself now.

'Stoned munchies,' agreed Zo. 'We'll get some popcorn.' They sat munching popcorn and watching movement and light, as they waited for the concert to begin. There was a silent warmth between them; relaxed as well as sensual. To Caro it seemed a vast dance drama was unfolding. She was fascinated by the red and green winking on the sound desk, the flashing of the Vari-lites, purple, pink, gold. The audience seemed a solid body, moving on impulse like a Mexican wave. Now whistling and heckling, now silent and rapt, as they waited for their heroine.

The performer, when she at last came on stage, was, as Zo had explained, a fashionable cultish androgyne with a fabulous voice and powerful presence. Caro was entranced. The figure on stage strutted and marched, crooned and smooched. Her voice was wonderful, her sex appeal assured. My goodness, thought Caro, I bet she's a terrible baggage.

A discussion she'd had with Ingrid about paying attention came back to her. She'd realized that she rarely did, she was always living either ahead or behind, never actually in the moment. Listening to this strange creature singing, she couldn't understand the words, the tunes, though she'd heard all the songs, she realized now, on the CD Jade played in her bedroom. But somehow it wasn't important what songs she was singing, what words were being said. What was important was the voice, the experience, the being there . . . the paying attention.

Zo too was deep in concentration. At one point her hand shot out and grabbed Caro's, squeezing it with excitement. Caro's whole body leapt in response. But a moment later Zo took her hand away, clapping and clicking her fingers. Caro, disappointed, ostentatiously crossed her legs and waggled her foot to the music.

As they left the hall, Zo put her arm round Caro's back to shield her from the public. She steered her and protected her from the crowd. Caro leaned into the taller body, enjoying being cared for.

Outside, as they approached her car, Caro didn't know what to say. It seemed there was some unspoken agreement. 'Well . . .' she tried, extending her hand '. . . that was wonderful . . . thank you. I'd . . . er . . . I'd . . . better get off. Can I give you a lift?'

Zo took the hand and pulled Caro up close. 'A lift,' she said with a raised eyebrow. 'I thought you were coming home with me?'

They drove to Zo's flat, an impressive one in Hampstead, paid for, Zo told her later, by her father. Zo took champagne from the fridge in the spacious, brightly painted kitchen and filled two glasses. Caro hovered nervously by the door. Zo came forward and gave her a glass. 'Cheers,' she said, chinking it with hers. They drank looking into each other's eyes. Then Zo leaned forward and touched Caro's lips with her own. Caro opened her mouth and received, to her surprise, a jet of warm champagne in it. She felt the sizzle of the drink down to her toes. She swayed a little with excitement.

'Come on,' said Zo taking her hand and pulling her into a high-ceilinged living room, with low futon-like couches and a vase of tulips on the paint-washed floor. She put on a CD and lit a joss stick. As she took a bag of dope from an oriental box and started to roll, the sound of the rich sensual voice from the concert filled the room. Caro felt her insides melting.

Zo sat down on the futon beside her and put the spliff to her lips. Caro drew on it then held her breath: it was like riding a bike, she remembered. After two or three drags she leaned back. Zo followed her, blowing the dope smoke gently over her. She kissed Caro's neck, exposed in this position, and undid the buttons on her jacket. Caro arched slightly so Zo could ease it off. Her eyes were still closed. She was too scared to open them. Zo held the champagne glass to Caro's lips and slid a hand behind her head, propping it slightly, so she could drink. Not a word was spoken. The intimacy was unbearable. Now Zo was unbuttoning Caro's silk shirt. In a moment she had slipped her arms round Caro's back and undone the clip on her brassiere. It passed crazily through Caro's head that she was much more adept than most men, particularly with the clothing. She wanted to laugh, but also to weep, as she felt the chilly air on her bare skin. Her breasts were tightening without even Zo's touch on them.

'Open your eyes,' said Zo gently.

Caro did, still fearful. In front of her knelt Zo, with her tee shirt off. Caro saw broad shoulders, small pointed breasts, a sturdy ribcage. Zo held herself proudly. Caro took a shaky breath. She said, 'I . . . don't . . . I've . . . never . . .' Zo put her hand to Caro's mouth and shook her head, then she pulled Caro on to the floor with her.

For a moment they looked at each other, both breathing fast, then they moved so that the tips of their breasts touched. Caro experienced the most complete ecstasy. A moment later they fell back clutching each other urgently. Zo kissed Caro's face and hair, her eyes, her nose, and finally her lips, thrusting her tongue deep into Caro's throat, pinning her shoulders to the floorboards. Caro pushed at Zo's jeans. She wanted her naked. Wanted to feel that smooth brown flesh between her thighs. Wanted to touch down the length of Zo. Moments later Zo's fingers were inside her. Up and up. Further than any cock. Caro shuddered and gasped. It was so . . . it was too . . . her back arched, her buttocks, clutched in Zo's other hand, left the ground. She rolled this way and that, clasping Zo, who, magnificently, rolled with her. They cried out and bit each other, desperate to be one. At last, Zo pushed Caro's arms over her head and lay fully on top of her. Their cunts met, the lips open to each other. Caro came and came. And Zo came with her.

85

18

LA was a town she had always hated, thought Delia, as she stripped out of clammy winter clothes and stepped into the shower. It was hotter than hell, even in February, but considerably less warm-hearted. She had made contact with countless Ansafones, been wished enough nice days to last her until death and eaten beansprouts until her teeth squeaked with them. Sean was out, she was relieved to see, gone, she hoped, on another attempt to see Sebastian. These had, so far, been failures.

As the water sluiced down her, reminding her that there was at least American plumbing to be thankful for, Delia considered her options. Sean had left many messages for Seb, then gone at last to the house in Laurel Canyon. He'd found a fortress among dusty palms, silent save for the gurglings of the pool and the machete of the Mexican gardener. It seemed, from the suspicion with which he was regarded, that the owners were out and his visit unwelcome. As Sean had no Spanish and the gardener, apparently, no English, no further progress had been made.

They had called everyone else who might help. Sean's publisher, Lloyd, in New York, acquaintances Sean had made while in LA, the MD at Delia's firm's headquarters, even Noelle, Sebastian's agent. The phone bill would be astronomical. BJ Kane's Ansafone had been stuck at a birthday jacuzzi for days. Perhaps BJ herself had drowned, thought Delia . . . if she'd ever existed.

The bedroom door banged and Sean came in looking hot and unhappy. Delia pulled her towelling wrap closer around her – she didn't want to give him ideas – and crossed to the fridge to take out some Perrier water. 'No go?' she said, already knowing the answer.

Sean's young face was wizened with disillusion. 'Nope. I reckon he's left town. He might have left me a message.'

'That's the business,' sighed Delia, with the sympathy of one who had only Sean's interests at heart. Privately she was grinding her pointed teeth in a total rage with both of them. 'Tell you what,' she said, 'why don't I try?'

Sean looked up with a shadow of hope. 'Go to the house?' he said doubtfully.

'At least my accent is familiar, and I speak Spanish,' laughed Delia, determined to lighten his mood. 'Maybe they won't find a woman so threatening.' The idea had come to her in the shower. She would present herself as herself, a publisher from England. She would say she had come on behalf of her firm, who were interested in Sebastian's biography.

That evening, when it had cooled down and the sudden dusk had fallen, Delia dressed and made up with care and ordered a taxi. The driver skimmed along Mulholland, showing Delia the satellite strips laid out below: really it was like being on a space station.

1198 Laurel Canyon was lit up when they arrived. Little green lights hovered in the palm trees and the pool was a grotto turquoise. Ordering the taxi to wait, Delia approached the electric gates and pressed the entrance buzzer.

'Hi,' came the treacly tones of BJ. 'Who's that?'

Delia cleared her throat, which was choked with disbelief. 'It's Delia Henderson,' she said, 'on a trip from England. We've never met but I'm a friend of Sebastian Radcliffe's.'

There was a silence on the other end of the intercom, then BJ's voice, less certain now, said, 'Are you alone?'

'Absolutely,' said Delia, adding for credibility's sake, 'I came in a cab.'

To her surprise the buzzer was pressed and the heavy gates swung open. She walked up the crackling white chip path, certain she would now confront Sebastian. The person standing at the door, however, was unmistakeably BJ. She was almost six feet tall and in the dim light looked about thirty. Honey-blond hair streaked back from a face tanned and California pretty. When she smiled, as she did now, nervously, her teeth were of a sparkling regularity not usually seen outside chewing gum adverts. She wore a silk shirt, open to display a more than adequate cleavage, over leopard-skin leggings, quite startlingly provincial.

'Delia?' she said uncertainly. 'I guess you'd better come in. Seb's not here right now.' This at least gave out hope that he would be later.

Delia entered the hall and was ushered into a long room with sliding doors out to the poolside. Everything in the room was white, the walls, the sofas, the carpets. Goodness, thought Delia, if you spilled red wine it would look like a murder.

'Can I get you something?' smiled BJ with Californian hospitality.

Delia shook her head, she was searching the room for signs of Sebastian. 'I'm fine, thanks. I'm sorry to trouble you. I have left messages.'

'Damn machine's gone wrong,' drawled BJ. 'Don't you just hate technology?'

Delia didn't, in fact, and thought with the use BJ's Ansafone got, it had probably died of exhaustion. 'Are you expecting Seb soon?' she asked, eager to get down to business.

'Well . . .' BJ's tanned brow furrowed and her blue eyes took on a wary look. 'I'm not real sure . . . he comes and goes.'

He certainly does, thought Delia. 'It's important I speak to him,' she said. 'I have an offer from my publishing house. We want him to do an autobiography.'

BJ's face lightened. 'Really! Oh, that's . . . he'll be so . . . things have been . . .' She turned away, her hand patting pointlessly at an overstuffed white cushion.

Delia decided to be frank. 'Look,' she said, 'I know Seb's had problems . . . the show in trouble and so on. But this could save him. We'd give an excellent advance.'

'You say you're a friend?' checked BJ.

'Mmhmm. A friend . . . of a friend. And fan. Oh yes. A great admirer.'

BJ relaxed a little and leaned forward confidentially. 'I guess I can trust you. Actually Seb isn't here at all.'

'At this house, you mean?'

'No. In LA. He hasn't been here for weeks.'

'But surely . . . Sean McCaffety met him here. They talked about working together . . .'

'Oh sure,' nodded BJ, 'he *was* here, for a couple of days over New Year's. Sean, yeah, Irish right? Seb thinks he's very talented.'

'Really,' said Delia in a vinegary tone. 'In that case, why isn't he pursuing this project?'

'Oh but he *is*,' BJ assured her. 'He's gone to Ireland.'

'Ireland!' exploded Delia. 'But the messages on your Ansafone said . . . you mean we've had a journey here for nothing!'

'I'm real sorry,' said BJ, looking woebegone. 'Seb's in a bad way. He needed to get some space for himself. He asked me to cover for him.'

'But why would you lie for him like that?' said Delia, knowing the answer. BJ's surgically corrected face slipped slightly. Delia saw now that she was forty . . . or even older. 'We go back,' she said bleakly.

'Back?' pressed Delia.

'Fifteen years,' said BJ, causing Delia a small gasp. 'We met at AA.' Delia started; so Seb was an alcoholic as well! Why hadn't Caro told her? 'He was here filming for several months,' continued BJ. 'We became close. He often visits.'

This man, thought Delia, really did have a girl in every town! Or at least someone to mother him. 'Well,' she said, trying to keep affront out of her tone, 'this is a serious offer . . .'

BJ nodded understandingly. 'I'd like to help . . . for Seb's sake . . .'

'He's hot right now,' Delia pursued, 'but who knows for how long . . . it's important that I find him.'

BJ sighed. 'I promised I wouldn't tell a soul, but I guess this is an emergency?' Delia agreed that it was, and scrabbled in her handbag for her personal organizer. BJ hesitantly gave her an address. 'It's just outside Dublin . . . a kind of retreat. He said he would do some recces.'

'Thanks,' said Delia. 'I guess I'll have to go there.'

BJ looked suddenly scared of what she'd revealed. 'You won't tell anyone else?' she urged. 'I couldn't bear to betray him.'

Too late, thought Delia, but she smiled at BJ. The poor thing wasn't very bright – Delia almost felt sorry for her. For all these women Sebastian had used. Used and then abandoned. 'Don't worry,' she said kindly. 'It's for his own good.'

As she tripped smartly back down the chalky path, aware that BJ was watching, she wondered if she'd warrant a chapter in the biography.

19

The waiting room at Celia Troubridge's veterinary surgery was full, Caro noted, as she struggled into her white coat. She sighed: she had wanted to get away early tonight, having promised Toni a visit. In the three days since her encounter with Zo, she had avoided her friend. But Zo had rung to say she was coming down at the weekend and Caro knew that Toni had to be tackled.

Zo had said, 'I'll stay at my parents'. I don't want to embarrass you.'

Caro, who had gone hot and trembly at the sound of Zo's voice, bringing back, as it did, the delicious thrill still locked in her body, had insisted that she wouldn't be embarrassed. Too late, she remembered Jade was coming for the weekend. Well they would have to go out . . . a barn . . . a car . . . the thought of not being able to make love with Zo was the most piercing agony.

Turning to her register she snapped her ballpoint pen and shook away the memory of Zo naked, bathing her, Caro, the morning after. She had run soapy hands over Caro's breasts, then rinsed them, with spongefuls of scented water. Caro, shy about her body in the daylight, had gradually allowed herself to uncoil. They had ended in the bath together.

'Yes, Mrs Wickes,' said Caro, 'it's Rocky again is it?' Mabel Wickes, a regular to the surgery, being an anxious parent, regarded her with troubled eyes. She would feel worse, thought Caro, if she knew what I was thinking.

Two hours later, hours punctuated for Caro with dreamy stares into the middle distance, where she could clearly see Zo's slender limbs in various heart-stopping poses, the last customer departed, carrying a crying kitten in a basket. ''E's hungry, thass all it is.'

Caro sympathized thoroughly.

She drove up to Toni's cottage feeling apprehensive. Toni could be so . . . scathing . . . dismissive – Caro could not bear it if she were to take this new development lightly. She might laugh mockingly. She might, of course, be horrified.

Toni was not at the door to greet her. Caro went through into the living room, surprised to see a circle of crystals on the rug and a joss stick burning. Some indistinct mystic music was playing. Then she heard Toni's voice murmuring and a phone being put down. A moment later Toni appeared at the door; she had obviously been crying.

'You look awful,' said Caro, taking in her friend's raw, makeupless face.

'You, by contrast, look blooming.' Toni tried to smile. 'Are you in love?'

Caro supposed she was but didn't intend to begin by saying so. 'What's happened?' she asked, deflecting the question. 'How's Jeremy?'

Toni grimaced and looked away. 'Distraught. He won't even go to work.' Caro recognized that this was serious. Jeremy was passionate about antiques, wouldn't miss an auction unless he was dying. Toni waved at the crystals. 'I've been doing a meditation for him . . .'

'Darryl hasn't come back then?' said Caro.

Toni's face wrinkled with distress. 'Rotten bastard,' she said. 'He's booked into a hotel in Stourbridge.'

'But have you found out why?'

Toni shrugged. 'It's over another man, of course.'

'Not Connor?' said Caro, suddenly alert to the pleasures of youthful flesh.

'No, no,' dismissed Toni, 'someone much more important. Someone Darryl was prepared to leave for.'

Caro was shocked. With all its ups and downs, Jeremy and Darryl's marriage was the most secure she knew of. 'So . . . is he with this . . . person?' she asked.

92

Toni shook her head. 'Apparently the man in question has disappeared. Darryl's convinced Jeremy has a hand in it.'

Another one, Caro thought but didn't say – suddenly four hundred missing men did not seem so unlikely. 'And has he?'

'He admits he went to see the man,' said Toni. 'Says he was desperate, couldn't resist it.'

'I tried that,' nodded Caro. 'It didn't work with Wendy.'

'Well, it looks as though it did this time. The bloke took off and hasn't been seen for some weeks. Darryl's furious. Swears he's going to find him.'

The thought of girlish, dependent Darryl finding the strength for a pilgrimage made Caro smile. 'He'll be back,' she said, thinking, he likes his comforts too much not to be.

'I don't know . . .' Toni looked scared. 'If it's love . . .' She left the thought hanging.

Caro put her hand to her breast. Yes. If it was love, anything could happen. Even Darryl might move mountains. She said hesitantly, 'Toni . . . there's something I have to talk to you about.' Toni looked up, for the first time really noticing her friend. 'Yes. All this had put you out of my mind.' She pulled Caro to the fire – the February evening was bitter – and said, 'Sit down and tell me all about it.'

Caro began nervously with some history. 'You see . . . since Seb left . . . it's been . . . I mean *I've* been . . . well, if it hadn't been for you and Jeremy . . .' Toni nodded as though she knew all this. 'Not being a couple suddenly . . . it's hard . . . people don't invite you out . . . I've been so terribly *lonely*.'

'Huh!' Toni snorted, indicating there was nothing about that state Caro could tell her.

'And then there's sex . . .' Toni sighed. 'I hadn't had any for so long . . . even before Seb finally went it was only on high days and holidays . . .'

'*Hadn't?*' Toni's eyebrows shot up. 'D'you mean you have now?'

Caro nodded apologetically. Toni made a small explosive

93

sound, as though pent-up surprise was escaping. 'Don't be offended,' Caro begged.

'Offended?' Toni gave a short laugh. 'Jealous, more like. I haven't had great sex for ages.' She paused. 'I take it, it was great?'

Caro saw Zo as she had been in the early-morning light. The long brown limbs as compact in sleep as in waking. The dark, self-contained triangle she, Caro, had touched and awoken; the caresses, tender yet passionate; the joy she had felt at Zo's pure, high cry . . . Oh, yes, it had been great. She let out her breath and nodded.

'Well,' said Toni, 'lucky you.'

'But what does it mean?' said Caro with anxiety. 'Do you think I'm a lesbian?'

Toni's eyebrows shot up, then she laughed, returning to her more vivacious self. 'We're all bisexual in my opinion.'

'But I'm terribly confused . . .' Caro pressed on. 'I've never thought about women . . . that way.' Toni smiled like an irritating sphinx. Caro said, 'Have *you* ever . . . ?'

''Course,' said Toni, chuckling now. 'Lots of times. In my "anything goes" days.' Caro wasn't aware that Toni had abandoned these. She also felt vaguely put out. Surely Toni should have told her?

'I suppose young Zo is the woman in question?'

'Well of course. How many lesbians do you think I know?' said Caro rather tartly.

Toni dropped her arm lightly on to her friend's shoulders. 'Be careful,' she said. 'It's deeper, more intricate with a woman.'

Caro looked up, searching Toni's face for an explanation. 'What are you saying?' she queried.

Toni gave her a quick squeeze. 'Nothing really. Just . . . you're very vulnerable right now . . . don't get involved too quickly.'

Caro felt the warning came too late. 'You asked me if I was in love,' she said. 'I'm afraid I may be.' Toni's face went dull. She's frightened of losing me, thought Caro. A man wouldn't matter but another woman . . .

Then Toni smiled and looked into Caro's eyes. 'It's ironic,' she said, 'just as I'm giving my wild ways up, it seems you're starting.'

'Mid-life crisis?' said Caro, smiling too.

'Who cares,' laughed Toni, 'enjoy it while you can. If I remember rightly, women are wonderful!'

'Mmm,' responded Caro, 'of that I'm not in doubt. But I don't know what Jade'll say about it.'

20

Her mother's sexuality was the last thing on Jade's mind as she pushed open the back door on Saturday. She was wondering if Warren would be in the kitchen. They had not communicated since the previous weekend and all week she had been unable to concentrate. Usually Oxford was compulsive, she had been totally in love with its feudal charisma, the charm of which fell on all her friends there. But these few days had seemed like a year. The gracious buildings were imprisoning, the lectures dull, the parties too. The drama was being played out elsewhere and she was missing her central role in it.

Allegra, her best friend and roommate, thought she was worried about her father's disappearance. She was especially caring of Jade because of this, hearing her lines for *An Inspector Calls* and inviting her out for sherry. Jade remained frustrated. The undergraduate men seemed callow and spoiled, lacking in real-world experience. Even rehearsals were without their usual glamour – it was only a play, after all.

The kitchen, she was sorry to see, was empty. Cindy came forward hopefully, wagging her tail and woofing with expectation. Jade gave her a perfunctory pat, then threw down her dufflebag and ran upstairs calling, 'Mum, I'm back, where is everybody?'

The spare room door stood ajar and through it Jade glimpsed a holdall. 'Hello,' she called and when there was no reply, pushed open the door and entered the bedroom. The bed was unmade, the duvet bundled untidily, clothes were scattered about, Jade trod on a sock, in the middle of the carpet was a pile of video cassettes which had tumbled over. The room was obviously inhabited. Puzzled, Jade checked her own room, which looked much as she had left it. Except, she now saw, for some open drawers with clothes hanging out of them. No wonder she'd felt restless in Oxford, she thought, plenty had been going on in her absence.

There was a ring at the front doorbell. Milkman, she thought, wondering if she had enough money to pay him. But when she opened the door, a middle-aged, seedy-looking man in flared trousers and a badly fitting toupee, lounged in the porch.

'Ello,' he began, breaking out in a professional smile. 'You must be Jade . . . I wonder if I could 'ave a word?'

'Are you selling something?' demanded Jade imperiously.

The man's smile widened, revealing nicotine-yellow teeth. 'No . . . no . . . I'm Charlie Barrett . . . from the *Warfleet Chronicle*? You must know my column . . . "Cheeky Charlie's Week"?'

Jade could hardly contain her contempt. 'I don't read it,' she said with a curling lip, 'but what do you want, anyway?'

Charlie's face snapped into business mode. 'A colleague of mine, Glyn Madoc, knows your mother. 'E mentioned your father's gone missin' from home. I thought you might want t' talk to me.'

Jade frowned, in an attempt to give her young face authority. 'Whatever would we want to do that for?'

Charlie said, 'Y' never know. Publicity might 'elp. Someone might know his whereabouts.'

The suggestion that they should advertise for her father seemed to Jade disgusting. 'I don't think so,' she said. 'It's no one else's business.'

'The thing is . . .' said Charlie, placing his scuffed Hush Puppy firmly in the doorway, 'we'll prob'ly run an article anyway. We know you've got 'is love child livin' 'ere. You see . . . local celebrity . . . it's in the public interest . . .'

At this moment Jade saw Warren appear round the corner of the drive, pushing a wailing Harry. Charlie saw him too and,

97

pulling out of his pocket a small Instamatic, began snapping furiously. Jade lunged at the camera shouting, 'Warren!'

Warren looked up, startled by the scuffle. Jade was hanging from Charlie's sleeve, while Charlie ineptly kicked out at her. Warren ran forward as Jade was shoved into the rockery. He caught Charlie by his lapels and head-butted him ferociously. The camera flew out of Charlie's grasp and splashed into the pond. Charlie himself crumpled to the ground clutching his skew-whiff toupee. 'Fucking 'ell,' he muttered.

Warren helped Jade up and together they went to rescue Harry, whose screams had now reached a crescendo. As they hurried to the front door, Charlie staggered up, grabbing at the pram, and shouting that he'd do them for assault . . . he was only doing his job . . . he'd make them bloody sorry!

Jade slammed the door and Warren lifted Harry from the pram, murmuring soothing phrases. They looked at each other, both heaving for breath and then both of them giggled.

They went through to the kitchen where Warren put the now recovered Harry into his bouncer and Jade went to the Aga to warm her freezing fingers. Warren filled the kettle and placed it on the hob, then got some bread slices out of the bread bin.

He's certainly made himself at home, thought Jade, a little resentfully. Somehow it made her redundant.

Warren said, 'You look starved. It's cold out today.' Jade nodded, blowing on her knuckles. Warren came closer and took her hands in his larger, warmer ones. He rubbed hers roughly. 'There was ice on the water barrel this morning,' he said. 'Bulbs'll get a shock, they think it's spring already.' Jade's throat had closed. The nearness of Warren and his intimate handling of her had made her thoroughly speechless. 'That Charlie Barrett's bin hangin' around for days,' said Warren. 'I seen him skulking about the hedge yesterday. Your Ma's not realized.'

'Where is she?' said Jade, suddenly worried Caro would bump into the venomous Charlie.

'I dunno,' said Warren, 'she went out before I was up this morning.'

'You mean . . .' started Jade '. . . it's *you* staying in the spare room?'

'Yeah,' grinned Warren. 'She asked me to stay 'cos Delia's still away. Seems she's tracked your Dad down to America.' The way he said 'America' made it sound properly New World and further away than a mere ride on a Boeing. Jade noticed this at the same time as feeling extremely put out. She drew away from Warren, reclaiming her space and rubbed at the place on her thigh where she had fallen. 'Did 'e hurt you?' said Warren with concern.

Jade shook her head. 'Horrible little peasant,' she said. Really she meant Warren.

'You don't mind do you?' he said now, sensitive to her rejection.

'Mind? Of course not. It's up to her.' She turned away and sharply filled the teapot.

Nothing more was said as they took their mugs of tea to the table. The awkward silence was not broken until the back door opened and Caro came in, flushed and breathless, struggling with bags from the supermarket. Warren leapt up to help her, quite one of the family, thought Jade meanly, and Caro, laughing, came to hug Jade, pressing her cold cheek against her. 'Darling, you're early,' she said, 'I wasn't expecting you till lunchtime.'

'I got a lift,' said Jade offhandedly, feeling she must correct the impression of eagerness.

They told Caro what had happened, chipping in with one another until a veneer of good humour was restored. Caro, however, looked unhappy. 'Oh dear,' she said, 'of course it must look odd. I hadn't thought of doorstepping.' She was thinking, with horror, how much worse it would look, if the press got wind of a Zo story.

As though on cue came the sound of a bike scattering gravel on the driveway. Caro hurried through to the front door, keen to forestall any social embarrassment. Her heart was thumping so loudly she was sure everyone must hear it. She threw open the door and watched Zo dismount, admiring again the tight trousers.

Zo saluted her and approached, helmet in hand, grinning with unashamed sexiness. Her face was glowing from the long drive down, her eyes sparkling with anticipation. Caro hardly had time to stammer 'Hello', when Zo caught her close and kissed her full on the lips, pressing her long legs against her.

Caro pushed her away, flustered. 'No . . . Jade's here . . .' She looked worriedly over Zo's shoulder afraid there might be prying eyes in the rhododendrons.

'Oh. Better behave myself then,' said Zo, contenting herself with a throaty growl at Caro's departing bottom.

They went into the kitchen, where introductions were made. It became clear Zo was staying to lunch when Caro began to prepare it. Jade flounced off, to change she said, and Warren took Harry for his nap. He now slept in the room adjoining Warren's.

Caro was chopping vegetables in a kind of frenzy. Zo came up behind her and slid her arms under Caro's so that her hands were on Caro's breasts. She squeezed them gently. Caro let out a small cry and dropped the knife. Zo's mouth descended and bit her nape. 'Still love me?' she murmured into Caro's neck. Caro felt her insides turn to jelly.

Upstairs, Warren put the sleepy Harry into his cot, watched him for a moment and then, satisfied that he would drop off, crossed the landing and knocked tentatively on Jade's door. Inside her room a CD was playing. It was the one Caro had recognized at the concert. After a moment Jade opened the door. 'Yes,' she said, eyeing Warren with hostility.

'Can I come in?' said Warren.

Jade opened the door wider and let him into the room, which she was tidying. Reclaiming really.

'You're angry with me,' Warren said, pushing the door to and standing with his back to it. Jade tossed her heavy hair so that her Indian earrings jingled. 'What have I done?' asked Warren.

Jade could have said, 'Invaded my home, upset my life, made me unsure of everything.' Instead she opened a cupboard and aggressively thrust some boots into it.

When she turned, Warren was leaning against the door, his

arms folded and a slight smile on his face. His gold-lashed eyes were narrowed against the window light which also picked out the fine line of his cheekbone. She was enraged at his easy beauty, his self-possession, what seemed to her his insolence. She crossed the room quickly and struck him on the face. He caught her wrist and bent it back, his eyes flashing angry amber. From below came Caro's voice, calling that lunch was ready.

21

Lunch had not been a success. It was a strained affair – everyone overly polite and avoiding eye contact. Caro apologized to Jade for not letting her know about Warren, Jade shrugged carelessly as though nothing could matter less. Zo passed people salt and water, alert to their needs: Caro's she assuaged by pressing her knee under the table. Warren was silent throughout and especially careful with his cutlery.

Afterwards Zo demanded a tour of Warfleet, and Caro offered to take her. Warren disappeared into the drawing room with a pile of cassettes. Jade was left to wander unhappily round the garden. She was puzzled by Zo's presence. She was an extra and unlooked-for player in the tragedy, usurping Jade's role as moral supporter.

Thoroughly disgruntled, she struck the icy ground with a stick she had picked up, then prodded the ice on the water barrel claimed by Warren. She poked it until it cracked into crazy paving and then, with malicious satisfaction, bored a hole in its centre through which brown water bubbled. She imagined Warren upended in the barrel like Clarence in the butt of Malmsey.

It was freezing in the garden, despite the bright sun, and calling Cindy, who was snuffling in the undergrowth of the frostily budded lilac, Jade went back to the warmth of the kitchen. She stomped about flinging dishes into the dishwasher. It was unlike Caro, she thought, with surprise and irritation, to leave the kitchen so untidy.

From the other room came the sound of Warren's video, loud music and the occasional scream; presumably it was a horror one. Jade refused to be tempted. She despised the video culture. It was fashionable among her friends at Oxford to decry it as the reason for the breakdown of society, kids brought up on violence etc. Trust Warren, yet again, to reveal the peasant in his nature.

She listened a moment outside the door then pushed it open and ignoring a piercing shriek from the television, marched across to the bookcase and removed several books ostentatiously. Warren did not look up, but she was aware that he hastily adjusted his position on the sofa, to make it seem less proprietorial. Turning slightly in his direction, she flicked through the books, as though searching for a quotation. Then sighing and shaking her head towards the screen, as though the cheap sound made proper thought impossible, she marched out again, the books clasped to her bosom. She smiled grimly as she climbed the stairs. That would show him. She glanced down to see what books she had picked up. They were *Howards End* and *Lady Chatterley's Lover*.

Zo and Caro did the tour of Warfleet in twenty minutes. Zo insisted they take the bike, she'd brought another helmet specially. Caro couldn't help wondering who had worn it before. But in the exhilaration of the ride, clasping Zo's warm leather waist, feeling their thighs wedged together, she forgot to be anxious and let herself be wild. It was like being in the movies.

She noticed a couple of disapproving stares as they roared down the High Street. Marsha Snelgrove stepped smartly back from the crossing as Zo throttled through the stripes. Caro hid her laughing face in Zo's taut back. Oh God, if she'd been recognized . . . ! The flying jacket was padded and warm, stretched across Zo's wide shoulders. Caro left her cheek there, enjoying the shelter from the wind. She felt safe for the first time in ages.

As Zo zoomed along the promenade, Caro shouted that they should stop for some tea. Zo taxied to a stop in front of the Delphinium Tearooms. They dismounted, Caro stiffly, and dangling their helmets, crossed from the bleak seaside to the foggy warmth of the Delphinium, with its open coal fire and steamy teapots.

103

They caused rather a stir as they entered. Teddy Forbes looked up from his paper and raised his eyebrows theatrically. He exchanged an oeillade with Rumer Petulengro, who had come down for a bun. She did Tarot upstairs on a Saturday. May Clark, who ran the Delphinium and was a kind soul, dodged between the feet and bags and showed them to a table. She sat them next to Jim and Peggy Bacon, who eyed Zo's buckled boots with alarm. They owned the High Street shoe shop.

Caro felt a hysterical urge to shout. In minutes her appearance would be known to 'le tout Warfleet'; it was too late now for caution. They ordered a pot of tea for two, a pleasure in itself, thought Caro, used for a long time to the lonely one-pot, and toasted teacakes with strawberry jam. Zo's appetite was prodigious. Caro watched with solicitous pleasure as she cleared the plate, then leaned forward and brushed a buttery crumb from the corner of Zo's mouth, aware that all eyes were upon her.

She began in a low voice to tell Zo the Sagas of Warfleet. The violent past, the smuggling and wrecking, the brave lifeboat men, the Cream Tea Wars . . . with a nod to May . . . the Masonic intrigues, the rival pubs, the petition against the new fish and chip shop. With each new subject Zo burst with giggles and exclamations. At last she said, 'You should write it down. They'd make wonderful stories.' Caro shook her head, holding up her hands to ward off the suggestion that she might have a talent for it. 'I'm serious,' Zo persisted. 'I told you, stories are hot. People have forgotten how to write them.' Caro filled up their cups, smiling indulgently. Zo said, 'I've brought some stuff down for you to read. I want reports by Friday.' Her voice had taken on a tough, businesslike edge. The change was, to Caro, quite startling.

The afternoon had clouded over by the time they left the teashop. They walked for a while along the prom, the seagulls wheeling above them. The sea was granite-grey today, the breakers by the pier end tremendous. Caro pointed out Jeremy's shop, Euroantiques. Connor stood glumly among them, staring out of the window. There was no sign of Jeremy.

Back at the house, Jade had fallen into a miserable sleep. She was jolted from it by the return of the bike. Looking out of her window, she was further affronted by the sight of her mother riding pillion.

The Radcliffe household fell into darkness early that night. At dinner, which Zo had helped Caro to cook while Jade laid the table with bad grace, Jade treated them to a monologue on the state of The Culture. Laziness. Fecklessness. Lack of Responsibility. No wonder the country was falling into disintegration. Many of her remarks were directed towards Warren, who sat pushing mangetouts round his plate, occasionally glancing wild-eyed at the doorway.

'I'm going out for the evening . . . if that's all right,' he said gruffly to Caro, as he helped clear plates.

'Fine,' she said, 'you've got your key.'

Jade trembled so with anger that she almost dropped the gravy. How dare he just escape like that! It was cowardly. Despicable!

She went to bed soon after, leaving her mother and Zo in the drawing room listening to records. Caro had asked, unaccountably, to borrow some of Jade's CDs, had mentioned one in particular.

Jade lay in bed wondering where Warren had gone. To some rave, she supposed, where he would be taking Ecstasy and dancing. Perhaps worse. She could not bear this thought and turned on to her side clutching the pillow. After a while she got up and removed her teddy bear from the chair. She got back into bed hugging him.

She must have slept because she didn't remember anything more until she was suddenly awake in darkness. She listened, holding her breath for the sound which had awoken her. A creaking floorboard. Yes, there it was again. She sat up, silently pushed back the bedclothes and crept to the door. She opened it a crack and peered into the blackness. She was sure she caught her mother's door closing. She stepped on to the landing, carefully avoiding the warning boards she had known from childhood.

Not a sound came from Caro's room. But, beneath the sill of Warren's door was a thin line of light. Jade was irresistibly drawn to it.

Carefully, carefully she opened the door. There was the sound of soft, even breathing. The light, she now saw, was from the bedside lamp. It fell on Warren's sleeping form, bathing the blond locks spread out on the pillow, the slightly swollen parted lips, the well-defined torso, with a sepia halo. Jade caught her breath, Warren had kicked the duvet to the floor and lay there quite naked. She saw the long shapely legs covered with gold-glinting down. The sleeping cock curled innocently between them, the arms flung out in peaceful abandon. He looked like a Raphael painting.

As if magnetized she drew closer and picked up the duvet. She thought he would be cold and she would cover him with it, but the tender gesture froze midway when Warren opened his eyes and looked at her. Without a word, he stretched out an arm and pulled Jade down to him. She half fell on to his chest and lay there for a moment quietly. Then she moved so that her body fell between Warren's warm open thighs. He put an arm around her back and held her tight. With his other hand he lifted her nightdress and let his cock slide into her. They stayed perfectly still, as if any move would explode the agony flowing between them. Then Jade cried out and Warren covered her mouth and caught a great mass of her hair in his teeth to smother his own cries of passion.

22

As the plane touched down at Dublin airport, a great feeling of relief took hold of Delia. It was good to be back on relatively familiar ground. She no longer felt at home in America. Beside her, Sean slept soundly, his nervy constitution exhausted by their travels. He had elected to go straight home, another relief to Delia.

She thought she would get to the refuge and book herself in before telephoning Caro. She hoped they were managing all right. To her surprise she found she'd missed Warfleet.

She had arranged a hire car at the airport and picked up a map at the same time. Sean pointed out the route into Wicklow. He declined a lift to his flat, off St Stephen's Green, saying he wouldn't subject her to Dublin's vicious one-way systems. He could be quite sweet really, and now she was getting rid of him she could see again the attractive young man she'd first invited to sleep with her. She promised to keep him in touch with everything that happened and see him on her way back to London. Almost satisfied, he climbed into a cab. His head lolled back in an instant.

Delia felt wonderfully free as she drove the Nissan Bluebird. The day was a bright one and if her tights had been clean and her clothes less slept in, she might have hummed to the radio. She couldn't wait for a hot tub to soak in.

Wicklow's mountains reared up before her, the purplish Sugarloaf dominating the horizon. Soon she turned off the main road and wove up muddy lanes, flanked by fields full of sheep. There was frost on the hedgerows. She passed farms and cottages of postcard cuteness interspersed with brutal breeze-block haciendas and stooping lean-tos of corrugated iron. There was a hillock dotted with tiny lambs; they made her think of Harry.

After an hour or so she began to look for signs to the retreat, a converted Benedictine monastery. A turning so tiny it was almost a track led to an ornate iron gate, through which she could see a great curve of drive and, above the trees, a tower.

She had called the retreat from LA, pretending to be a lady writer with a major novel to finish. In retrospect she felt this was rather dull; she should have pleaded a writer's block, or at least a nervous breakdown . . . but the soft Irish voice at the end of the phone had been completely understanding.

Now, standing in the vast vaulted hall, with its stained-glass windows, she felt a draining of confidence. The coloured glass cast wonderful lozenges on the tiles, but the stern-faced saints seemed to judge her.

She had to ring a little bell on the carved oak desk several times before anyone appeared. Then a small round person, who introduced himself as Father Doyle, came through a Gothic arch to greet her. His voice was the soft, accommodating one from the telephone, but Delia could not shake off the impression that everything about her was being noted and possibly found wanting.

Her room, however, was divine. Literally, in fact, as Father Doyle explained to her it had once held sacred relics. Its high-ceilinged whiteness reminded Delia of Italy and the view from its pointed windows was, in every direction, spectacular. As soon as Father Doyle had gone, after pointing out the no smoking sign and explaining about the heating, she threw herself down on the gracefully ancient bed, which creaked slightly but otherwise stood fast, and stripped off the offending tights and other sticky garments. A few moments later she was fast asleep, rolled up in the Irish lace counterpane.

When she woke up it was dusky and for the moment she couldn't remember where she was. She disentangled herself from the bed and fumbled for a light switch, then hurried to close the shutters as she was lit up in her underwear. The outside world looked misty and interesting. There was water, she could just make out – she'd explore the grounds later. Her watch told her it was 8.00 AM, LA time, she remembered. She adjusted it to four o'clock and pulled on jeans and a sweater.

A notice outside the door told her not to whistle, sing or talk in the corridors and to respect the privacy of other guests. She walked down the polished wooden floor on tiptoe and wished she had bought some espadrilles.

The hall was deserted. Through huge double doors she could see the refectory, with a long table laid out for dining. So, the guests did sometimes get together. She pushed at another door which swung back to reveal a library, leather armchairs around an empty grate and important-looking books from floor to ceiling. A third door led into a sitting room with chintzy furniture and a television. It too was cold and empty. There was not a sound and although the little bell still stood on the desk, Delia hesitated to ring it. It seemed an affront to the other guests, who obviously took privacy seriously.

Supper, her first opportunity to corner Sebastian – she was still not sure how she would do this: an exposé at the refectory table was unthinkable – would not be for some time, she was sure. She decided she would have a walk outside, get to know the territory.

A fine mizzle was falling. This was what the Irish called 'the soft air', Delia supposed. She pulled her scarf closer and stepped down through a beautiful stone terraced garden – how pretty it must look in the summer, she thought – to an ornamental lake. The water stretched for some distance. It was dotted with reedy islands and on the other side were woods of birch. A light mist lay on top of the ripples. It was still and very calming.

As Delia gazed, two swans glided out of the mist and made a serene progress across the water. They glowed like mother-of-pearl in the half-light. They were together yet with distance between. They mated for life, remembered Delia. Suddenly she felt tears running down her face. Her whole body convulsed and great sobs broke out of her. She clutched at her ribcage from where the pain seemed to come. What on earth was the matter?

Was it the swans? But she had never craved that kind of partnership. Never wanted to bond with another for life. She prized her independence, her separateness, surely . . . ?

Rubbing her wet face with her sleeve, she turned away from the ethereal creatures, fading now on the darkening lake, and stumbled back up the stone steps to the house, from which cheerful yellow light now beamed. Her one thought was the telephone. She must get back in touch with reality.

In the bedroom the phone extension rang and rang. Eventually Zo put out an arm and picked it up. 'Hello,' she said sleepily.

'It's Delia,' came an anxious voice, sounding far away. 'Hello, hello Caro . . . ?'

Zo shook herself quickly awake. 'It's Zo,' she corrected. 'I'm . . . er . . . visiting.'

'Oh,' said the voice, turning sharper. 'Is everything all right?'

'Fine. Fine,' said Zo. 'How's LA?'

'I'm not in LA. I'm in Ireland.'

'Ireland,' repeated Zo.

'It's a long story,' said Delia, sounding exasperated. 'Look, my money's going to run out. Just tell Caro that I'm still on the hunt, oh . . . and how's Harry?'

'Gorgeous,' said Zo. 'He's got two teeth.'

'Two!' exclaimed Delia, as the pips went.

Zo replaced the phone and turned over, spooning herself around Caro's warm, sleeping body. They had taken advantage of Jade and Warren's absence on a walk to steal a few hours in bed. Zo slid her arms round Caro so that her hands cupped Caro's belly. She massaged softly, hoping Caro would wake. The time before the young ones got back was precious.

Delia put down the phone and stood in the booth for some moments. There had been something unsettling about the conversation. What was Zo doing there and how had Harry managed to get *two* teeth in her absence? She realized, with dismay, that what she was feeling was homesick. She must be jet-lagged, she decided, to be having all these contradictory and destructive emotions. What she needed was a good hot meal. With relief, she heard the gong banging.

The gaggle of eccentrics who collected at the refectory table made Delia's heart sink further. They seemed like parodies of Artists, with their baggy clothes and unkempt hair. There was not a sign of Sebastian. She realized she had been depending upon him for moral support. He, at least, would be 'like' her.

Everyone served themselves from large earthenware pots, left over, Delia supposed, from the days of the monastery. The food, however, was good and plentiful. The Artists ate greedily: there was no sense of denial.

Delia had been introduced by Father Doyle. She had opted, when booking, for a nom de plume, Dorothea Harrison, but she need not have worried, as few took any notice. A booming man, shovelling through a large plateful of meat, asked her what she did, and when she said wrote novels, looked resigned and turned his attention to a tureen of vegetables. Delia was unusually hungry. In LA she had been super-conscious of diet and had halved every portion she'd been given – a legacy from her anorexic days when the server had been her mother – but here she fed herself generously, drank the cold spring water and was grateful.

After dinner she wandered from room to room, searching for Sebastian. A fire had been lit in the library, but the booming man had taken up residence there and she flinched from conversation. A couple of people were watching television, but the room was chilly and uninviting. She discovered, at reception, a list of those who were in retreat. Sebastian's name was not on it, but that didn't mean anything, she reassured herself: he, like her, could be using a false one. There again, there were more names on the list than people she had met, so maybe he had dinner in his room, couldn't stand the company. Sean's book was set in Dublin, but had scenes also in the country nearby – maybe Seb had gone out on a 'recce'. Running through these options made Delia suddenly weary. The search, she had to admit, was taking it out of her. If this was another red herring . . .

111

She climbed the great oak stairs to her room, aware of every dragging footstep. When she entered again the big bare bedroom she was aware of how small she felt in it. She took Sebastian's photo out of her wallet and propped it up on the mantelpiece. The half-shielded, laughing eyes challenged her.

The smile seemed seductive but had something sad in it too . . . shivering, she turned away. At this moment she'd be glad to have even Sean. She contented herself with a hot water bottle she found in the bottom of the closet.

Caro and Zo were making love when they heard the back door open. Zo held herself off for a moment but Caro whispered, 'Don't stop,' and pulled Zo's sweat-streaked body back down to her. They climaxed quickly, murmuring brokenly into each other's neck, then lay still, holding each other soundlessly and listening for Jade and Warren. Laughter came from downstairs and the sound of Harry's chuckles.

'Jade's cheered up,' whispered Zo.

In the light filtering through the half-drawn curtains, Caro could catch her gappy grin and the twinkle in her eyes. 'This makes me nervous,' she whispered back. 'I'd rather tell her before she finds out. I feel like a naughty schoolgirl.'

'Go easy,' said Zo, 'she's only a kid.' Caro couldn't help laughing at Zo's assumption of maturity. 'I'm twenty-nine,' said Zo, 'that's old. Besides, I'm very experienced.'

Caro had to admit that she was. Beside Zo she felt like a novice, despite having twenty years on her. 'Must you go tonight?' she pleaded, and when Zo nodded, caught her head in her hands and kissed her almost angrily.

Zo took Caro's hands and held them away, nibbling softly at the fingers. She looked into Caro's searching eyes, seeing her anxiety about age, sex, Sebastian, Jade . . . seeing her fear of losing. 'Don't worry,' she smiled, 'I'll be back.' She laid her head on Caro's breast, calming the frightened heartbeat. 'We've got plenty of time,' she said gently.

112

23

Across the boggy water meadow pitted with cow hoof puddles, came two small boys. One carried a jam jar and a net and the other a ghetto blaster. Oasis roared across the muddy bank, startling a couple of coots, as the boys made camp at the water's edge.

'This is a good place,' said Dave. 'We found a whole lot 'ere las' year.' The boys' half-term project was to gather evidence of seasonal change. Dave had decided on frogspawn.

'Iss too cold,' said Sidney, hanging back.

'Don't be wet,' said Dave, splashing into the water. The muddy bubbles burst over his expensive trainers and soaked his rolled-up tracksuit bottoms. 'Chuck us that,' he said, indicating a broken length of branch on the bank. He poked about in the shallows while Sidney followed more gingerly, holding his jeans bunched out of the water.

Dave sloshed out of the little bay and rounded a jutting tree root. Sidney stood irresolutely watching.

''Ere,' Dave shouted, 'come and look at this!'

'Have you found some?' called Sidney hopefully. He picked his way past the tree to where Dave was standing. In the water was a cloth-coloured hump with sinister-looking indentations. 'Iss a dead dog,' opined Sidney standing well back.

'Less 'ave a look,' urged Dave, prodding the bundle with his stick.

'Might be maggotty,' considered Sidney.

'Use 'em for bait,' said Dave, not one to let an opportunity pass. He bent down and dug the pointed end of the stick into the fabric, which, rotten with water, tore across quickly.

Purplish-white flesh appeared through the rent and even Dave was taken aback, standing up to reconsider. "S a body,' he said, having got his breath and his courage back.

'Nah,' said Sidney, 'you're windin' me up.'

'Look for yourself,' said Dave, taking a step or two back.

Sidney came up the bank, slipping and sliding in the mud, and bent forward to look at the sliver. 'Yeah,' he said at last, 'bloody 'ell.'

"Elp me,' said Dave bending again and tugging at the hump.

'What you gonna do?' said Sidney looking worried.

'Get it out, 'course. We wanna 'ave a proper look at it.'

The two boys heaved at the sodden lump, falling back into the mud as it suddenly gave way and surfaced.

'Uurrgh, it touched me!' screamed Sidney, divided between excitement and horror.

'Fuckin' sissy,' dismissed Dave. He kicked the body with his foot, forcing it to roll over. It fell like a dummy into a semi-sitting position. The two boys stared at the face, bloated and partially scavenged. One eyeball was missing. 'Iss a bloke,' stated Dave. 'I reckon.'

Sidney nodded, taking in the torn trousers. 'Le's see if 'is willy's still there,' he said.

Nudging each other on they approached the body and with the stick at arm's length, ripped into the trousers. A pale sad penis appeared, dark crinkly hair bursting above it. The boys whooped and swapped the stick between them, taking turns to poke at it. After a while they got bored with this and started to chuck pebbles at the genitals, screeching with laughter when they scored a bullseye.

'Less keep 'im,' said Sidney.

'What, don't tell?'

'Yeah,' urged his friend. 'We can charge for lookin' at 'im.'

'Huh,' laughed Dave, 'won't Jason be sick. We'll put 'im back under the tree. Iss dark there, no one'll find 'im.'

They buffeted the body with their trainers until it rolled back into the water, then towed it with the stick hooked through a

114

hole back to the tangle of tree root. They shoved with their feet until they'd wedged it in tight; a bit of material tore off and floated free, causing them both to shudder. Sidney punished the corpse by poking at its other eyeball.

'Iss gettin' late,' said Dave, 'less go now.' Neither boy wanted to be around the spot as the early night fell.

'Swear not t' tell,' said Sidney, as they squelched up the bank. 'If you do they'll take it away from us.'

They scampered across the field. Partners in crime. Dreading what their mothers would say about the state of their clothing.

24

The *Warfleet Chronicle* came out on Tuesdays and Mrs Strongitharm always brought it up when she came to do the cleaning. Caro was coming into the kitchen with a pile of washing when Mrs S. plonked it down on the table. 'Seen that?' she said with relish. Caro glanced over the page; the usual articles about horse maiming and capsized fishing boats met her eye. 'Page three,' said Mrs Strongitharm, obligingly turning to it.

MYSTERY OF WARFLEET MEDIA MAN, blared the headline. Below it was a blurred photo of what appeared to be an arm. Looking closer, Caro saw by the thongs that it was Jade's. Charlie must have salvaged a negative. With mounting dismay she read the article, bylined by Charlie Barrett, which described the disappearance of Seb and Charlie's encounter with 'Radcliffe's daughter, Jade, (19)', in particularly vivid language. Harry was referred to as Seb's 'love-child with librarian (32)' and Caro as 'estranged wife (50)', which unreasonably enraged her.

Mrs Strongitharm stood by the Aga with folded arms. Her face was arranged in a Job's comforter type of smile. There was nothing quite as satisfactory as being the bearer of bad tidings. 'You'll 'ave the police up,' she said. The implication in the article was clearly that there'd been a cover-up, though by whom, Charlie didn't specify.

Caro bunged washing indiscriminately into the front-loader. 'The windows need doing today,' she said, 'the sun makes them look very smeary.' This indirect criticism produced a snort from Mrs Strongitharm, but she shifted her bulk from the Aga.

As Caro was hanging out the washing a little later, Sergeant Plummer appeared on his bicycle. He stopped at the back gate and laboriously chained his bike to it, then entered, politely closing the gate, and touched his brow to Caro. 'Mornin' Mrs Radcliffe,' he said. 'Have you got a moment?'

'Of course. Come in,' said Caro, wiping her hands. 'I suppose it's about that article.'

'In a way,' said Sergeant Plummer, taking everything in his own time.

He accepted a cup of tea and a biscuit, patted Cindy and cleared his throat. 'You see . . . it's not so much what it said . . . we all know Charlie, he has t' make a story . . . the problem is . . .' He paused. Caro wondered if he was about to warn her that they were bringing in a mechanical digger to excavate the back garden, but after surveying the ceiling for so long she began to worry about cobwebs, Sergeant Plummer continued, 'Charlie's made a charge, against your daughter . . . we're forced to examine the evidence.'

'What charge?' demanded Caro.

'Assault. And damage to property.'

'Well really!' Caro exploded.

'It was worse. 'E wanted GBH. We managed to dissuade him.'

'That wretched man,' cried Caro, her annoyance over the mis-quoted age coming back to her. 'He trespassed on our property, forced his way in, attacked and threatened my daughter . . . !'

'If there are any witnesses . . . ?' suggested Sergeant Plummer, looking encouragingly at Caro.

'Certainly,' said Caro, 'there's Warren Peabody.'

'Well now, Warren's record is not that dependable,' said the sergeant. 'And Charlie's named him, too.'

'It's his word against theirs,' said Caro firmly.

Sergeant Plummer sighed. 'Next time your daughter's home, 'ave them pop down and see me, eh? We'll try to get it sorted.'

After he had gone, Caro sank down heavily in the wicker chair and dropped her head to her hands. Cindy raised a sleepy eyelid and seeing tears plop between Caro's fingers, struggled across and laid her head on her knees, sighing sympathetically. Caro had thought the tears were over. Instead she felt more disturbed than

117

ever. If only she could get away . . . she felt suddenly constricted by her life here.

Zo, she thought suddenly, she'd go and see Zo. They had arranged to meet midweek. And it was almost Wednesday.

Without thinking further, she scribbled a note to Warren, 'Called to London . . . friend in distress . . . probably see you later', forked out Mrs Strongitharm's outrageous twenty-five quid, scrubbed her face and applied some colour, and climbed into the car, dressed in an assortment of Jade's clothing. It crossed her mind that if Jade had noticed missing articles surfacing on her mother, she had said nothing.

She parked the car on a meter opposite Zo's office and crossed over, already feeling better. The girl at reception told her, however, that Zo was 'working from home today'. Caro was taken aback. Zo hadn't mentioned working from home – there again, why should she? Hampstead was not that far, after all: she returned to the car and drove up there. She had a moment of doubt as she parked the car. Suppose Zo felt uncomfortable, tracked to her home. She might think Caro was intrusive? The desire to see her was so overwhelming, though, that she dismissed the feeling as her usual paranoia and set off up the road, a silly smile spreading over her features.

As she neared Zo's house she heard a door open and through the branches of a forsythia bush saw that it was Zo's door and a young woman was descending the steps. She had short dark hair and a denim jacket – Caro knew before she saw Zo a couple of paces behind that this was one of Zo's lovers. She stood frozen still behind the bush as the couple emerged on to the pavement, talking and laughing. Zo was the taller and she put her arm around the other girl, hugging her close. Caro thought her heart would burst as they swung jauntily along the road, disappearing at the corner.

She staggered against the wall and hung there for a moment, certain she would be sick into a clutter of dustbins and bottles. After a long time she straightened, grateful for the prickly twigs that stung her face and brought her back to reality. She managed to walk, with several stops, back to the car . . . it was important to get away . . . but once in it, she sat for another few minutes with her head flopped on to the steering wheel. Never had she experienced such shock. Not even with Sebastian.

She could not go home, of that she was sure. How could she appear normal? Toni was out of the question – her warning came back to Caro now, bringing a wave of humiliation. At last she drove, recklessly it seemed, as she could hardly see the road, to Hampstead Heath, where she wandered about like a lost soul, staring at the ponds and ducks and people who were all in couples.

She waited until it was dark. She had a plan. Not so much a plan perhaps as a compulsion. She would go back to the flat and watch again. She had to know for certain. Even as she returned to the car, she knew she was being ridiculous. A woman of fifty . . . as Charlie had pointed out . . . behaving like an adolescent! She seemed to be on automatic pilot, though, and nothing would deflect this other being from pursuing its awful purpose.

She parked between street lights and crept back to her bush. She'd intended merely to watch and wait, but when she saw a light on in Zo's upper room, she knew she would ring the door-bell. 'Catch them at it', was her thought. She wanted to see Zo's embarrassment and shock. Wanted her to feel as she had.

She marched up the steps, preparing her face and excuse (the dentist). Zo would have to invite her in: Caro almost enjoyed imagining her expression. She put her finger on the bell and pushed hard. Now, she thought, they would be scrambling into their clothes, perhaps tossing down the remains of champagne, complaining a little at the nuisance. Each thought hit the dagger in her gut, but she couldn't resist twisting it.

She heard feet tripping down the stairs. A light went on in the hall and the door was opened. Zo stood there in a vest and cutoff jeans. Caro wanted her terribly.

'God!' said Zo, 'what a great surprise. I was just going to ring you.'

She pulled the stunned Caro over the threshold and hugged her. Caro's speech had flown, she stood inside Zo's embrace, her

119

heart and head whirling. 'Can you stay?' Zo was saying. 'I can make some food. I wish I'd got something special.'

She drew Caro up the stairs and into her flat. Mozart was playing and the fire was on, manuscripts were scattered on the desk – clearly Zo had been working. Now Zo was in the kitchen, clinking glasses and opening the fridge. She seemed unaware of Caro's state and chattered on about the pile of work . . . the phone at the office . . . the strain of reading . . . needing glasses . . . the marvel of Caro's appearance. She returned with two glasses and gave one to Caro, smiling into her eyes. Caro took the glass and burst into desperate, howling tears. Zo looked astonished. She retrieved the glass and guided Caro to the fire, saying worriedly, 'Darling, darling . . . what is it?'

Caro heaved and gasped but could not speak. Zo held her and stroked her back, saying, 'Hush now. Hush now. Tell me.'

At last Caro looked up and choking between words, said, 'I thought . . . you had . . . someone . . . here . . .'

Zo looked puzzled. 'Yes?' she said. 'So what?'

'I . . . came . . . by . . . earlier . . .' The words tailed away as Caro saw Zo realize what she meant.

'And,' said Zo, 'you saw me with Mel?'

Caro nodded.

A kind of resigned grimace crossed Zo's face. She groaned slightly and moved apart from Caro.

'Who is Mel?' said Caro. Zo shook her head, but Caro went on relentlessly. 'She's your lover, isn't she? The owner of the other helmet.'

Zo gave a short laugh then, after a pause, said, '*Was* my lover. Isn't now. Not for a long time.'

'But you seemed so . . .'

'Intimate?' Zo finished for her. 'We are. We know each other well. I'll always love her.' Caro's head collapsed. Her body shook. She had been right then. Zo knelt on the rug and hugged Caro's knees. She said, 'You'd have had to know sooner or later. But it's no threat to us. As for the helmet, you couldn't be more wrong . . . she's terrified of the motorbike.'

Caro leaned back and sighed. She no longer knew what to believe. She was exhausted. Zo too leaned away. She looked at Caro and said, 'But if she was still my lover, would it matter?'

'*Matter!*' said Caro, 'if you *knew* what I'd been *through* . . .' She meant with Sebastian.

'I won't betray you,' said Zo, 'but I won't be possessed by you either.'

Caro said sulkily, 'I don't understand.'

'I love you,' said Zo, 'I'm committed to you. In my book that means for ever.'

'Did you say that to Mel?' Caro accused.

'Yes,' replied Zo, 'that's why we're still friends.'

'I don't want to be your friend,' said Caro.

Zo laughed and took Caro's hands. 'Not for a long time yet,' she said. 'We're still very much lovers.'

She pulled Caro towards her and kissed her neck and face. Tiny nuzzly kisses. As Caro calmed down, Zo said softly, 'It's not me you're looking for, it's yourself. I'm willing to help you find it.'

Caro clung to her, fighting to understand. There was something in Zo that she wanted. More than her nearness and her warmth, more than her hands on her body and her tongue inside it. But for now those things would do. Slowly the giddiness of desire took them over . . . they slipped down to the rug and made love to each other with passion.

25

Jade's rehearsals had gone well that week. She saw herself now as Nina in *The Seagull*, someone changed by her real-life experience.

On Wednesday Caro phoned to tell her a real Inspector had called. Jade was surprised but unimpressed. Sergeant Plummer didn't have a significant role – he was the buffoon of low comedy. Caro had sounded worried, though. 'Are you busy this afternoon?' she'd asked tentatively. 'I'm in London. I thought I might drive up and see you.'

'About Sergeant Plummer?' said Jade.

'Not just him . . . there's something else . . .'

'Okay,' said Jade, intrigued now.

Caro had had a challenging day. She'd woken at 5.00 AM, cramped and cold on Zo's floor. The fire had died down and although Zo still held her, even the youthful furnace of her body had chilled. They had crawled to the futon and pulled the duvet up. Caro's teeth had been chattering and it took a lot of cuddling and sleepy chubbing from Zo, for her to unclench them and fall asleep again.

This morning Zo had kissed her tenderly and promised to be in touch soon. But Caro had a residue of doubt (how could she leave Zo to the temptations of London? She wanted to watch her every moment of the day) and serious intimations of mortality.

She took those to Ingrid later. So much had happened since their last session, Caro hardly knew where to begin. Ingrid waited, finger poised on temple, then said, 'So you're coming to terms with the notion of death. That is normal at fifty.'

Was everyone, Caro wondered, in a conspiracy with Charlie?

'It's more,' she tried to explain, 'that Zo reminds me of something I've lost . . . or perhaps haven't found yet.'

'Yourself as a separate person,' suggested Ingrid, echoing what Zo had said last evening. They were right, thought Caro, she'd been daughter, mother and wife first. Her years of devotion to Seb's needs and desires went through her head. But for once he wasn't mentioned.

She met Jade for tea in the fake antique lounge of the Randolph Hotel. It was full, as usual, of Americans. A lady harpist plucked at 'Greensleeves' in the corner. Caro was dressed rather oddly, thought Jade, recognizing one or two garments. She decided not to query it, however, and chatted about rehearsals until Earl Grey tea and scones with jam and cream were delivered.

The air of English cosiness was shattered a moment later by the news Caro, in a low voice, delivered.

'You *what*!' said Jade, looking round swiftly to see if anyone else had heard her mother declare herself a pervert. But the Texans at the next table, with their Burberrys and maps, went on murmuring about the Cotswolds.

'Toni says everyone's bisexual . . .' Caro tried, but Jade cut her off, hissing, 'Mother, don't be disgusting!'

Caro suddenly became angry. 'There's nothing disgusting about it,' she said, quite loudly now. 'Love is wonderful wherever you find it.'

Jade had gone dark red. She pushed a splodge of jam round her plate – she was thinking of Warren. A deep shame invaded her . . . love might be wonderful but it was also very embarrassing. That her mother was prepared to reveal this unsuitable passion, shocked her. There was no way she'd tell about Warren.

Looking at her daughter's closed and mutinous face, Caro was filled with despair. Would this desire of the younger to destroy the older go on, biblically, generation to generation? Surely they could break the pattern. 'Darling, won't you try to understand?' she begged.

Jade looked tearful. 'Don't talk about it any more,' she choked. 'I've got an important run-through.'

Caro sighed and called for the bill. She had a certain sympathy with Jade . . . mothers didn't rush off and have lesbian affairs and expose them in Oxford tearooms. They stayed home, cooked and shopped, grew old with a grey shawl around them. Too bad, she thought, amazed at how little guilt she felt. Ingrid's words of that morning came back to her: 'In the end we are all alone. We have to find our own salvation.'

26

It was clear to Delia within twenty-four hours that Sebastian was not at the refuge. She suspected he never had been and decided to tackle Father Doyle about it at the earliest opportunity. This proved to be difficult, as he was never around. It seemed he materialized, liked a ghostly janitor, only when people were arriving. Meanwhile, the days slipped by, as the place hypnotized her with its peace and lulled her with its beauty. She found herself wandering in the grounds, the only place she could smoke (and hum), as though she hadn't any pressure to get back. As though she wasn't on a job, but really in retreat. She almost got a notebook for some jotting.

The artists had separated out more now into individual personalities. The booming man was Homer Gilliray, a literary critic: he held forth on The Culture at every mealtime. Delia listened at first, with an attempt at politeness, but found herself in constant disagreement. She assumed after a while that he simply had no taste, an opinion borne out when she dipped into one of his books, from which he was constantly quoting. There was a painter called Bryan, who by contrast never said a word – Delia imagined his subjects were onanistic – a sculptor, who looked like a slab of granite himself, a poet or two, and several intense young women who held conversations over dinner about the creative process. They irritated Delia and she dealt with them rather as though they were her own writers, saying snappishly that it didn't matter a toss whether you word-processed or wrote in Braille, it was what you were saying that counted. This comment caused a silence at the refectory table. Delia bit her napkin and reminded herself that she too, was supposed to be an Artist.

125

Truthfully she hardly gave work a thought. Homer demanded to know, one evening, what she thought of the nominations for a coming literary prize. Delia had no answer. Despite the fact that one of her authors was on the shortlist, she'd forgotten about it. This search had taken over her life. Had become, in fact, an obsession.

She tried to draw the guests, one by one, on the subject of Sebastian. '. . . He's got these dark, sort of brooding eyes . . . longish hair . . . a wolfish smile . . .' She realized, with an inward cackle, that she was describing Heathcliff. At night she lay sleepless and cold in her bed. She conjured images of Seb as the Byronic devil of romance, and moved her own hands around her body, as much to keep warm as anything. Nothing satisfied her. There was an ache inside her that began in her bowel and rose to her throat. She was empty and wanted to be full. She pressed her palms on her flat stomach and knew it wasn't sex she wanted, it was love. Love and healing.

She pounced on Father Doyle as he came out of his sanctuary one evening with an armful of Guinness bottles. Father Doyle's cherry-pink lips folded inwards and his face took on a distant look. 'We never discuss our guests,' he said, 'it isn't at all our policy.'

'No, no, of course . . .' said Delia hastily, 'it's just that he's a friend . . . We agreed we'd meet here. I'm surprised and a little puzzled.'

'Things in life are puzzling,' said Father Doyle, in the manner of a confessor, 'people's behaviour especially. You seem troubled, Dorothea. In your soul? You know,' he became confidential, 'the Buddhists believe we must accept life as it is and not be continually searching.' He rolled away, as though his feet were on casters, leaving Delia standing speechless. It was almost as though he knew about her quest. Yet who could have told him?

She decided, as she sank into a musty leather armchair in the library with *The Tibetan Book of the Dead* on her lap, that his remark was purely coincidental. Anything else was too uncomfortable.

The *Book of the Dead* seemed very bossy and instructive. When I die, thought Delia, I shall not want to be told how to do it. The image of death merged for a moment with that of the swans on the lake. Twin souls to eternity. Delia shivered.

Other guests had come into the room while she was reading. She shifted restlessly, certain a discussion about the pros and cons of the daisy wheel would shortly begin. They were like baby birds, she thought, fed, cosseted. 'Quickly, prop me up,' one might cry, 'I feel the start of an epic poem!'

To her surprise a reading circle was formed and she was invited to join it. She realized with slow dismay that people were preparing to read from their own work. Her thoughts flew to Sean's manuscript in her briefcase. Could she safely pass it off as her own? Maybe somebody here would know him? There was no choice, however, if she were to keep up her front of lady writer, to withdraw now would seem strange, so, feeling a wretched imposter, she went to get it.

The loose circle shifted and sighed. The body language told of fear of exposure. Delia too, was nervous. She might get away with pretending the work was her own, but what about its quality? Thank goodness, she thought, Homer Gilliray hadn't appeared.

With coughs and trembly voices people began. Delia set her face, determined to show none of the boredom and annoyance she knew would soon overtake her. The first piece was a description of a wood in spring. It was good. Delia relaxed – she might even enjoy this. The second reader apologized in advance for work in progress and stammered out the discovery, in his thriller, of a body. There were some stunning images and Delia began to be genuinely interested. The third reader, too, acting out various parts in a play, was lively and entertaining. Others followed more quickly and Delia was amazed and delighted by the standard of work. At last a young poet read a poem about the lake and the swans and Delia was moved almost unbearably. It touched so nearly the feelings she had had, it was all she could do not to weep again.

When her turn came she took Sean's pages and shuffled them, trying desperately to hit upon a paragraph of competing standard. Halfway through a description of a terrorist's funeral, she choked to a stop and tears ran down her face. She cried for shame. At herself for the sham she was perpetrating and for the whole of her beastly industry that lived off and despised these creative, original people. The circle stared at her, round-eyed and sympathetic. They didn't attempt to interfere, this was the effect, after all, that art intended. Delia gathered her papers and ran from the room, feeling her empty insides unravelling.

27

Surrounded by little screwed-up pieces of paper, Caro sat in what used to be known as Sebastian's study. *The Cream Tea Wars* was not coming nicely. Perhaps, she thought, as she stared in despair at the empty sheet of A4, it was the title that was lacking. How about *Jam in the Eye* or *A Storm in a Teacup*? She bellowed softly and lit a cigarette, her tenth that day – she, who until the last year, hadn't smoked since she was pregnant. She'd polished off Zo's reports in no time at all. It had been a pleasure thumbing through the undiscovered work, trying out pithy critical phrases. This, though, was different and certainly made her more appreciative of the work she had been reading.

Zo phoned at lunchtime. Caro, locked in creative anguish, was almost dismissive with her. Zo said, 'Delia's back. She rang me this morning.'

'Mmm,' said Caro, still thinking of concise and witty titles, then collecting herself. 'Oh. Delia! Did she find anything?'

'Apparently not. Says the trail's gone cold and she's exhausted.'

'Ah,' said Caro, remembering this was the effect Seb had on most people.

'She's staying a couple of days in town. Sorting out business. There's this awards do. Do you want to come?'

'Awards?' said Caro vaguely.

'The Guthrie-Scott,' said Zo, as though this was self-explanatory, 'bigger than the Booker. Monday night. I'd like to escort you.'

'Well . . .' said Caro, pleased now, 'but won't it look strange . . . two women . . . ?'

129

'Who gives a damn,' said Zo, 'they'll all be pissed as farts. Seven o'clock. The Savoy. Black tie.'

'Oh Lord,' sighed Caro, 'I haven't got one.'

She phoned Toni straight away and demanded that they went shopping. Toni sounded glum but cheered up at the promise of an expedition and they agreed to meet at the Delphinium for coffee. Caro felt strange walking into the café she'd just been trying to create on paper. It was rather like returning to the scene of the crime. The place was weekday empty, only Marsha Snelgrove sat in a corner booth, finishing a Welsh rarebit.

Toni breezed in, wearing a cape with occult mandalas scattered over it. She drew up her chair and launched into the latest news of Jeremy and Darryl. The latter was still away, though in sporadic touch and the former had returned to work, though without his usual spirit. 'Honestly. He passed up the chance of some Bicker-staff plates and a marvellous Spring Fayre in Canterbury!'

'Oh dear,' murmured Caro, sympathetic but preoccupied with long or short and what on earth shoes to go with it?

'That's not the half of it,' said Toni, conspiratorially lowering her tone. 'I've got some more of the story out of him. Apparently he didn't just go to see this man – Guy, his name is. Jeremy told him that he had Aids, and Darryl didn't know about it.'

'No!' Caro was shocked into total attention.

'Yes,' nodded Toni grimly. 'I warned him about karma back-firing.'

'So . . .' Caro tried to follow. 'The man . . . Guy . . . he would think he might have it too?'

'Well wouldn't you?' said Toni forcefully. 'I'd be off like a shot to get tested.'

'Yes . . .' agreed Caro, 'but then he'd find out that he didn't . . .'

'He'd think he'd been lucky and steer well clear. The way they carry on, he wouldn't even tell Darryl.'

'. . . And Jeremy would bank on that,' nodded Caro.

'Right. But not of course on Darryl's going after him.'

They sat in silence digesting this leg of the intrigue. It was all so tragic, thought Caro. When love went wrong, there was nothing you could do to halt it.

Laurel Hopcraft swept through the door, bringing a great swirl of sea breeze with her. She eyed Toni and Caro and then joined Marsha Snelgrove. The two fell to watching and whispering and Caro said in a low voice, 'I think we should go. The vice squad are on to us.'

They walked along the gusty front, pretty today with neatly laid out spring flowerbeds and gleams of sudden sharp sunlight.

'Romany's first, I think,' said Toni, taking charge of the couture. Caro began to demur – Romany's was the most expensive shop in town – but Toni overrode all objections, saying it was Caro's first public appearance with Zo and she must rise to the occasion.

Staring at herself displayed in slightly sagging underwear in the full-length dressing-room mirror, Caro wondered again what Zo saw in her. Her tummy was round, a legacy from Jade, her flesh soft-looking. Her breasts were still good, full and plump. It made Zo chuckle that they stood to attention like a nubile girl's, when she ran her long fingers over them. Caro felt a blush rising and covered up, struggling into a tight little cocktail number.

Toni made the decision for her in the end. A discreet but sexy Issey Miyake gown in a subtle greenish colour. 'Good with your skin,' she said firmly, steering Caro to the till. 'I'll do your hair on the day for you.'

Caro was appalled at the price, but having handed over her credit card, got enthused and gladly followed Toni to Jim and Peggy Bacon's High Street Heels, where Peggy, with pursed lips, sold them some intricate high-heeled gold sandals. Toni thought she had a bag that would match, so they went back to her house for a gin and tonic.

The first view Delia had of her flat filled her with depression. Why had she never noticed how bleak and comfortless it was? Perhaps because she was so little in it. She thought with nostalgia

131

of Wendy's little house in Warfleet. Cramped as it was, she'd got used to its homely atmosphere.

She dumped her bag and made ready to go to the office. There was a pile of work waiting, Zo had assured her, and besides that, this wretched award. Her writer would be expecting her undivided attention. Normally she would have been on the phone for days, lobbying for him. She hoped Zo had been a good lieutenant.

The office staff greeted her indifferently, as though hardly aware she'd been away. Her London clothes felt stiff after the loose skirts she had affected as part of her disguise in Ireland. Zo was cheerful, however, and pleased to see her. She kept breaking into little giggles as she answered Delia's questions on Warfleet, Harry, Caro. Delia wondered if she was 'on' something. She reassumed control of her desk, shoving Zo's papers out of the way, and with sinking spirit began her telephoning.

The sitting room in Toni's house had undergone another mystic renovation, Caro saw with mild alarm. Shamanistic symbols hung from the nails where bold slashes of paint had previously riveted the eye. The fireplace was as full of candles as a Catholic shrine, incense cones and oil burners littered the mantelpiece and on the sofa, the *I-Ching* jostled with a set of Egyptian Tarot cards and a book about the Medicine Wheel. Toni was clearly leaving nothing to chance.

'I've had Rumer round,' said Toni offhandedly, sweeping a space for Caro. 'She did some interesting stuff with a smudge stick.'

'I thought you didn't approve of her,' said Caro, meaning that she herself didn't.

'Oh, I don't know,' said Toni, keeping her tone light. 'She's a bit commercial. But she knows her stuff. I think she's a genuine psychic.'

While Caro absorbed this altered perspective, Toni mixed large G & Ts. She handed Caro hers with a laugh. 'I've given up meat and cigs. Drink'll be the last thing.'

Caro looked at her friend closely. Toni's hair was showing flecks of grey – she hadn't rinsed it lately. Her face was without makeup and had a thin-skinned, vulnerable look. Her clothes, too, were unusual. Apart from the flamboyant cape, Toni wore leggings, leg warmers and a long dark beatnikish sweater. Heavy wooden beads with astral signs dangling from them decorated her neck and wrists. It was amazing, thought Caro, how someone you knew well, saw all the time, could change so much without your noticing.

She said, chastened, 'I feel rather out of touch with you. I've been so obsessed with this Zo thing.'

Toni smiled kindly, looking at once like her familiar self. 'I understand,' she said. 'It'll be like that for a while. But I'm still here when you need me.'

Caro wanted to ask her what these changes meant, but instead she said, 'Can you do my Tarot?'

Toni laughed and picked up the beautiful glowing pack. She gave them to Caro to shuffle, saying, 'Remember, I'm only a novice.'

Delia slammed down the phone and sighed heavily. She'd been round the Guthrie-Scott network and pitched heavily for her client. She'd encountered everything from indifference to sexual frenzy. 'I *love* his work,' gushed the features editor. 'So full of sensual ardour. Is that what he's like in real life?'

'I haven't had the pleasure,' snapped Delia. 'What do you want, a pair of his jockey shorts?'

During this, the client himself had faxed that he had spent all morning trying to get through. Zo waved the fax under her nose with a sympathetic grimace. By the time Delia called him, he was in a state of suicidal melancholy. The book was shit. It would never win. Judges must be mad to shortlist it. He would never write another word. Where the hell had she been, anyway?

Her last call had been to Briar, on Sean's behalf. She hadn't seen him before leaving Ireland. Couldn't stomach it really. He'd

133

sounded so disappointed on the phone, that, as her last coin dropped, she promised she'd move heaven and earth for him in England. Briar had been brusque, even rude, when Delia reached her. She seemed to be eating and answered in sloppy monosyllables, chewing noisily through them. She'd ended by saying she didn't think the project was for her: the new MD's directive was 'wall-to-wall fanny'.

Delia adjusted the crotch of her own pantihose – the constricting Lycra had been giving her indigestion all day: she'd put on weight in Ireland. Zo came in with two cups of tea and sat at her desk in the shared space, looking invitingly at Delia. 'Tell all,' she said with her gappy grin, but somehow Delia couldn't. She shook her head, feeling close to tears, and took a great gulp of scalding tea to give an excuse to her wateriness.

Zo said, 'Much has happened since you left.' Delia tried to look engaged. 'Blythe Fitzallan's threatening to leave, she's got a new agent . . .' Delia grunted '. . . Morgan Freeman's late with delivery . . .' Delia sighed '. . . says he's got a block . . . We had a crisis meeting on the cover of *Forever Embers*, you were missed, but I said you had gynae problems . . .' Delia snorted '. . . Laurel Hopcraft sent us a first draft . . . it's not bad. I thought I might take her on . . .' Delia raised her eyebrows. '. . . Oh . . . and, I've engaged Caro, usual rates, to read for us.'

Delia started, then checked, 'Caro Radcliffe?'

'She's sound,' nodded Zo, 'did a sample. Great!'

Delia had a strong sense that she was losing her grip. Any one of these news items would normally have sent her into a spin. Strangely, though, for a self-defined workaholic, she hardly seemed to care.

Zo said, 'And there's one other thing . . .' She smiled, almost shyly. 'I've fallen in love.'

Delia looked up with ironic eyebrows: she was used to the parade through the office of Zo's besotted girlies. 'No,' cautioned Zo, 'it's serious.'

'It always is,' said Delia, ungivingly.

'It's Caro,' said Zo bluntly.

Delia almost dropped her tea. 'What!' she spluttered. 'But does she know?'

'Oh yes,' said Zo, 'she returns it.'

'But what about Sebastian?' demanded Delia, feeling affronted for him.

'She couldn't care less. He made his bed.'

Delia writhed uncomfortably. It was partly the tights and partly unusually conflicting emotions. The first, to her confusion, was relief. Sebastian was free. The second, as she looked at Zo, was an overwhelming envy. She carefully replaced the tea on the desk. She had to admit, this was serious.

28

The testing of Warren had begun as soon as Jade had left War-fleet. She didn't answer his calls and had made no promise of when she would return, pleading pressure of rehearsal. It was obvious to Jade why this trial was necessary. She was like the Lady of Shalott and Warren must prove he was Lancelot if he wanted further favours. Now she had conquered him, his attraction for her should be lessened, she felt; out of his presence she could dismiss the sexual charge, relegate him to a curious object.

Her mother's visit was an unlooked-for spoke and had shaken her to her platform soles. Desperate for a confidante, she'd at last told Allegra, who'd shrugged it off, laughing. Middle-aged women did peculiar things. Her mother was on the change wasn't she? This did not reassure Jade and she brought a new tremulousness to her role as Sheila Birling.

As the first night approached she focused all her energies on the play and tried to exclude real-life emotional tangles. Caro sent her a good luck card, promising she and Zo would come and see the production, if Jade so wanted. Jade stuck the card in her dressing-room mirror, after Tipp-Exing out the reference to Zo. There was nothing from Warren, she was disappointed to see. She felt he had failed at the first jump – he could easily have got the date from Caro.

She was terribly nervous as she made up. Her entire peer group would be at the show, people she needed to impress. Her hands smoothing on Nine and Five trembled. On the quarter there was a knock at her door. 'Come in,' she said, expecting the stage manager. A large bunch of tulips was thrust into the room.

Behind them came Warren. Jade's heart began beating very fast. She dropped the stick of greasepaint and pulled her loose wrap close to her throat. 'What are you doing here?' she croaked.

'Your Mum lent me the car,' explained Warren, grinning charmingly. 'Thought I'd surprise you.' He'd certainly succeeded in that, thought Jade, terrified another member of the cast would enter. 'You look beautiful,' said Warren, putting out a finger to stroke her bobbed wig.

She smacked his hand away, saying, 'You shouldn't be here after the half. I'll . . . get the ASM to find you a seat.'

'I'm looking forward to seeing you,' said Warren, not at all abashed by her rebuff. 'I'll come round after, shall I?'

Jade almost said, No, you must go straight home. She thought wildly of excuses she could offer, but, finding none, agreed lamely. Warren backed out, still smiling. No doubt he put her bizarre manner down to stage fright, thought Jade, as the door closed. Punters had great reverence for artistic temperament.

As the curtain rose, Jade clutched her prop champagne glass. Her first gay laugh had a crack in it, it was all she could do to begin the line: 'I should jolly well think not, Gerald . . .'

In a moment between lines she scanned the audience, but the bright stage lights made all faces a blur and she could not tell where Warren was sitting. As the scene progressed she settled into her stride, even began to enjoy it. She scored a couple of laughs and her confidence rose. Let Warren see what a star she was, how far beyond his ambitions. By the time she came to her last impassioned speech, '. . . I remember what he said, how he looked, what he made me feel. Fire and blood and anguish . . .' she was triumphant.

In Jade's dressing room, friends and members of the cast gathered to drink champagne and congratulate each other. Jade, flushed and giggly, filled their glasses. She saw Warren slide in and stand by the door, but did not go to him, staying surrounded by the *jeunesse dorée*, the centre of all attention. She flirted very obviously with the director, Neil, an Oxford luminary who'd been courting her for some time. Leaning to kiss him she slyly

137

monitored Warren's response. He was staring at her with eyes very black; there was exciting anger and pain in them.

People began to drift away. There was a party at Neil's flat. At last only Jade and Warren remained in the room. Jade turned her back, gathering glasses and downing the dregs of champagne in them.

'Well. Did you enjoy it?' she said in a careless tone.

Warren said stiffly, 'You were very good.'

'Aren't you going to ask me how I learn all those lines?' laughed Jade mockingly. 'Most people who aren't in the business do. Poor dears. Still it's hardly surprising. The average IQ in this country is less than a hundred.'

'I suppose you mean mine is,' charged Warren dully.

''Course not,' said Jade airily, facing him with an arch look on her face. 'Yours is at least a hundred and two.'

'Unlike your posh friends,' said Warren, looking at her directly.

Jade's smile faltered a fraction, but she could not stop. 'You have to be clever to be here at all,' she said. 'I would have thought that was obvious.' She started to undo the buttons on her flapper frock, reaching for her wrap with an ostentatious modesty.

She saw in the mirror Warren kick the door shut and cross the room to behind her. He looked into her eyes in the mirror and for a long moment she was pinned as the room seemed to go dark around her. Then Warren gripped her shoulders and turned her around. She raised an arm to fend him off but, as though she were a straw, he lifted her on to the dressing table and wrenched her legs apart pressing himself between them.

'Do you want me?' he breathed hoarsely, his hands now tugging beneath her frock.

'Warren . . .' she said weakly, shivering with fearful longing. He was unzipping his jeans and a moment later she felt his cock touch her thigh.

'Do you? Do you want me?' he urged.

She looked at him with eyes opaque with feeling. She wanted him more than she had ever wanted anything, but she could not say so. He withdrew to an arm's length so that she could see what

138

she was missing. Now, as she grabbed at him, it was he who was mocking. 'Tell me,' he said, twisting his mouth, 'tell me, or I won't.'

'I . . . want . . . you,' she choked, straining him to her.

He shoved into her savagely, and she fell back on the dressing table, crushing the tubes of makeup. She bound her legs round the small of his back and bucking with him begged him to fuck her, fuck her . . . ! Their cries of rage and release were heard all over the building.

29

Assured by Toni that she looked fabulous, Caro entered the foyer of the Savoy Hotel with some confidence. The dress did indeed suit her, she saw in the mirror of the expensive-smelling powder room, and her hair, teased by Toni into a burnished chignon and set off with fake gold Cleopatra earrings (Toni's, from what she now claimed was a previous life), looked eye-catchingly elegant. She giggled a little. People would think she was someone. Already the paparazzi crowding the steps had lifted their cameras, only to lower them again, glancing at each other, uncertain. She had sailed by, head high, affecting a regal indifference. She was three minutes late to meet Zo which was, she felt, nice timing.

At first in the crowded foyer Caro could not make her out, then a tall figure in evening dress came towards her and Caro's heart turned over. Zo had taken black tie literally. She gave a low whistle as she took in Caro's appearance. 'Very classy,' she said, her eyes dancing approval. 'Aren't I a lucky fellow?' Then she grinned her famous grin and took Caro's arm, guiding her to the champagne reception.

Shepherded by her tall, assured youth, the Page of Cups according to Toni's reading of her Tarot, Caro suffered none of the apprehension she had expected. This was, after all, a very public appearance. A declaration of sorts. Not that anyone here knew her, of course. Sebastian had occasionally attended these events, but she had never gone with him. She recognized many famous faces, though, like the photographers, could not be sure she hadn't mistaken them. Few had names for her. Zo seemed to know everyone and chattered unself-consciously, introducing Caro to right and left as though proud to display her.

At last they came upon Delia's group. And Caro and Delia smiled with relief at one another. Delia said, 'Caro, this is Nigel Waddle and his wife Amy. Nigel, I'm sure you know, is on the shortlist.' Caro nodded; she'd been briefed by Zo, even dipped into his novel, which she'd found pompous and predictable. Zo said it was bound to win.

Delia pulled at her arm in a quiet moment and said, 'How's Harry? I'm sorry I've been so long away. I'll be down tomorrow.' Caro reassured her quickly, feeling Warfleet talk was out of place here.

They were called in to dinner and sat at a large round table near the award rostrum. Nigel took this as a positive sign: he and Delia exchanged nods and nervous smiles. The others at the table were Nigel's agent Patsy and her tiny husband, a well-known barrister and his tiny wife, and a left-wing politician, Ted Sainsbury, invited, presumably, to make up the numbers.

After several glasses of champagne Caro no longer felt out of her depth. She discussed topics of the day with extravagance, asserting all sorts of opinions. Zo, across the table, occasionally winked at her. Delia, Caro thought, looked ill and not at ease. She played with her food and drank only Perrier water. By her side Nigel drank vast quantities of wine and said little: he hardly touched his pheasant. Ted Sainsbury polished off everything on his plate, ate Caro's chocolate mousse, and sat back with a hefty sigh to light a cigar. He, at least, had enjoyed himself.

A lull came as the toastmaster called the toasts and then the hush of terror fell as the chairman of the Guthrie-Scott rose to take the microphone. Caro paid little attention to his speech, she was watching people's faces. How hard they were working to keep casual, unmoved. They indicated that if they won they would be pleased but not amazed, if they lost, disappointed but not destroyed. How very sophisticated, she thought.

Now the judge was opening an envelope. 'And the winner is . . .' pause '. . . Nigel Waddle.'

Delia's table exploded in loud applause. Nigel, red-faced, stood in a confused way. Amy had gone to the loo, so Delia and Patsy set him on his tottering way to the platform. At the microphone he seemed about to burst into tears, but collected himself and thanked many people, including God, for his success and then stumbled through dwindling applause back to the table.

Relief descended on the gathering. Whatever its outcome the pressure was over for another year and everyone was free to joke and drink and gossip. Nigel was patted on the back and his hand was wrung by passers-by. Delia was smiling, for the first time relaxed, and Amy, who'd shopped all day for this moment, had a minor tantrum because she'd been queuing in the ladies and missed it. At the next table a group of men were smashing glasses and singing. They seemed to have strayed in from a different occasion – a stag night perhaps. But as Patsy explained to Caro, they were a group of security men, engaged these days to police bookstores.

Ted had been fondling her thigh for some time, so Caro was not sorry to be told the party was leaving. They were going to a hastily convened gathering at Nigel's house. Amy had laid in micro-waveable finger food in anticipation. She would boil up a quail's egg or two for those who'd been too anxious to eat dinner.

The Waddles' house was in a Victorian terrace in Notting Hill Gate. It was furnished from Conran and the Portobello Road and had the odd sign of previous affluence. Perhaps, thought Caro, she too could learn to write to earn her living. The prospect was attractive, though she saw that to win prizes she would have to curb her imagination. Zo, who'd done sterling work with Nigel, at last could come to her and they sat on a sofa holding hands and floating on each other's perfume.

Delia had watched them all evening. Caro looked wonderful, she thought, love obviously suited her. Zo, too, had shining skin and breathed an aura of wellbeing. Envy in Delia had turned to hope. Maybe she too could find happiness. Nigel, totally recovered from his previous gloom, was being boisterous in the kitchen, Patsy was lurching about in a stupor of self-praise, Amy was whirling with bottles and plates, Delia felt she could absent herself without attracting attention.

She climbed the stairs to the Waddles' bedroom to collect her coat. A great pile lay on the bed and she began to search through them without enthusiasm. She heard the door behind her close but took no notice until she was clasped from behind and grappled to the bed, her face ground into mounds of fake fur and her arms pinned beneath her. It was Ted Sainsbury, as she could soon tell from his northern vowel sounds and the Hennessy's on his breath.

'You're so sexy,' he grunted, rucking up her tight skirt. 'God, why are you so sexy?'

Delia didn't feel this required an answer and struggled round to face him. 'What the hell are you doing?' she demanded.

But Ted, now snuffling in her breasts, was too far gone to notice. He was tearing at her tights; she was wearing no knickers and one of his hands had got between her buttocks and was pawing desperately for enlodgement. 'We've got to fuck. You know I'm right. You felt the charge between us.'

Delia had felt nothing of the kind and said so, at the same time grabbing a handful of Ted's overlong grey hair and yanking his head off her bosom.

'But you've been staring at me all evening,' he said in a slurry, aggrieved voice.

This was too much for Delia, who had, as far as she knew, barely acknowledged him. 'Get off me, you horrible little ape!' she cried and pushed him hard, her fragile arms finding remarkable strength suddenly.

Ted fell in a heap on the floor, dragging coats and wraps down with him. Delia stepped over the writhing bundle and, picking up her own jacket, headed smartly out of the door. On the stairs she paused to recover her breath, and to adjust her clothing. This was, she knew, the final straw. The nail in her career's coffin.

30

Slipping the key into Wendy's lock next day, Delia experienced sudden liberation. The events of the previous night had pinpointed something she'd been circling for weeks, a kind of disgust for the life she had been leading. She almost thanked Ted Sainsbury.

The hall felt cold and unused. Though it was only afternoon, she switched on a light; the day was overcast. She had not warned Warren of her return, thinking she would surprise him later when Caro was back. Would carry him away with Harry. Halfway up the stairs one of Harry's toys had been dropped. It was a small woolly lamb. She picked it up and cradled it to her, humming softly. It was like the lambs in Ireland.

In the bedroom she took the framed photo of Wendy on her graduation out of a drawer and stood it on the tallboy. It was a photo she herself had taken. Wendy had been giggling and embarrassed in her plumage. Unlike Delia, who'd relished every moment of the ceremony, paraded swishingly about in her cap and gown with large horn-rimmed specs bought for the occasion. How the tables were turned, she thought now, smiling wryly.

She unpacked, showered, then went to the telephone. Caro answered, saying she had just returned herself and what a marvellous evening. Delia did not disagree, but asked if it was convenient to come round soon and pick up Warren and the baby.

'They're out,' Caro said, 'probably gone to his Mum's, besides I want to hear about your travels. Look, I'm going to the Health Club for a couple of hours, why don't you come with me?'

* * *

'The Spa' health and fitness club harked back to the days when Warfleet had really been one. It was run by Sunny Delgardo, a woman in her fifties dedicated to the idea that nobody need look it, who belonged to old Warfleet money. Her family had once been in ice cream. The club was popular with the Am-drams crowd and Caro had been a desultory visitor. Recently reawakened to the beauty of muscle tone, she'd begun to go more often.

Now as she and Delia stripped off for the sunbed, she stole covert looks at Delia's trim, perky figure. Her skin was pale fawn as though it never lost its tan completely. Her breasts were generous, ending in neat brown points. Caro's own nipples, which she hastily hid, were dark red and bruised, where last night Zo had sucked them. They climbed aboard their ultra-violet cradles and lying under the gentle heat began, with awkwardness at first, to talk to one another.

To avoid confusion Delia said, 'Zo's told me about you and her.'

'Oh,' said Caro, falling dumb. She wondered what exactly Zo had said. She supposed Delia was used to it.

'You don't mind my saying?'

Caro, to whom no sentence was complete without mention of Zo, said that on the contrary, she was relieved. She noticed as Delia went on with her tale that she managed to mention Sebastian almost as frequently. The couple did a circuit of the gym where Delia, still talking, pedalled furiously on the exercise bike leaving Caro flagging, then had a jacuzzi, which was brief, as Delia claimed they were unhygienic.

Exhausted, they sat wrapped in towelling robes in the basket chairs of the juice bar. It was quite crowded. Caro spied Laurel Hopcraft downing a stiff tomato juice – God that woman was everywhere – Evelyn Antrobus from the kindergarten and Fenella Pepper, who was being manicured. The blood red she was having painted on her nails would give her husband a coronary. The towelling dressing gowns were great levellers, Caro noted gratefully, inflating each body to a shapeless white bolster. One such, slumped in a swinging basket seat, she realized, was Jeremy. She waved and smiled but he seemed not to notice. He was staring at his bare legs with unblinking misery. She must, she thought, go and speak to him in a moment.

'So,' she said, taking a sip of her Banana Smoothie, 'after all that we're none the wiser on Sebastian's whereabouts?'

'No,' agreed Delia, feeling criticized, 'but at least we know where he isn't.'

At this point Marsha Snelgrove entered with the *Warfleet Chronicle* under her arm. She sat a few yards away and opened the paper. Caro's eye fell on the front-page headline: BODY FOUND ON RIPPLE BANK. POLICE COMPLETELY BAFFLED.

Delia saw the announcement at almost the same time and across the room Jeremy too, had looked up. All three stared at the paper. Not one of them moved. They were frozen still in terror.

31

BODY FOUND ON RIPPLE
BANK. POLICE COMPLETELY
BAFFLED.

The bizarrely decorated body of a man was
found in a hole on the bank of the River Ripple yesterday. Police are puzzled as although
death by drowning has been confirmed, the
circumstances give rise to suspicion. 'The
man may have been a New Age traveller or
member of some obscure sect,' said Sergeant
Plummer. 'He appeared to have taken part in
cabalistic rituals.' The discovery was made
by Mrs Enid Lucas, who had moored her
narrow boat near by. She said it was, 'Very
upsetting.'

Warren had the paper spread out on Wendy's kitchen table. Harry
gurgled close by in his playpen. The two of them had been
delivered to Honeysuckle Cottage by Caro on her way up to
London. She had seemed tense and preoccupied. Delia was in
bed feeling poorly. Warren sighed and pushed the paper from
him. He thought it unlikely his Dad had been involved in 'cabalistic rituals', but knew this would not deter his mother, who
would be on the phone directly. He wondered if the body was
Sebastian's – he seemed a more likely candidate for membership
of some artistically decadent sect. Perhaps he should call Jade:
surely she would want to know? Perhaps the article was the root
of Caro's odd behaviour? His hand hovered over the telephone,

but Jade would be in lectures now and he was done with leaving messages.

He stood staring at the garden. Grape hyacinths had nosed their way out now and daffodils, dispelling the impression of tidiness. He'd promised Delia he'd look after the borders. He felt a great need to get his hands on something real. Soil or wood. Jade was right in a way. Technology had divorced man from nature.

He swung the chirruping Harry into his pram, wrapped him up well and pushed him out into the garden. He parked the pram on the little patio, then went to the shed and assembled fork, trowel, secateurs. With a sense of purpose he rolled up his sleeves . . . he never felt the cold . . . and set about turning the soil and weeding. Soon new bushes would have to go in, a visit to the garden centre. Glancing back at Harry peacefully cooing at the sky, Warren thought, 'If only Jade were in the house and not Delia. We'd be a proper family.'

The bedroom curtains were closed against the light as Delia lay, half stupefied by painkillers, on the bed. The shock of the article had left her drained and brought on an early period. With the blood, her belief in Sebastian flowed away. If, after all her efforts, he should be dead! And if only she were next of kin! Instead, she had to rely on Caro to instigate enquiries. The suspense might kill her, she thought, rolling over to grope for another Nurofen.

Caro was twitching on Ingrid's couch after telling her what had happened. Ingrid said, 'This time, did you phone the police?'

'I spoke to Sergeant Plummer,' nodded Caro, the good girl. 'He said the body was being held in Stourbridge. It couldn't be seen until forensic had completed.' As an afterthought she added, 'He asked if Seb had ever been in the Masons.'

In fact, the revelations of the strange state of the body had rather reassured her. She could no more imagine Sebastian as a warlock than she could see him as Brown Owl. Apart from anything else he'd be too lazy. Delia had been practically hysterical,

148

though, hence Caro's call to the police station. This morning she'd had her mother on the phone. Cynthia had said there was a tiny piece in the *Daily Mail* sent in by a . . . she searched the paper . . . Charlie Barrett. It seemed to imply Seb might have been drowned? Would it be on 'Crime Watch'?

Caro was glad to escape from Ingrid that day. There was too much practical to be done to give time to inner feelings. She was going to have lunch with Zo, but first she must phone Jade. She would have to come home and help her.

Jeremy had gone straight round to Toni's with the paper. The description in it had put him instantly in mind of certain S & M practices fashionable with gays at the moment. Suppose Guy had been involved, or the victim of some orgy? Toni could not see the connection, but sensed that Jeremy's real concern stemmed from fear that Guy might have committed suicide. 'It's all my fault,' he kept moaning, his head in his hands and a large gin untouched beside him. 'I never meant to kill anybody.'

He was frightened to return home in case Darryl was there, drunk and abusive. More had gone on between them over this than even Toni had realized. She said briskly, 'You must go and see the body. Put your mind at rest.'

Jeremy gave a sort of howl and collapsed sideways. He was too frightened, Toni managed to get out of him, frightened it might be Guy, frightened of what Darryl would do if it were.

Toni hugged him fiercely while her mind raced over possibilities. Perhaps she could go? In disguise? But did Jeremy have a photo? One thing was certain, Jeremy was her beloved baby and she would defend his interests to the death. She must come up with a solution.

With sudden clarity she said, 'We'll hold a seance.'

'Wha'?' said Jeremy blurrily.

'Contact the dead man's spirit,' said Toni, enthused now. 'Rumer should be able to do it.'

Jeremy looked up from her lap, rubbing at his runny nose.

'What good will that do?' he asked rather petulantly. He was scared of all this psychic nonsense Toni was getting into.

'We'll find out who he is, of course,' she asserted now, 'or more to the point, who he isn't.'

Sergeant Plummer had been inundated with calls since the *Chronicle* had come out. They were really crawling out of the woodwork this time. He was expecting one from Mrs Peabody – he longed to tell her to forget her old man, she was still an attractive woman – and was dealing with the usual pot pourri of freaks. The Radcliffes were more interesting, as was a strange call from a coin box, a man attempting to disguise his voice; he was sure it was Darryl Willoughby. Until forensic had examined everything there was little he could do. The newspaper, and Plummer himself, had omitted some of the more succulent details. The genitals, for instance, had been cut off, the nipples pierced, the face had been painted Red Indian style and there was a toy arrow thrust from ear to ear. The hair, which stood out all round the head, was fantastically woven with beads and feathers. He looked like some sort of medicine man, opined the police photographer. They'd have to clean him up, thought Sergeant Plummer, before he could ask anyone to identify him.

In the school playground Sidney's gang gathered. Policed by Dave they huddled behind the bike shed, each one displaying the bloodied wrist which was the mark of brotherhood.

'Thing is,' said Sidney, strutting in front of his troops, 'there's no way they can trace nothin' to us. Unless . . .' he paused and Dave stepped forward menacingly, 'someone talks.'

The boys stared down mutely. Playing with the body, stripping and decorating it, had been a disgusting sort of fun. In its discovery, it was deeply shaming. None was bold enough to challenge Sidney, though. He and Dave were famous for wreaking nasty revenge on quislings. Dave had recently demonstrated his bloodlust by cutting up live frogs in the playground. And then there was that kitten . . .

The electronic bell shrilled above them and quickly they nodded and joined their scratched wrists in a human totem. Blood to blood. Must be honoured. Let it not be forgotten.

32

That night Toni held a seance. Those who gathered in the dimmed sitting room were not exactly 'le tout Warfleet', but a mixed bunch of people in need of comfort. Toni had marshalled Jeremy, Caro and Jade, who'd arrived at teatime on being summoned, Warren and Mrs Peabody, Zo to be supportive, and Rumer Petulengro. The circle sat apprehensively round Toni's extended dinning table, unsure whether to behave as though in church or at a social function. Toni alone looked at ease and expectant.

Rumer got their attention with a clap of her hands. 'Have any of you done this before?'

Mrs Peabody and Warren shyly raised their hands. The others looked down, or away, or at the Peabodys, surprised and embarrassed. Warren, with a straight face, pressed his thigh to Jade's. Her hand had already run up his and rested lightly on his crotch.

'Now,' said Rumer, bossily. 'I want you to hold hands and *concentrate*. All hands on the table please.'

Jade reluctantly abandoned Warren's buttons and followed the command. Zo was the last to obey, leaving Caro rather pink. Under the table a confusion of intertwined boots reigned.

'I may go into a trance,' warned Rumer. 'Please don't break the circle or attempt to assist me in any way. Above all, don't panic.' Toni frowned at Jeremy. He, particularly, should take this advice. Jeremy was looking quite alert, as if the relief at hand was better than the awful uncertainty.

'Can we close our eyes please,' said Rumer, in a more spiritual voice. 'We will have a few moments' silence to tap into the subconscious.' A nervous quiet fell, punctuated only by people's breathing, the odd cough and the ticking of the clock. Zo stole a look at Caro through slitted eyes and winked surreptitiously.

Rumer's breathing became charged and several people half opened their eyes to look at her. She lolled back with her mouth slightly open. Above her the crystal drops on Toni's fake chandelier tinkled softly like wind chimes. Rumer began in a hoarse voice to speak staccato phrases: 'Feathers . . . yes . . . arrows . . . war paint . . .'

'It'll be her spirit guide,' whispered Toni, 'they're often Indians.'

'Water,' crooned Rumer, 'water . . . water . . .' Toni pushed a carafe and glass closer to her, but Rumer ignored them, going on, 'Down . . . down . . . water . . . drown.'

Caro was having her usual difficulty in paying attention. She was very aware of Zo's knee against her own and the delightful frissons its pressure caused her, but her mind wandered round the room, taking in the detail – Rumer's catarrhal breathing, for instance, Jade's bitten nails, the hands moving on the grandfather clock – but somehow not the whole picture. She wondered if the drowned man had been paying attention. She would want to if she'd been dying. Had he truly experienced that last waterlogged moment?

Rumer's voice became more urgent. 'Yes . . . yes . . .' she shouted, 'have you a name for us?'

The table tappers grew tense. This was the moment. The glass on the table top slowly began to move. Around the edge of the table Rumer had placed the letters of the alphabet. All eyes were riveted to the glass as it slid across towards them. 'S' it approached, causing Caro to hold her breath, then 'E', then 'Y'. Jeremy at this point almost fainted. The glass seemed confused. It spun and then moved faster, going to 'E' again, then 'N', then 'G', then 'B', then 'L'. Now it was whizzing round and round, dizzying those watching. They moved their arms quickly out of the way, frightened of what they had provoked. Suddenly there was the sound of a great gale in the room. The french windows blew open, the curtains streamed out, clothing and hair stood on end. Jeremy cried, 'Oh God,' and clutched Toni, Zo put her arm round Caro, Jade buried her head in Warren's shoulder, Mrs Peabody ducked on to his lap. Rumer fell on to the table foaming from the nostrils. The glass shot off the table and smashed to splinters in the stone fireplace.

Delia woke with a start. A great noise had roused her. A sort of whoosh of air. It was dark and, still drugged, she was confused. She felt for her watch: its luminous dial told her it was nine-thirty. She scrambled out of bed and, pulling on her dressing gown, switched on the light. The hallway was silent. She listened outside Warren's door, then opened it. His room was empty. Downstairs, too, was in darkness, but in the kitchen was a note from Warren saying he'd popped out for an hour. She ran to the Ansafone, hoping for Caro's voice. She must have found out something by now! But it registered no messages. She dialled Caro's number and heard it ring with a hollow sound. 'Come on, come on,' she said out loud, now in a kind of panic. No one answered and after a long few moments, Delia replaced the phone with a shaking hand. She must go round, she knew. She could not wait here for deliverance. Caro's back door was always left open – at the worst she would just stay until her return. She had to know what had happened.

As she flung on her clothes, old jeans, a shirt, a bulky sweater, she suddenly remembered Harry. Wild-eyed she stumbled into his nursery. He lay on his side in his cot, one fist in his mouth, sleeping sweetly. With a cry of relief she caught him up and swaddling his limp form in blankets, hurried down the stairs with him.

She started the car and backed out of the cul-de-sac. Beside her, in his carrycot, Harry grunted sleepily, startled by the cold. She drove as one possessed to Caro's house, which was also, she soon saw, in darkness. In the driveway she juddered to a halt and, clasping the woolly Harry in her arms, rushed around to the side of the house and turned the back door handle. The door swung open, creaking slightly. On the kitchen table a candle flickered. By its light she could just make out a dark shape in the wicker chair by the Aga. She stepped forward, strangely unafraid and catching up the candle, moved closer to the figure. The light fell on the sleeping man's face. It wasn't Heathcliff or Byron. But it was Sebastian Radcliffe.

The moment, frozen in time, seemed to last for ever. But at last the wind died away, the windows blew shut, and the room was restored to normal.

The circle sat up feeling rather sheepish about its communal display of terror. Only Rumer remained face down, a thin trail of snot hanging from her nose. She appeared to be sleeping.

Zo said, 'What now. Ectoplasm?'

'Don't mock. You've seen the power,' Toni rebuked her sharply.

The others fell to discussing the letters the glass had chosen. They didn't make sense as anyone's name, said Jeremy with relief.

'What was your Dad called?' asked Jade of Warren.

'Andy,' said Mrs Peabody.

Caro, paying attention, said shouldn't they do something about Rumer? Toni went to make some tea. It was clear the seance was ended.

When Sebastian opened his eyes and saw before him a candlelit mother and baby, he thought for a moment he was in heaven. He blinked himself properly awake as the apparition moved closer, bending down to him. He focused on a face, beautiful in the tallow glow, with a wide mouth and passionate eyes. The chubby baby in her arms smiled at him merrily. The woman, if woman she was, spoke, calling his name softly. He put out a hand and encountered the baby's damp, waving fist. It was real then. The woman took his hand and held it saying, 'I'm sorry to startle you. I'm Delia Henderson. I've been looking for you.'

In his bemused state he thought it must be a joke. This angel had been looking for him? He shook his head trying to clear it and to speak, but his tongue seemed swollen and he couldn't get started. Now she put a hand on his forehead and said, 'You have a temperature. I'm going to make you a toddy.' Her hand was cool and smooth and felt divine. He whimpered when she removed it.

Delia put Harry back in his carrycot. She filled the kettle and placed it on the hot range. She could see Sebastian was in a fever. Wandering. Lost. This was not the time for further revelation.

She found whisky on the drinks trolley and honey in the larder. She added a Beechams for good measure. His haunted face begged for sleep and this brew should certainly do it. She fed it to him, gently propping his head. He gazed at her in wonder and gratitude, his dark eyes burning out of lined bluish hollows. 'Bed now,' she said as he finished, 'lean on me.' She hoisted him out of the chair – though tall he seemed light – and pulling his arm round her neck guided him to the door, followed by helpful woofs from Cindy.

In the hallway he tried to speak again. Perhaps, she thought, to tell her which way. But she hushed him and together they limped up the stairs to what she knew was the marital bedroom. She had a qualm as she led him over the threshold, but suppressed it, thinking this, after all, would be where he was most familiar.

As carefully as if he were china, she laid him on the bed, shading the small lamp away from him. She drew the curtains and took off his shoes, then pulling up the blankets still favoured by Caro, she got in beside him and held him close, rocking him, as if he, and not Harry, were the baby.

33

Caro sat by Seb's bed holding his hand in hers. Seb was asleep, or at least had his eyes closed. Caro's visits to the cottage hospital were, for the most part, silent. Dr Robinson said pneumonia, had prescribed antibiotics and complete rest, moved heaven and earth to get this bed. Soon Seb's convalescence would begin – so, Caro knew, would the problems.

Seb remembered jigsaw fragments. Dublin airport where he'd been arrested. He'd taken things in the café without paying. The Gardai thought he was drunk. But next morning he was still dazed and they'd sectioned him to Grange Gorman. Then there was a dead patch. He thought he'd had shock treatment. Would occasionally rub his temples, as if they were sore. Caro was reminded of Ingrid.

She had discussed this return with her. 'I feel terribly guilty,' she agonized, chewing at her knuckles, 'because, of course, I don't want him.' Ingrid reassured her that under the circumstances, that was perfectly natural. 'But I won't see him go without care,' said Caro. 'He's had a nervous breakdown. I can't just turn him away.' Ingrid said perhaps there were some halfway measures.

Now, looking out of the hospital window on to a field of spring cabbage, vibrant green in the otherwise grey day, Caro could not imagine what these would be. Seb seemed totally dependent. Sometimes she caught him looking at her with a puzzled expression, as though he was trying to work out why she was there. The only time his face came to life was when Delia, with flowers, entered.

Caro sighed and pressed the limp, dry hand. Cynthia was

threatening to visit, but the Easter holidays would begin soon and Jade would be home to discuss it.

The discovery of her father's return was like a bad old B movie playing and re-playing in Jade's head. Scene One, the door of the kitchen opened and in spilled the party from the seance, high on nervous laughter. 'Strong drink!' cried Zo, reaching for the whisky bottle which stood on the kitchen table. Caro got glasses, the others leaned on chairs or collapsed, shrieking Rumer's phrases: 'All hands on the table! Water, water . . .' 'Bet she'll have a terrible headache,' chortled Zo. Their giggles were cut short by a cry from Harry. They stared at him as though he were a super-natural manifestation. Eventually Warren picked him up and said he needed changing. Jade went with him to find a nappy. In the hall they stopped and kissed, probing each other's mouth for reassurance. Suddenly aware they were observed – this bit always played in slow motion – they turned and saw Delia on the stairs. She looked pale enough to be a ghost, but the smile on her face was beatific.

In Scene Two farcical elements entered, and Jade did not wish to remember them. To distract herself she reeled Scene One of the movie through again, stopping this time at a close-up of her father's face. His eyes, when he had finally woken, had been milky with confusion – he had not seemed to know them. King Lear, thought Jade, immediately embracing the casting of herself as Cordelia. Fear shivered through her again: for the first time her father had seemed to her really missing and the discovery had been upsetting.

She wandered across Magdalen Bridge, chewing a braid and wondering how she would tell Warren her news. He'd been so tender before she'd left, his lovemaking as urgent as ever and inspired in the back seat of the car. She shook the beaded braid away as if to forswear childish habits. Next time he called her she would have to tell him.

34

'What?' said Warren. 'What did you say?'

'I'm pregnant,' said Jade blankly. 'I did a test. Three times. Jesus.'

Warren clutched the phone hard and leaned back against the wall of the booth: he felt dizzy. 'Bu ... but ... how?' he stammered.

'I'm not on the pill,' said Jade accusingly.

'You never said.'

'You never asked!'

The line went quiet. Then Warren laughed. Delight had surprised him. 'I'm glad,' he said. 'Glad! Glad!'

'What!' said Jade. 'Are you crazy?'

'Yeah,' said Warren, 'with love. We made a baby!'

'It isn't a baby, it's a collection of cells,' Jade corrected coldly. 'You surely don't think I'm going to *have* it?'

'Why not?' said Warren. 'We could get married.'

'I'm in the middle of studying for a degree. I haven't got time to get married.'

'I'm not talking about this on the phone,' said Warren, 'I need to see you. I'm coming up tomorrow.'

He replaced the phone and did a brief breakdance. His heart was full to bursting. Of course Jade needed reassurance, that he was pleased, would stand by her. One look into his face tomorrow would tell her. He needed to share this astonishing news. He'd go to the pub ... find Dean, Travis, Lee, his mates from the estate ... he hadn't seen them for ages.

* * *

159

Warren was coming by coach and Jade had promised to meet him at the bus station. This was preferable to having him arrive in her room. Though Allegra had heard by now a version of the story, she had yet to encounter the real Warren. In Jade's tale he was a piratical stud, a cross between Robin Hood and Long John Silver. The bus was late, and Jade, wearing unsuitable clothes, shivered in the sharp March wind. She bought a coffee from an instant machine and stood clutching it for warmth as she waited with the other poorly dressed disadvantaged.

Despite herself she was glad to see Warren. His smile was irresistible, the way it lit up his honey-warm eyes. He kissed her cold nose and pulled her close to him. As ever in his presence, she was weakened by need. She wanted to take him straight to bed, feel his body inside her. Instead, there was this other thing inside her . . . She said, 'We'll go and have tea. The Randolph.' She knew its false grandeur would intimidate Warren.

He did seem uneasy as they were shown into the lounge. Jade's lip curled a little. She was able, in these surroundings, to regain her scorn for his uncouthness. She almost laughed out loud at the thought of their being married. As they waited for tea to be delivered she said, 'I've got to get rid of it.'

Warren gave her a disbelieving look. Then he laughed. 'Don't be silly.'

'I'm not joking,' she hissed. 'There's no way I'm having this baby.'

'But . . .' Warren looked hurt now, 'I'll stand by you . . . I've said . . .'

'That's not the point.' Jade's voice rose, she hastily converted her shriek to a laugh. The Randolph lounge seemed to be the place for scenes of emotional disturbance. 'Look,' she said, in a more reasonable tone, 'Allegra says it costs about three hundred quid. Can you get it for me?'

Warren stared at the Axminster carpet. His arms dangled help-lessly between his knees and his face had taken on a frozen look.

'Have you gone deaf?' said Jade after a few moments.

Warren shook his head, as though he had, or as though he

160

were a dog, trying to dislodge an unwelcome burr in his ear. It was a distressed, unco-ordinated movement. He said, 'We've got to talk about it. After all, I am the father.'

Jade gave a small sneer of laughter. 'You surely can't think you have rights in this! Did you really imagine I was going to have it?'

The sheer incredulity of her tone branded him as though he were a steer or a slave. He looked at her for the first time right in the eye. 'I did,' he said slowly.

Jade was silenced. She felt half amazed and half shamed. In that moment she realized that Warren truly loved her. It made him horribly attractive. She said in a voice so low it was almost a whisper, 'Have you got enough money to pay for a room?'

In the swagged bed Warren stripped Jade with care and she held his head to her breast, sliding a nipple into his mouth. His lips pulled on it as he stroked her gently from neck to thigh, running his long fingers into every nook and crevice. By the time he was ready to enter her, she was wet and open, spreading around him like moist seaweed, tangling with his limbs and sucking him in as though she wanted him to drive out the demon in her. They fucked with an athletic desperation. Warren was at his most fervent, Jade matched him in abandon. At last they fell across each other, exhausted and bloodied, still murmuring incoherently as they nuzzled at each other. When Warren woke up a little later, Jade was sitting at the bottom of the bed smoking a cigarette. She said, 'I'm still not going to have it.'

35

Sergeant Plummer pushed his bike down Cherry Tree Walk and leaned it against the battered fence of number thirty-nine. 'Could do with a nail or two,' he noted to himself as he pushed open the gate and walked up the weedy concrete path. This body business was disturbing. The man now rested at the mortuary, but despite the initial interest no one had come forward to claim him. For once he had not even heard from Jean Peabody.

He lifted the small brass galleon knocker and let it fall, thinking these were the sort of jobs he hated most, seeing the pain and distress on people's faces.

Jean Peabody opened the door. She seemed startled to see him. 'Is it about Warren?' she began, in a worried voice. 'He was going to come down, honest . . . but he's been so busy.'

'It's all right, Jean,' said Sergeant Plummer gruffly, presuming on their long acquaintance. 'Charlie's decided to drop the charge. As long as he can interview Mr Radcliffe.'

Jean nodded with relief, as though the matter had now passed into hands more capable than hers. 'Thanks for letting me know,' she nodded.

'There's another thing, Jean . . . this body?'

'Come inside, won't you?' she said hastily. She didn't wish to discuss bodies on the doorstep.

In the overheated living room he took off his cap and undid the buttons on his tunic. Jean Peabody came back with tea and cake, exclaiming over the fact that it was, 'Only Marks and Spencer's.'

'You've not rung us, Jean,' he remarked, slowly stirring in two sugars.

162

Mrs Peabody averted her eyes and smoothed at her skirt. He saw she had taken off her pinny in the kitchen. 'No,' she said quietly, 'not this time.'

Sergeant Plummer nodded gravely. 'I come t' put your mind at rest. This man's altogether wrong. Doesn't fit your description.'

They were both silent for a moment, reviewing the many photos of Andy Peabody she had pressed upon the station. Jean said, 'I knew it wasn't 'im.' She paused, then continued with a choke in her voice. 'I've 'ad a postcard from 'im.' Plummer looked up in surprise. Jean said quickly, 'I know I shoulda told you, I 'aven't told a soul. It's Warren I'm worried about. It would so upset 'im.'

She got up and crossed to her knitting bag. Out of a jumble of needles and wools she produced a lurid postcard. ''S Australia,' she said briefly, handing it to the sergeant. On the other side of the blue-skied picture of the Barrier Reef, he read, 'Bet you're surprised to hear from me? Well they always sent the black sheep to Australia! I'm courting a young lady here, who's crazy enough to want to marry me. How about a divorce? No hard feelings. Andy.'

Sergeant Plummer felt his throat constrict with pain for her. He cleared it and said heartily, 'Well Jean, it must be a relief to know?'

Jean was staring out of the window. She looked very frail against the cruel spring light. Plummer rose and rather awkwardly put his arm round her. 'Divorce him, Jean,' he said, 'quick as possible. It's not too late to start again.'

She gave him a pitying smile. 'With five children?'

He wouldn't mind, he thought. A ready-made family could make some man happy. Lick of paint and some DIY would soon see the house spanking. And it would do that young Warren good to feel a man's influence.

For ten days after the seance, Jeremy wrestled with his guilt and fear. Far from putting his mind at rest, the seance had increased the pictorial terrors. He conjured Guy's face, imagining it as

163

eyeless now. He made endless anagrams in his head of the letters he remembered. At night he lay awake, listening to the unaccustomed sounds of an empty house. Did the windows rattle like that when Darryl slept beside him? On one occasion, tortured by Ancient Mariner images of drowned men, their bones picked white by water scavengers, he resorted to a night light. He lay for hours staring into its greenish flame, a tiny hope in the darkness.

At last he could stand it no longer and rang Toni, asking her if she would accompany him to view the body in the mortuary.

Sergeant Plummer let them into the breeze-block building. It was cold inside and both of them shivered. 'It's a complete mystery,' said the sergeant, with a slight air of desperation. 'We've had the usual phone calls but they've all been dead ends . . . Oh, excuse me, I didn't mean that to sound like a pun.' He coughed to cover his bad taste, then continued, 'Somebody must know him. He might be someone who lives alone. Or has been doing recently.' He spoke in the present tense as though out of respect for the spirit of the dead man which might be hovering, listening.

The body was on a table behind a pockmarked screen. Toni took a quick glance at the uncovered head then looked to Jeremy to see if there was any recognition. Jeremy was staring at the pale water-bloated flesh with its one eye pointed skywards. The whole face seemed lopsided, as though frozen in a malicious wink. He shook his head slowly but seemed more disappointed than relieved. Perhaps, thought Toni, he had wanted it to be Guy. Wanted to put an end to it.

Sergeant Plummer sighed and drew the greyish sheet up over the body. It would have to go back to the freezer. 'What made you think you might know him, Mr Taylor?' he asked Jeremy, who was in the grip of a fit of shuddering.

'Oh . . . er . . . a friend. A friend . . . of a . . . friend. That is . . . an acquaintance . . . is missing,' said Jeremy, summoning every ounce of amateur dramatic skill. 'Just a chance really . . .

he's probably gone on holiday.' He finished with a laugh which
would not have convinced even the loyal audience of the Warfleet
Players. Toni steered him out of the room before he could do
further damage.

36

The bar of the Admiral Nelson buzzed with speculation. Rumer was there, queen bee in the centre of the healing circle. They sat, as though still in meditation, in a circle round her table. Stories of the dead man circulated in the group. It was believed he'd been horribly mutilated.

'Have those hippies been through?' demanded Fenella Pepper.

'Trussed up like a chicken,' said Laurel Hopcraft.

'Red Indian,' said Rumer firmly.

They all turned as Toni and Jeremy Taylor entered the bar. Jeremy looked pale and shaky, his face was blotchy as though he had been weeping. Toni nodded to the circle then shovelled Jeremy into a button-backed booth and made her way to the bar for a couple of stiff whiskies. Warren Peabody lounged there with a group of youths. Pints of lager were being consumed at great speed. Warren was flushed and excited-looking. He half-acknowledged Toni, then turned his back, it seemed deliberately.

Toni glanced back to check on Jeremy. He looked wretched, still leaning, as awkwardly as she had placed him, against the padded seat back; like an abandoned teddy bear, she thought, flung down in a childish rage.

They'd had a bear in common when they were children. He was called Dr Spock in defiance of their mother's obsessive devotion to the guru. Toni had done many terrible things to Dr Spock. Once he had been found with his head down the lavatory. Jeremy had always rescued him, bandaged his wounds, cuddled him back to life. Now he himself was in need of resuscitating. Toni's heart clenched with pity for him and rage at the faithless Darryl. She'd like to stick *his* head down the lavatory. She turned

166

sharply back to the bar as the barman slapped down the whiskies.

Warren certainly did not want Toni to hear the group's conversation. He laughed loudly to cover a remark of Carl's about a lorry load of videos he was expecting to shift for fifty quid apiece. As Toni returned to her seat, he relaxed and leaned against the bar again.

'Are you in?' demanded Carl. He was the hard man of the estate – he'd once dropped four tabs of acid in one go, and was planning a rob, a ram-raid of High Street Heels which had just had a large delivery of trainers.

Warren hesitated, then nodded. He caught the warning glances of Dean and Lee. 'Yeah,' he said boldly, 'I'll do it.'

'You,' challenged Carl, turning on Travis who had gone quiet, under cover of downing his lager.

Travis shrugged. ''M on probation.'

'So?' charged Carl belligerently. Travis shrugged again, indicating that he had run out of words on the subject. 'You an' me then,' said Carl, throwing a contemptuous grin towards Warren.

The deal was sealed with some blow round at Carl's house. Tracie, his girlfriend, glowered at the gang as they trooped in with Carl. But he told her to fuck off to bed and, with a long-suffering sigh, she did so.

Travis took Warren aside in the kitchen and said, 'What are you getting mixed up with him for? You know he's a tithead.'

Warren tossed his hair back and said pointedly, 'You're smoking his stash.' He paused, then said less insolently, 'Besides, I need the money.'

The youths passed the spliff gravely between them and gradually sank into a stoned silence, nodding and occasionally beating time to the drum'n'bass that blasted from Carl's stereo. One by one they sloped off into the dark estate encountering cats, marital discord, the occasional cruising Panda. When the others had all gone Carl and Warren got down to serious planning.

37

At two-thirty in the morning on a Sunday towards the end
of March there was a bomb-like explosion in Warfleet High
Street. The plate-glass front of High Street Heels splintered into
a million crystal fragments, flying through the frosty night air
like winged icicles. The heavy RSJ Jim was having installed
crashed down, bringing with it breeze-blocks and mortar. The
air was a stew of plaster dust and through it ran a dark figure,
its unlaced trainers making a light slapping sound on the
pavement. A second later an alarm bell split the tinkles and
crashes. It rang shatteringly through the now still darkness.
For a long time no one came. People were used to sudden in-
trusions of noise, car alarms, sirens. They turned over cursing
and pressed the bedclothes closer. At length a police car sauntered by. It stopped some yards beyond the shop front and
slowly a young policeman got out. He approached the
gaping crash site gingerly. Raiders these days tended to be
armed. In the hollowed shop front a Bedford van was
rammed. The roof was crushed by a ton of fallen masonry. The
passenger side was empty; on the driver's side a man lay over
the steering wheel. His head streamed with blood. He was out
cold, maybe dead, thought PC Armitage, as he turned over
Warren Peabody.

Jean Peabody had to go to the station. Warren had come round,
he was concussed and being attended by the police doctor. 'We
'aven't got a solicitor,' she said, agitatedly twisting the ends of
her headscarf.

'Don't worry, Jean.' Sergeant Plummer dropped a comforting

hand on her shoulder, letting it rest there slightly longer than was necessary. 'We'll take care of it.'

Jean stared vacantly up at the kindly pink face fringed in greying gingery hair and burst into tears. 'It's the shock,' she excused herself, distractedly sipping at the mug of tea the sergeant had given her. 'He's bin so good lately. What with Harry and Mrs Radcliffe . . . I don't know what got into him.'

'Stupid young fool,' said Sergeant Plummer feelingly.

Jim Bacon was shaking his head. 'Wonder he wasn't killed. That RSJ was only resting there, the builders were coming in this morning.' The van, ramming into the shop window, had brought down the whole of the front wall Jim was in the process of rebuilding. 'It's subsidence you see, the whole place was on the slide. I don't know what the insurance will say about this.' He sat down rather heavily, as though buckling beneath the weight of further forms to fill in.

Jean was allowed to see Warren for a moment. He looked sheepishly at her, still dazed. There was a long ugly gash on his forehead. 'Oh, Warren,' she cried, flinging herself at him.

'Don't, Ma,' he said, 'I'm all right. Really.' He paused. 'I'm sorry.'

Sergeant Plummer had to cough to relieve the lump in his throat. Pity the birch had gone, he thought, he could have larruped young Warren.

As soon as he could stand, Warren was cautioned and carted down to the cells. Plummer was intending to take a statement later. 'I'll run you home, Jean,' he said to Mrs Peabody, who was standing hopelessly in the interview room. With her coat on over her nightie, she looked like a refugee from a war-torn country.

'You're very kind,' she said in a thin voice, looking at him directly now and registering the concern in his nice blue eyes. You deserve some kindness, he thought to himself, but he didn't say anything.

The panic in Jade's voice when Caro relayed these events over the phone next day was, to Caro, mystifying. She was surprised when Jade said she must come home immediately.

169

Replacing the phone, she thought, 'Of course, she's worried about Sebastian.' For her, Jade's visit would be a relief. Cynthia was descending in the morning.

Delia came to the door with Harry in her arms. He gurgled, parting his lips in a smile which showed two tiny bottom teeth, and held out his hands to Jade, who stood on the doorstep.

'Can I come in?' said Jade awkwardly to Delia's arched eyebrows.

Delia stood back to let her pass, then followed her through to the kitchen. 'You've heard about Warren, I guess,' she said, one-handedly filling the kettle and placing it on a burner. Jade nodded dumbly. Then, with an effort, said, 'It must make it difficult for you . . . with Harry.'

'I don't mind,' smiled Delia, shifting the baby with more enthusiasm than expertise on to her other shoulder. 'Any excuse not to go into work. As a matter of fact, he's quite jolly.' Harry drooled happily, spreading sticky slobber over Delia's once immaculate collar. Jade was too consumed with her own drama to notice Delia's change of attitude, she merely nodded and murmured something about it being a good thing Delia had Zo to deputize for her. Delia gave a barking laugh. 'Only too ready.'

She made tea and asked Jade what brought her home mid-week. Jade looked at her teacup with its whirlpool of brown liquid. She was reminded of the river on her first walk with Warren. Now she felt it would be a happy fate to be sucked into it. Her lips trembled and as she raised the cup to them, two large tears squeezed from her eyes and plopped into the Darjeeling.

'Jade, you're crying,' stated Delia, still matter-of-factly. 'Tell me what's wrong.' Her tone would brook no prevarication and Jade found herself stuttering out the whole sorry story.

'He was doing the robbery for me,' she finished, clutching her head and sobbing openly now. It was a suitably operatic ending.

Delia clicked her teeth. 'Lordy lord. Have you told anyone else?'

Jade shook her head and raised her hands to push her heavy

170

wet locks out of her face. Her jewels tinkled like a herd of Tibetan goats. 'I came to you first,' she said, 'you're the only one I can tell. Ma would have a fit. Or do something mad, like want to keep it.'

'Is that so mad?' said Delia softly.

Jade looked at her in surprise. 'I thought you'd understand . . .' she said plaintively.

Delia looked at Jade as though through the wrong end of a telescope. Jade's small, hunched body could have been hers very recently. Now a great space was between them. A space filled with Sebastian . . . and Harry. She said gently, 'I do understand. And of course I'll help you. But . . . it's some time since . . . I don't quite know . . .'

'Could you lend me the money at least?' said Jade. She asked very humbly.

'Yes,' responded Delia, 'if you're absolutely certain.' Jade nodded slowly.

'I've just had a thought,' said Delia, as she showed Jade to the door. 'I went to see Briar, you know . . . your Dad's ex-girl friday? She'd just had a termination.' Delia didn't mention whose child Briar had been sluicing away. She didn't think it appropriate. 'She'd have an up-to-date clinic number. Why don't you call and see her?'

Jade nodded and set off to the gate. She turned when she got to it. Delia, standing framed in the doorway, held up the laughing Harry's hand and waggled it in a goodbye gesture.

38

There was a powwow over Sebastian's bed in the hospital next day. The consultant had said he could go home and the question was where to take him.

Cynthia and Jade took it for granted that Seb would return to Four Trees. Caro was uncomfortably aware that she didn't. Delia was adamant that Seb must come to Honeysuckle Cottage. She was prepared to take time off to nurse him. Jade was appalled that there was even a question. Daddy belonged with Mummy. Four Trees was his home. Caro said warily that of course that was true . . . she paused, recalling a dream she'd had in which she had visited Seb and asked to be set free. He had smiled at her like an understanding friend and given his blessing for her to start her life over. She realized the others were staring at her and continued, bolstered by the memory . . . but there again their relationship was over.

Cynthia dropped the grapes she was eating and appeared about to faint at this news. Caro was glad they were in a public place. It prevented Cynthia giving full space to her melodramatic instincts. Jade, however, burst into tears. This was the very conspiracy she had feared. Zo had perverted Caro. Delia patted Jade, knowing her problem was largely hormonal, and said calmly that she agreed with Caro. If Seb came with her, he could get to know his son. Cynthia choked on her reviving glass of Lucozade.

At this point a long sob came from the pillow end of the bed. Sebastian was crying. The women were shocked into speechlessness. They exchanged shifty glances. 'Home,' said Sebastian and pointed to Delia. The women were moved by his terrible need. None of them could resist him.

Caro went home very relieved. Zo would be busy now she was to shoulder Delia's load; her visits to Warfleet would be limited. But she, Caro, could go up to Hampstead . . . two or three days at a time, why not? The only thing that stood in the way was Cindy. Perhaps Delia could be persuaded . . . ?

Cynthia said she was going straight to bed. She felt, she claimed, sickened. At the foot of the stairs she made time to deliver to Caro a monologue on her deficiencies as a wife. Caro was silent; she knew Cynthia was really referring to her deficiencies as a daughter.

Jade said she was going to London for a couple of days. Caro had told her Warren had been released on police bail, pending his court appearance, but she did not want to see him. 'Say hello to Zo,' said Caro. 'Maybe you can stay with her.'

Later that day Delia went to the hospital and collected Sebastian and his suitcase. She put him in the downstairs back room she had prepared for him. From his bed he would be able to see the garden and Harry in his pram. Neighbouring cats would come and go. Delia pictured neighbours chatting over the fence as she hung out the washing. The little house would be full of life as it had never been when Wendy had lived in it.

39

Jade had decided to see Briar in person. She had never been to her father's office and was curious. She wondered, as she walked from the tube, what Sebastian would do for a job now. He was clearly unsuited to the anxieties of an executive position.

She had telephoned Briar to say she was coming. Briar had been short on the phone, even off-putting. She had seemed resistant to a meeting, though Jade had not mentioned her business. When the receptionist had stopped filing her nails long enough to press some buttons and connect with Briar's office, Jade had heard the grudging voice saying that she'd better be sent up then.

Jade had met Briar once or twice at Four Trees and remembered her as a bouncy Tiggerish type of person. She was unprepared for the doughnut she saw exploding over the swivelling desk chair. Briar was eating egg salad and there was a smear of mayonnaise on one of her chins. She gave Jade a malevolent look and said, spitting small mouthfuls of egg on to the glass desktop, 'Make it quick, I've got a meeting in three minutes.'

'Dad's back,' said Jade. 'I think the company's been notified.'

Briar shrugged as though she couldn't care less. 'Poor sod,' she said. 'He's washed up. It's no good you coming to plead for him.'

'No,' said Jade. 'It's not about that . . . it's . . .'

'Want a job?' demanded Briar suddenly.

Startled, Jade shook her head. 'I haven't got my degree yet,' she said.

Briar gave a horsy snort, almost inhaling egg salad. 'Don't bother,' she said, 'if you want to get into television. These days it's run by car salesmen from Essex.'

Jade said, 'Actually, Delia told me to get in touch with you. I need an address. Of a clinic.' Briar stared at her unhelpfully. Jade hoped she was not going to have to resort to sign language to make her meaning clear. Briar's door stood wide open to a world full of Essex car salesmen.

A young man with a tea trolley came in, but Briar waved him away, saying sharply, 'And shut the door after you.' When the boy had gone, Briar turned a furious face on Jade. 'How dare you come here making allegations! Is this some sort of blackmail?'

Jade hurriedly said that it was nothing of the kind. She had no interest in Briar's private life. She was in trouble herself and just wanted a telephone number. Briar subsided back over her seat and pulled her Filofax towards her. 'You never know what these sleazeball journalists will come out with,' she cautioned. 'You don't want your Dad's affairs all over the papers.'

Jade agreed that she did not, though she was puzzled by Briar's reference. She forgot it an instant later when Briar pushed a slip of paper over the desk. There was a name and a telephone number. 'Dr Greenbaum,' said Briar in a stage whisper, 'tell him I said. He'll look after you.' Jade looked up and met her eyes. There was knowledge and sadness in them. She looked for a moment like a small intelligent monkey in a rhino's coating. Briar's telephone shrilled and she picked up the receiver indicating that the interview was over. As she left the room, Jade heard Briar behind her, chortling and bandying gossip as though their moment of truth had never happened.

40

Jade couldn't be seen by Dr Greenbaum until the following day, but was assured by the receptionist, in coded language, that as her case was urgent, she could go straight to the clinic if the doctor was satisfied. Satisfied she could pay, Jade supposed she meant. Allegra had dissuaded her from the Infirmary in Oxford, saying the National Health took for ever and besides, her geography classmate's best friend had been in for one, and it had been all over Oxford.

Jade decided to follow Caro's advice and see if she could stay with Zo. It was time, she felt, she had a face-to-face with her. She called from the station and then again from a pub in Hampstead. Each time the engaged tone sounded. Zo was a talker after all. Or perhaps her phone was off the hook – Jade imagined she had a mobile. She had left it late to find anywhere else to stay, so took a chance on going round anyway.

The front door of Zo's house opened as Jade came up the path. A boy with a bike was coming out. Jade held the door open for him as he struggled with the handlebars, then slipped in as he gratefully wheeled it down the steps. Jade climbed the stairs to the top floor, hearing all the way the latest Tina Turner record.

The music was coming from 1A, Zo's flat. The front door was ajar and through it Jade saw a blur of candlelight. She pushed the door until it opened enough for her to enter. The lobby, off which the sitting room led, was empty, as was the softly brilliant sitting room. A couple of empty wine glasses stood on the floor by the fur hearthrug. Jade wandered into the kitchen where the remains of a meal lay on the table. Two plates, she noted.

'Hello,' she called uncertainly, returning to the lobby. There was only one door left to try, since the bathroom door was wide open. The bedroom door was not quite shut and a sliver of light showed down the crack. Tentatively, Jade nudged it. It swung wide displaying the kingsize bed. Upon it lay Zo, completely naked. Below her writhed another body. For a moment Jade thought it was Caro, then some blond curls appeared to the side of Zo's shoulder. The two women were oblivious to her as they shuddered to their climax. Then, as they rolled apart, Zo looked up and saw Jade's staring face. 'Oh Christ,' she said softly.

Zo made camomile tea and gave it to Jade, who'd been very sick in the lavatory. Zo's new secretary, Millie, had hurriedly dressed and gone. There had been whispered arrangements in the lobby. Jade lay on the sofa and sipped at the medicinal brew. Zo came across and put a cold damp flannel on her forehead. She was saying something, but Jade couldn't concentrate on it. This wasn't the face-to-face she'd had in mind, acting the heavy father.

'What have you eaten?' Zo repeated.

Jade's eyes were closed. Without thinking, she blurted, 'I'm pregnant. I'm getting rid of it tomorrow.' She turned her head away as Zo's warm hand brushed back the heavy locks on her forehead.

'Does Caro know?' said Zo.

Jade's eyes shot open. She turned and glared at Zo. 'You're not to tell her!'

Zo smiled ironically. 'Seems we've both got a secret.'

'Blackmail!' spat Jade, pushing Zo's healing hand away.

Zo's face went rather hard. 'Silly girl,' she said quietly, 'we could be friends. I could be a help to you.'

'You've twisted my mother's mind!' cried Jade childishly, 'I hate what you've done to her!'

Zo sighed and withdrew, sitting cross-legged on the floor. Jade sat up, blood coming back to her face. She stared at Zo judgementally. There was nothing contrite about her. Nothing guilty or apologetic. Her body language was relaxed. Her face, as Jade gazed, assumed a slight smile with a question mark in it.

'How could you?' Jade accused. 'She loves you!'

Zo nodded. 'And I love her. This was . . .' she shrugged '. . . just sex.' Jade made a spitting sound. 'Well, what about you?' countered Zo. 'Did you love the man who made you pregnant?' Jade looked away. 'You did,' pressed Zo, 'I'll bet. And yet you won't have his baby.'

'It's none of your business,' snapped Jade.

'Just pointing out that love is complicated.'

'At least I was faithful,' said Jade, summoning great disdain.

Zo laughed. 'So straight,' she said. 'Sex isn't important. Scratching an itch.' Jade threw her a disgusted look. ''S true,' said Zo firmly, 'love's what counts. And what you do with it.'

Jade looked away quickly. An image of Warren's stricken face, his eyes black with misery, had reared in her head. She remembered a puppy she'd had when she'd been little. It had been run over, and Jade, returning from school, had found it whimpering in the gutter. She would never forget its hurt eyes, turned to her for help in its dying agony. A groan broke from her. Her heart began to pump nastily and she squeezed her hands over it.

'Going to be sick again?' said Zo, jumping to her feet. 'Head between legs and breathe deeply.' With girl guide efficiency she manipulated Jade's body. When the crisis was past, she went for brandy. 'Want me to come with you tomorrow?' she said, holding the glass to Jade's lips. 'Often work at home Friday.'

Jade looked into Zo's frank face. The eyes were kind, she saw. It would be good to be loved by Zo. Reassuring. She nodded slowly. Zo grinned, revealing her charming teeth. 'Better?' she said, putting a friendly hand on Jade's shoulder. Jade looked down, ashamed to be so needy. 'Don't worry about your Mum. She'll be fine.' Zo paused. 'She doesn't know it yet, but I'm only a stepping stone for her.' There was regret in Zo's voice as she said this, but when Jade looked up, she was smiling. Zo was a brave person, she thought, she'd learnt to take life as she found it.

'Thanks,' she said. 'My appointment's ten-thirty.'

'Bed now,' said Zo. 'Have you got toothbrush, nightie?' Jade fished about in her dufflebag as Zo unrolled the futon.

'Great kit,' said Zo, as Jade fetched out a froth of red and black lace nightie. 'Sleep well, sweet dreams. I'll wake you in the morning.'

When Zo collected Jade from the clinic in Hendon next day, Jade was a chastened woman. 'How was it?' asked Zo sympathetically. The last time she had seen Jade was as she was wheeled into the operating theatre.

'He asked me if I was reading Stendhal,' said Jade in a small voice.

'What?' said Zo.

'As I was going under. *Le Rouge et le Noir*. It was because of my nightie.'

Funny, thought Zo, the details you remember. 'Come back with me for the night. See how you're feeling tomorrow.'

The thought of the warm room and being nursed was attractive. Jade smiled at Zo: she didn't need persuading.

41

Delia was in her element. All her organizational skills, so useful at the office, were recycled into caring. Sebastian gazed at her humbly. He didn't like her to be out of his room for long, so she took to reading manuscripts at a desk there. He delighted in the garden, bursting with green and gold thanks to Warren's tending. He even seemed entranced by Harry who was at his most playful. Delia had explained to him, simply, his relationship with the baby. Sebastian accepted everything with a kind of wonder.

Slowly he began to speak of what had happened to him. How the stress of his rocky job, coupled with the nightmare of his private life, had finally broken his mind. The turning point had been New Year's Eve. Unbeknown to Caro, he had often begun new affairs on the stroke of twelve. He'd run away, terrified of the thought of another liaison.

The sentences were at first disjointed. He would lose his way and look to Delia for help. 'You were in LA, staying with BJ . . .' she would prompt gently. He didn't query how she knew these things, thinking perhaps, in his confusion, that he had already told her. But as his memory, wiped it seemed by the shock of treatment, returned, he became curious about Delia's part in his story.

She told him of her long search and the reason behind it. Once, as she spoke of Wendy, long slow tears ran from Sebastian's eyes. She held his heaving shoulders and thought how changed Wendy would have found him. The jungle spirit the other women had loved him for was gone now, leaving a helpless dependence she found irresistible. He was like a large baby, she thought, as she helped him to the lavatory or ran his bath. A sexy one, too. Often as she arranged him in bed, smoothing down the covers, her hand would brush against an erection. Was this what she'd been searching for, she wondered, a child man, innocent and erotic? She longed to touch him as a woman, but held back, knowing the right moment would present itself.

At night, after Warren had gone and Harry was in bed, Delia had him to herself. In the dimly glowing room she would read aloud to him. One night, as they listened to *La Bohème*, he reached out to her. She went to the bed and let his arms pull her down. His hands touched her hair, caressing it. She lay still, calm, feeling the rightness. After a while she got up and undressed, letting the clothes drop to the floor. She stood naked in front of him, feeling rather than seeing the intensity of his dark eyes. She felt like a piece of sculpture.

He touched her at first as though she were indeed a precious object, stroking her body with reverence. She let him explore her, then gently drew him over her, looking up into the face she had followed so many miles, recognizing each line upon it. As the weight of his body pressed down on her, she remembered her feeling of emptiness and laughed out loud. This was what she had been waiting for. She opened her legs and let Sebastian into her. They moved together slowly, inexorably, and at last, ecstatically. Afterwards they lay quiet, their bones melted into each other. An innocent joy surrounded them. It was as if they had both been reborn, but this time found life palatable.

42

On the third day Cynthia rose again from the dead and announced that she might as well go home now as there was nothing more she could do.

Caro, standing with lightly boiled egg on breakfast tray, was overtaken by a wretchedly familiar feeling; a surge of guilty pity for her mother's need to be needed. She stared now at the small girlish figure in its lilac knit, hair as blond as when she was twenty, waist as small, probably, mouth set in a mulish rose-coloured line, and said resignedly, 'No Mum, stay a few days more. I'm glad of your company.'

Cynthia's face relaxed. She almost permitted herself to smile but instead took the tray from Caro, admired the embroidered cloth and asked if there wasn't any honey.

In the hours when Cynthia 'rested' or attended to her rigorous toilette, Caro worked on her short story. One of the things Zo had in preparation was an anthology of women's work and she had held out the possibility of Caro's being included in it. When she worked well, Caro discovered, nothing else mattered. For simple cash, she had increased her hours as Celia Troubridge's right-hand man, graduating from form filling and bill giving to clipping claws and administering shots of antibiotic. She considered putting Four Trees on the market, but knew she couldn't do this without consulting Jade and Sebastian.

She hadn't heard from Jade since she'd gone to London, though Zo had called and mentioned Jade had stayed the night and she felt some breakthrough had been made. Caro was grateful, she didn't want stress between her daughter and her lover. Perhaps

Jade was growing up at last, accepting that Caro was not solely her mother.

Seb she saw fairly frequently. Mostly, it was true, urged by Cynthia, who seemed convinced a reunion was inevitable. 'But Mother,' said Caro, with her eyebrows taking on an angle of exasperation, 'you can see how happy he is with Delia.'

'It's temporary,' insisted Cynthia, 'an aberration. After all, he hasn't the full use of his wits yet.' Caro would turn aside to hide a despairing giggle. No matter what Ingrid's advice, she still found it impossible to talk to her mother.

The matter of Harry was more serious. It took some days of consideration. Finally, in triumph, Cynthia announced that Caro must adopt him. 'Think how lovely it would be. A baby in the house. It would draw you back together.' Caro turned cold at the thought. She wanted neither a baby, nor Sebastian. That chapter had ended.

She rang Toni to ask if she would take Cynthia off her hands for an afternoon so she could go up to town. Toni said she'd love to, but she was going to see the Dalai Lama. 'Why don't you come?' she said. 'Heaven knows you could use some spiritual insight.'

'I have Ingrid,' responded Caro tartly. 'That's all the insight I can deal with.'

Sitting by the open french windows, looking out on to the sunlit garden of Honeysuckle Cottage, Caro drank a second cup of tea reluctantly. Cynthia was in full flood, describing some friend of hers who'd had shock treatment. 'Turned her into a cauliflower. Didn't know me, and I'm her oldest friend. Still has trouble with numbers.'

Seb's dark eyes would engage with Cynthia's, then flicker back to the garden where Delia was walking Harry up and down in his pram, pointing out the flowers. He's in love with her, thought Caro, with great relief, I hope to God she returns it. The solicitous way in which Delia, re-entering, bent over Seb and rearranged his blanket, the complicit look which passed

183

between them, the touch of hands as Delia departed, told Caro she did.

'Come on, Mother,' she said briskly, 'drink up. I'm due at the surgery at five.'

Delia called from the kitchen, 'If you have things to do, leave Cynthia here. She's very welcome.'

Caro went into the kitchen. 'Really?' she said with disbelief.

'She keeps Seb amused. I still have a certain amount of reading.'

'What will you do if Warren goes to prison? It'll make things awfully difficult for you.'

'Stay home and be mother,' said Delia. 'I find I like it.'

'Well,' said Caro, still unwilling to burden Delia, 'perhaps tomorrow? I have to go up to town. I'd like to stay on and see Zo.'

'Have you resolved anything?' asked Delia.

'What do you mean?' said Caro.

'About how you'll live? Surely you don't want to go on at Four Trees?'

Delia was as usual one step ahead, thought Caro. She said, 'I have thought of selling. I could go to London. Live with Zo.'

'Mmm,' said Delia noncommittally. 'Well, you stay up tomorrow and have a look round. There's a lot of cheap stuff on the market.'

It seemed that Ingrid agreed with Delia. 'You've never really known your own boundaries,' she asserted.

'I had a flat when I was a student,' responded Caro hotly.

'That's not exactly what I mean,' sighed Ingrid. 'You've been co-dependent all your life. Don't you feel it's time to break the habit?'

After lunching with Zo, Caro took her key and walked about Hampstead. She noticed several 'For Sale' signs on property close to Zo's and eventually went into an estate agent's and collected a pile of literature. A studio flat, photo white walls and huge skylights, looked interesting. The prices shocked her. She'd almost forgotten Seb and Jade, nor had she mentioned this plan to Zo. After all it had barely formed yet. In the meantime, she gathered up the papers: she'd go and view some property.

43

The case of The Crown versus Warren Peabody was to be tried at Stourbridge Crown Court shortly after Easter. Caro was to appear as a witness for the defence, as was Delia. They would testify to Warren's good character. Jade had elected to stay in Oxford for the holidays. She was studying hard for her Part Twos, she said, and didn't want the disturbance.

Easter had been cold and hard. Caro had spent much of it in bed with Zo, when not out flat-hunting. Four Trees was on the market, though so far there had been little interest.

The day of the trial was fine and bright, however, and as Caro and Delia approached the court, with its self-important curlicued façade, they saw le tout Warfleet hurrying in. 'One would think it was an auto da fé,' said Delia.

'Yes,' agreed Caro, noting the predatory eagerness of the crowd. It would be useful for her story.

Jean Peabody got out of a taxi. She was wearing a lime-green suit obviously bought for the occasion. Beside her, Caro and Delia in their dowdy anoraks, felt shabby. Delia had at least taken Warren shopping, thinking it unsuitable that he appear in court in jeans and a leather jacket.

When he was brought into the dock, she wondered if she had done right. Warren seemed diminished by the dark suit and tie. Shorn of his glamorous locks, he looked like a pollarded tree. A felled hero.

Despite their horror of the courtroom Lee and Travis had turned up to be supportive. They nudged each other and gestured at Warren. Privately they thought he was crazy to have taken all the blame. Carl had been the instigator. Maybe he was scared to implicate Carl, who was known to have a squad of revengers.

The others who filled the public gallery were 'friends' of Jim and Peggy. They ranged from Rumer, who'd years ago predicted Warren would 'come to no good', to Laurel, who sat on the youth advisory board, and Jeremy, who secretly fancied Warren. Toni was there, dressed even more eccentrically in orange and, Caro saw with dismay, with her head shaved, Fenella Pepper, representing the church in a large purple hat, Teddy Forbes, whispering with Marsha Snelgrove, and May Clark from the Delphinium, one of the few, probably, on Warren's side. Squeezing in at the last moment, notepad poised, was Charlie Barrett.

'Oh, my God,' said Delia, peering through the door.

'Quite,' said Caro.

It was, as Hugh Jessop for the prosecution announced, 'an open-and-shut case'.

'More of a down-and-out one,' whispered Marsha waggishly, causing Teddy Forbes to giggle loudly.

Eric Antrobus, for the defence, appeared to lack conviction in his case. As though aware he was on the wrong side, he seemed anxious to join in the general condemnation. Caro and Delia and a newly assigned social worker spoke for Warren. Kind-hearted, good with babies, deprived background etc, etc. At the last remark Jean Peabody was heard to click her teeth loudly. Delia spoke in clear ringing tones, drawing a slight echo from the overbearing spandrels of the ceiling. Caro was nervous and stammered. She was trying hard not to notice details – Fenella Pepper's purple turban, the way the light from the high windows fell on the faces in the public seats turning them into Hogarthian grotesques, the judge's wig in need of a perm – and to concentrate on the questions. By the end of the session she had a migraine.

Warren was subdued throughout. Called upon to give evidence in his own defence, he agreed, in monosyllables, that he was guilty. The jury was out for ten minutes. The judge sentenced Warren to two years' detention in view of his previous record.

Warren looked up only once and his eyes went straight to Caro and Delia. He seemed to search the space around them, but it was empty, and a moment later he dropped his gaze and his head. He was led away to the cells. In the absurd handcuffs, thought Caro, he looked like a serf who had stolen a sheep and was being sent to the gallows.

On the steps outside gaggles of people had lingered. It might be a wedding, or a christening, thought Caro, people wearing their best clothes and talking cheerfully. She almost expected sherry and cake to be handed round. She moved between the groups with her new observer's ear, hearing Laurel Hopcraft saying it was the last government's fault. Youth had no hope. The Tories had created a lost generation. Teddy Forbes thought it was all down to 'E'. 'Loosens the moral centres of the brain,' he asserted, nodding his toupeed head so vigorously, Caro feared for his own grip. The only drug she had ever known Warren to take was Nurofen. Toni opined that the sentence was draconian: Warren would benefit more from counselling and aromatherapy. Rumer shrugged her shoulders. 'It was in the cards,' she said darkly. Around Jeremy and Marsha Snelgrove the talk was of the Warfleet Players' summer production. Marsha thought *The Trial*; Jeremy thought that might be construed as insensitive.

Jim and Peggy Bacon stood glumly to one side. Theirs was a pyrrhic victory. They had nothing against Warren, he'd even done a bit of part-time work unloading for them. Jean was one of their best customers. They felt guiltily responsible for this hiatus in the community.

Jean Peabody, in tears, was being comforted by Sergeant Plummer. As Caro and Delia passed, Caro heard him say, 'There there, Jean. He'll be out in fourteen months with good behaviour.'

Toni came across and Caro felt almost embarrassed to speak to her. She glanced round to see if others had noticed the outlandish costume. Toni herself, however, seemed completely at ease in her Buddhist drapes and open-toed sandals. On her forehead was a small red dot, put there, Caro supposed, by the Dalai Lama.

'It's a shame,' said Toni. 'He's not a bad lad.'

'What I can't understand,' said Caro, 'is why he did it? I mean he had money, a job, any of us would have helped him . . .' She tailed into puzzled silence. Delia looked down at her scuffed pumps and said nothing.

A car drew up beneath the steps and a man got out. It was Darryl Willoughby. Toni saw him first and turned straight to her brother. Jeremy was in animated conversation with Laurel Hopcraft, but when he saw Darryl, over her head, he stopped. His face went white and he swayed. A moment later he was stumbling down the steps into Darryl's arms. The two of them clung together. Darryl appeared to be weeping. Toni started towards them, but Caro put a restraining hand on her arm; there was no place for Toni in that reunion. 'Wait,' she said softly.

Jeremy and Darryl half fell down the steps towards the parked car. Somehow they got in and Darryl drove, in an uncertain line, away.

'Well!' said Toni.

44

Side by side in the rococo bed lay Jeremy and Darryl. Darryl's cock rested limply on his thigh; Jeremy's too had subsided. They had made love with a commitment they had not felt for years. Odd, thought Jeremy, what it took to rekindle passion. Love he was not in any doubt about. He had always loved Darryl.

Darryl said, 'I need a drink.'

'So it begins again,' sighed Jeremy inwardly. 'There's champagne in the fridge,' he said in a bright tone.

'Did you keep it there in case?' asked Darryl sardonically. They toasted each other in Jeremy's antique crystal, then Darryl said, 'You might as well know, I found Guy.'

Jeremy clutched the crystal goblet as though he would crush it. 'You're not . . . you're not going to him?' he managed to whisper.

Darryl ignored the question, saying instead, 'He's in London. He's got Aids.'

The word fell brutally through the air between them. Jeremy let it lie for a moment then began to shake his head. 'No,' he said, 'no. He just thinks he has. You see I told him that I . . .'

Darryl cut him short. 'You don't understand. I found him in hospital. St Mary's. He's been diagnosed. He was receiving treatment.' Jeremy put his glass down shakily. Toni's words about bad karma came back to him. 'The prognosis isn't good,' Darryl was saying. 'His T-cell count is very low.'

Terror took hold of Jeremy. He said, 'Have you been tested?'

Darryl did not meet his eyes. He sipped his champagne and said at length, in a flat voice, 'No. I was too frightened.'

Jeremy let his breath out slowly. So, there was still hope. He gulped back the champagne, letting the radiance of optimism fill his body.

Darryl said, 'He only found out because you lied to him. He went and got himself tested.' There was no anger in Darryl's voice, only a hollow irony. There was a pause. Jeremy refilled their glasses, glad he was not to be attacked for his craven behaviour. After a sip or two Darryl continued, 'Guy may be too ill to care for himself. I feel I must do something.'

'Yes, of course.' Jeremy nodded emphatically. Provided he was not going to lose Darryl, one way or the other, he knew he could put up with anything. '*We* must do something.' He would speak to Toni. She was into this holistic business. Anything money could buy . . .

Darryl slumped against a cherub. Now he had told his story he seemed exhausted. Jeremy stroked his thigh, still muscular and youthful despite Darryl's forty-something years. Suppose, thought Jeremy, he were to get ill, his beautiful boyish body wasted away? No, he would not see that. He bent and took Darryl's cock in his mouth. He would suck the life back into him.

45

Stourbridge prison where Warren was held was a red-brick castle-shaped building. It had turrets and battlements and although Jade had given up experiencing her life as a series of literary interludes, she could not help but think of *The Prisoner of Zenda*.

Warren had written to her and asked her to visit him. She didn't want to much, as the guilt she felt for her part in the affair was still very much with her. She had blocked it to some extent by throwing all her energy into work. Her tutor thought if she kept it up, a First was certain.

Warren had regained some of his rakish, heroic quality in the blue prison denim. His face was tanned and his eyes were a sunny gold as they crinkled into a smile. His hair, grown now, curled softly on his collar. Jade longed to stretch out her hand and touch it. She resisted, however, as she knew where the gesture would lead her.

'Been working in the garden,' volunteered Warren in answer to her admiring look. He stretched out his fine hands and Jade saw that they had a healthy residue of soil upon them. 'Better than mechanics,' said Warren, 'making things grow.' Jade nodded, then turned away, a lump in her throat. Warren caught her hands which rested on her side of the table. They twitched like white mice inside his lion's paws. 'Jade,' he said, 'I wanted to see you. I wanted to say it's all right. It wasn't your fault. You're not to feel bad about it.'

Jade's lips trembled uncontrollably and tears spilled over her cheeks. Her whole body convulsed and she sobbed and sobbed for what was lost, while Warren squeezed her hands gently. A prison guard came over and bent to the table. 'Everything all right?' he said briskly. Warren nodded and fetched out a hanky. It was incongruously white and laundered, Jade noticed, as she buried her nose in it. Surely it should have been a grimy rag – none of the scene lived up to pictorial expectation.

'All right?' said Warren, as she looked with watery eyes over the hanky. She nodded and brushed away wet strands of hair. 'You've had it cut,' said Warren.

'It looked childish,' she explained.

Warren gave a half-smile. 'I liked it,' he said.

Jade took a deep breath, and said, 'Of course, you know about the baby.'

'Delia told me,' said Warren.

'I'm sorry I didn't write,' said Jade humbly. 'I just couldn't, somehow.'

Warren shrugged as though it was water under the bridge. There was a pause, then Warren lifted the conversation. 'Delia's been very good. Visits a lot. Makes me cakes.' He delivered the information laughingly.

'Delia?' checked Jade, in a disbelieving tone.

'She's changed a lot,' agreed Warren. 'Hardly ever goes up to town any more. She an' your Dad are so happy.' He lowered his long lashes as if he suddenly felt he had improper knowledge of Jade's family.

Jade was not put out, only curious. 'What about Mum?' she queried. 'Does she come?'

'Now and then,' nodded Warren. 'She's more . . . distant. She's very wrapped up in her London life. She's having a story published.'

Now Jade *was* bemused. How had she not known? Had Caro even mentioned it? She couldn't remember. There was a poignant irony in Warren's knowing more about her family than she knew herself. How quickly life moves on, she thought. My life. The events of the spring seemed much further than a few months away. She was already another person. Out of touch with the small town, absorbed into global doings.

'I've been busy,' she said by way of excuse, though Warren had

193

not demanded it. He pressed her hands again and said, 'That's good. You're clever. You should work at it.'

How could he be so selfless, wondered Jade, looking at him. For a moment their eyes met and a leap of the old desire flooded into them. They held hands tightly until it had passed, then Warren said, 'I do understand.'

Jade said, 'Perhaps when you get out . . .'

But Warren shook his head. 'It was never right. We're after different things. You don't want to go through that again.'

Jade had to agree that she did not. She nodded and dropped her eyes from his tawny gaze. She felt very much his junior.

A bell rang and people began to shuffle to their feet. Visiting time was over. Jade gathered her jacket and stood up. Warren stood too. He looked down on her with a benevolent smile. 'Well, goodbye then.'

'Goodbye,' she said, extending her hand. He pulled her in and kissed the top of her head. She felt like a dismissed child.

At the doorway she turned for a last look. Warren was staring after her with a look of such sadness that Jade's breath almost stopped. 'Warren,' she wanted to scream, 'I love you!' Instead she turned and fled the room, her throat choked with the tears that would flow as soon as she reached the daylight. She knew it was the last time she'd see him.

46

In the early summer Zo was made executive editor. She rang Caro with the news and to command her to a celebration. 'What about Delia?' said Caro nervously, wondering who else would support Sebastian. She could almost see Zo's shrug.

'Nigel Waddle refuses to be edited by anyone but me. Nothing I can do about it.' It had been the final straw, Zo explained, as Delia's attention had been less and less engaged, her appearances at the office more and more scanty.

Caro could not take the situation so lightly, but she went up to town for the celebration anyway. Zo was at her most cheerful and expansive. She was full of plans for their future life as they ate their way through goat's cheese and rocket at Hugo's, a club favoured by the literary 'in' crowd. Caro felt for the first time uncomfortable in her company. Perhaps it was the place, she thought, looking at the surrounding tables full of chattering young literati. It was right for Zo. Useful. Trendy. Ruthless. She suppressed the thought as disloyal and smiled as Zo refilled her champagne flute. 'Here's to your great success,' she said, lifting it.

'Yours too,' grinned Zo, clinking it. 'First novel on the bestseller list.'

Caro grimaced. 'Hold on. The story's not out yet.'

'Start now,' said Zo. 'As your editor, I'm insisting on it.' A tough note had come into her voice.

Caro thought, 'She'll get what she wants, no matter what.'

It had been accepted that Caro would find a flat reasonably close to Zo's. Zo had even helped her look. The light, bright studio Caro had first seen was still a favourite. Unspoken between them was the knowledge that both needed their freedom. Caro no longer looked for signs of Zo's infidelity. She knew in her blood that there were other women – perhaps some in this restaurant now – and while it would never cease to matter, she had, in a way, come to terms with it.

At first, when she was certain, she had been distraught. She had wept in Ingrid's office about commitment.

'But,' said Ingrid, 'you say she's editing your work. Surely that is committed?'

'I don't mean that,' moaned Caro, 'I mean to the relationship. How can I be if she isn't? I must be committed to something.'

'How about yourself?' suggested Ingrid. 'I think it's time we increased your visits. Shall we say three times weekly?'

After the dinner they had a grand night of passion, high on success and champagne. Zo, ingenious as ever, licked and bit and stroked and sucked. Caro too had come on in technique. The piercing sweetness she still felt as Zo came over her penetrating fingers, drove her now to her own prolonged orgasm. She revelled in sex in a shameless way she had never achieved when younger.

Next morning, aching in every muscle, she looked down at Zo's sleeping face and had to smile. Zo looked so contented. Like a well-fed cat. Or something more exotic, a tiger, always eager for the chase. Yet Zo loved her, she knew. In her care Caro could become the artist she was in her soul. She really couldn't ask for any better.

47

It was true that Delia was worried about money. She had laughed out loud, thrown back her head and shown the deep throat and pointed teeth that gave Sebastian so much pleasure, when she had heard Zo's news. 'I was so relieved. The strain was awful,' she told Caro.

'What did Seb say?' asked Caro, worried for them both.

'That it would give us more time together. I've been thinking,' she went on, 'what if we moved to Four Trees? If I sold my flat and Wendy's house, there'd be enough to pay you your share. You could have your nice studio in London.'

Caro thought for a moment – the garden, Cindy, her past life – then said, 'That's a good idea, that's a very good idea. But how will you manage it?' She was thinking of the cost of heating in winter, even with the faithful Aga.

'Mmm,' said Delia. 'I know.'

In fact, she had a sort of plan. It had come to her the previous week, when Jeremy had come round to discuss with Seb the Warfleet Arts Society's poetry competition. Seb was to be one of the judges. Jeremy had been saying how hard it was for young poets these days. Low book sales, little sponsorship, day jobs with no time to work; something should be done about it.

Delia saw rows and rows of lettuces and leeks laid out in the Four Trees garden. She saw dried flowers in whitewashed rooms, herbs and jars of pickles and jams. She saw herself presiding at a scrubbed table, around which sat grateful artists. A retreat like the one in Ireland! The combined qualifications of herself and Sebastian made them the perfect couple for the job. She had become aware recently that she wanted another child. Harry she thought of as almost her own, but she wanted to feel Seb's seed growing inside her. And what better way to provide for them all? She would apply for a grant immediately.

As had become her habit, she accustomed Sebastian to the idea slowly. He had grown immeasurably in health and strength, but sudden changes in his routine could bring a wild look to his eyes and forewarn of panic.

He and Delia took long clifftop walks together. The wind blew away fears and Sebastian's face would take on a shining look which Delia loved. His hair was long now and streaked with white, it streamed behind him as he strode, leaning occasionally on a favourite thorn, giving him the look of a grizzled troubadour. The Knight of Swords, Toni would have said. Delia, wearing a humdrum collection of country clothes, hopped and skipped beside him. He liked the idea of the retreat, though he said the responsibility scared him. She decided not to tell him of her plan to have a child. Instead she visited a clinic in Stourbridge and secretly had her coil removed.

She encouraged Seb to get more involved in Warfleet affairs. She could tolerate the occasional coffee morning, had made good friends, Toni among them, but found the petty politics of Warfleet beyond her. Seb embraced them with enthusiasm, perhaps as a pale shadow of his life in television. As he took up commitments and causes some of his old fire returned.

Spring shuffled chillily into summer and in May came an unexpected heatwave. Their nights together became trips of sensual wonder. Sometimes in the hours of languorous lovemaking, Delia felt their spirits leave them and merge in air, over and above the coupling of their bodies. There was never any question of the relationship. From the moment he had opened his eyes to her, Seb had adored Delia. She was everything in life to him and he demonstrated it night after night, filling her pale body with his ardour. In June she knew that she was pregnant.

48

Bill Plummer and Jean Peabody were married as soon as her 'quickie' divorce came through. It was a glorious day in late summer and le tout Warfleet assisted at the celebration. Jean Peabody was overcome at the turnout. 'I never knew I 'ad so many well-wishers,' she kept saying, as she plucked convulsively at her hat. Delia, who was giving her a hand, heaved her already considerable tummy to the other side of Jean's hem and resisted saying that it was the same crowd which had been audience to her son's humiliation.

As Jean walked up the aisle of St Peter and Paul there were nods and murmurs of approval. She did look nice, thought Delia, pleased at the powder-blue frock and jacket, the hat with the little spotted veil. She'd persuaded Jean for once to go to Romany's. Sergeant Plummer, in a constricting new collar, turned his head with difficulty to watch his bride. He nearly popped his buttons with admiration. Gone was the fragile mouse he'd encountered so many times at the station. He no longer feared she would break if he touched her. This woman, though slight, seemed solid. Her face beneath the coy veil was blushing and smiling. Jean was, to him, a revelation.

Reverend Pepper sped through the service as though mindful that he had two christenings to go. Besides, people were eager to get to the sherry. At Four Trees, where Delia had offered to hold the reception, the recently mown lawns and full-leafed trees bore heated summer scents over the glittering gathering.

Caro and Zo had come from London. Caro was staying with Zo while the conveyancing of the flat she was buying was completed. They both looked very smart, thought Delia. Caro was wearing fashionable linen, Zo, at her new executive level, had abandoned leathers for silk shirts and designer breeches. Delia's own costume was rather improvised. She had rushed towards pregnancy eating enough for three and examining with delight her daily expansion in the mirror. Though barely four months pregnant, she really must shop for proper maternity wear. The thought of smocks filled her with excitement.

The news of her condition had been broken to Caro some weeks ago by telephone. This was the first time the two women had met since and they looked at each other warily.

'You don't mind?' said Delia, when Zo had dragged Seb off to see her latest toy, a customized Toyota Celica.

Caro shook her head. Actually, she didn't. 'It suits you,' she said, noticing for the first time Delia's tiny freckles. With her clear eyes and lightly flushed cheeks, she was the picture of wellbeing.

'I'm happy,' said Delia, smiling, 'are you?'

Caro thought for a moment then smiled back. 'If I have a good day on the novel,' she said, 'I'm delirious.' The two women laughed, understanding each other perfectly.

Laurel Hopcraft approached and Delia went to see about food. 'So, you're a writer now,' said Laurel with a contemptuous smile. 'How's it going?'

'Very well,' said Caro firmly.

Laurel looked rattled, as though she had prepared herself for a discourse on the pain of conception. 'Lucky you,' she said, somehow managing to imply that nothing worthy was ever achieved without agony. 'I saw that story.' Caro said nothing, wondering if Laurel had recognized herself and was throwing down a gauntlet. But Laurel said only, 'Good observation. Some of the characters were over the top.' Her attention was distracted by a nearby tray of glasses. She had avoided, Caro was well aware, saying that she liked it.

Toni got hold of Caro as the finger food circulated. 'I'm thinking of starting a holistic centre,' she said, 'with Rumer. Shiatsu, counselling, aromatherapy. Rumer will do crystal healing.'

Caro regarded her friend with great affection. Toni's hair had grown into grey feathery tendrils. She looked like an owl, or, when her brows came together, an eagle. 'Great idea,' she said warmly.

'Mmm,' said Toni, 'we can give a hand here when it gets going. Delia's asked me to give yoga sessions.'

Beyond Toni, Caro could see Jeremy and Darryl circling the party. Darryl teetered, as usual very drunk, as he was swept by Marsha Snelgrove, in full medieval costume, into a whirling farandole. Jeremy looked a little strained, Caro thought, though he covered it with his usual bonhomie. She was glad Toni had found something else upon which to focus her energies.

The cutting of the cake was announced and Jean and Bill came forward amid applause. The table was set under the largest of the four trees from which the house took its name. It was an old oak and the sunlight filtered ethereally down through its canopy of whispering green. Jean and Bill Plummer kissed and were caught in a spectacular beam for a moment. The knife plunged into the cake and a cheer arose. Caro looked at Zo and Delia at Sebastian. Though they were in neither case married, the moment was poignant. They were committed, for as long as it lasted, to a binding union.

49

The following May, as predicted by her tutor, Jade received a First. She had kept her head down and worked and worked. Allegra was astonished. She departed with a Third and a husband, as she expected.

Caro invited Jade for a celebratory dinner. It took place in the large light studio which had been her first choice. The balmy summer night entered through the skylight and bathed the candlelit table at which they sat. Zo was elsewhere, so for once Jade had her mother to herself.

Caro was telling Jade about her novel, soon to be published. 'Zo wants to enter it for the Whitbread,' she laughed deprecatingly, '– ever the mad optimist.'

'I don't know,' said Jade, 'your stories were brilliant.'

There was a hint of envy in her tone and Caro said quickly, 'But what about you, darling? Have you decided on anything yet?'

Jade hesitated, as if uncertain how her mother would receive her newly formed Plan for Life. At last she decided on bald presentation and declared, 'Briar's offered me a job. I think I might take it.'

'Briar!' exclaimed Caro, her tone telling Jade everything.

'She's not as bad as you think, Ma. Dad treated her shabbily.'

'She threw her cap at him from the start,' said Caro huffily.

'In that case,' said Jade, 'she got her comeuppance. Dad only shacked up with her to stop her taking his job. He was on the skids already.'

Caro fell silent; what Jade said could be true. It would be entirely in keeping with Sebastian's former tactics. 'What exactly has she offered you?' she said, after a pause to recover ground.

202

'Researcher.'

Caro had to laugh. How the wheel had come full circle.

'Good salary. Prospects for promotion.' Jade built on her advantage.

Not while Briar's in the job, thought Caro, but Jade was tough. 'Well,' she said, 'it's your life. But I think you should talk to Daddy about it.'

Jade had every intention of interrogating Seb and she went down to Warfleet at the weekend. The day was warm and she decided to walk from the station, savouring the changes in the little town a year had brought. The Delphinium Tearooms was shuttered up, she noticed, and Jeremy and Darryl's Euroantiques now bore the name Pulman Photography. A different young man slouched in the window. In the High Street, Jim and Peggy's emporium had expanded to a Shoe Supermarket. She was amused to see, prominently displayed, a pair of boots buckled and zipped like those Zo had worn first in Warfleet.

She still got a shock when Delia, not Caro, opened the door of Four Trees. Delia, grown plumper since the birth of Alex that January. Jade was glad he was a boy. She didn't have to feel jealous. Delia agreed with her. She didn't want the competition of another woman in Sebastian's life.

Part of the attraction of Four Trees to Jade was the mystery of whom one might meet there. The retreat was funded by various Euro schemes and artists came from all over. Homer Gilliray had recently made an application.

This weekend some American students were running a workshop. Delia steered Jade past the former sitting room, from which came barks and squeals, through to the kitchen, now two rooms knocked into one but still cosily centred on the Aga. Alex was cooing in his crib, kicking his legs in the air and catching his toes in chubby fingers. Harry was in the garden on his tricycle.

'Sit, sit,' said Delia. 'I've made tea.' She plonked down a tray with cheese scones and ginger cake just taken from the oven. Jade, whose current diet consisted of yoghurt and tofu, crumbled a morsel of cake and hid it beneath her teacup. In her opinion Delia had let herself go. Her hair was no longer a shining cap but an undyed shock in need of ruling. Combs stuck in at eccentric angles did nothing for the image, nor did the Laura Ashley frock which disguised a full-breasted, wide-hipped body. She might be a cornucopia to Sebastian, as he displayed in his habit of laying hands on her whenever she came within reach, but to Jade she seemed closely related to a bag lady. She compared her with Caro, as she had recently seen her. Bobbed hair. Svelte shape clothed in leather slacks and Nicole Farhi sweater. It was almost as though they'd changed places.

Delia was gossiping on about life in Warfleet. 'Jeremy and Darryl moved to Stourbridge . . . closer to Guy for nursing . . . Connor . . . married Genevieve Dudicort-Roussel . . . everyone astonished . . . Rumer and Toni . . . Natural Healing Centre . . . Old Mill on the river, Delphinium closed . . . May not well . . .' etc, etc. From the general she moved seamlessly to the particular and her obsessions at Four Trees. '. . . Yoga swami . . . terrible row . . . Celia Troubridge . . . one of the cats . . . Irish poet . . . absolute disgrace . . . made a pass at Jean Peabody . . .'

'What?' interrupted Jade. 'Jean Peabody?'

'Umhumm,' confirmed Delia. 'You know she comes in to clean and shop.'

'I thought she got married?' said Jade with careful vagueness.

'Oh yes, last summer, to Sergeant Plummer. Jean's changed a lot. They're very happy. Warren's out, you know.' Jade put her cup down rather heavily. Delia chose not to notice and went on, 'Yes. He's fine. Got a job at that safari park over at Tolleymarsh's.'

Jade stared at Harry circling a patch of lawn with determination. She had seen pictures of the Tolleymarsh estate. The marquis had opened it to the public to help pay off death duties. That would be good for Warren, she thought, dealing with young animals. Tending them. Watching them grow.

Delia dropped a hand lightly on her head. 'You'll stay to dinner? Seb'll be back soon, he's at a Medieval Society meeting.'

* * *

Dinner took place at the long stripped pine refectory table provided by Jeremy and Darryl. Seb sat in the carver and Delia in the basket chair at the foot, with the Americans scattered in between. Jade sat at the carver end so that she could talk to her father.

Seb's eyes became rather vacant at the mention of Briar. He had, Jade decided, blanked out a lot of his former life. He thought the job was a good idea, though. Questioned her about pay, insisted that she see his lawyer about a contract. 'Television's a vicious world,' he said. 'Get what you want in writing.'

Several of the young Americans paid attention to Jade. She was, as she knew, very beautiful. She looked at them through slitted eyes, wondering if there was one she would sleep with. She decided not. Her life had been without sexual complication for some time and on balance she preferred it that way. It disturbed her to see Delia and Seb so wound about each other. Seb's eyes followed Delia wherever she moved. She lost no opportunity to graze him as she passed. It was as if they were in a voluptuous conspiracy, could hardly wait until the meal was done and they could shut the door of their darkened room and strip each other's clothes off.

Jade went to bed alone. A tiny room in the attic. She lay awake thinking of Warren. A few miles down the road, yet far, far away in reality.

50

"Ere, Jean,' said Sergeant Plummer to his wife. 'Remember that body?'

'Body, Bill?' said Jean with concern; she didn't approve of his bringing his work home. 'What body?'

'Must've been eighteen months ago. Fished it out of the river.'

'Oh yes,' said Jean, 'I do recall. It was when you first come round.' They smiled at each other shyly, both turning a little pink. Neither could have imagined how much more pleasant that event was going to make their lives. It crossed Jean's mind that whoever he was, he didn't die for nothing.

'What about it?' she said, coming across to the armchair where Bill sat reading the *Warfleet Chronicle*.

'Look at this,' he said. He pointed to the personal column in the classifieds.

> Recently returned from Canada and seeking
> information about the whereabouts of my
> brother, Len Butcher, last seen in Warfleet
> the Christmas before last.

'Ooh er,' said Jean, impressed, 'what makes you think it's him?'

'Just a hunch,' said the sergeant modestly.

At the station next day he telephoned the number given in the advert and spoke to Marjory Alsopp née Butcher. She confirmed that Len was her brother, but that they'd been out of touch for two years. The last time they'd communicated was when she sent him some thermal underwear for Christmas.

Well he wasn't found in that, thought the sergeant grimly.

'It was strange he never phoned Christmas,' went on Marjory in a hybrid accent combining Warfleet with the Rockies. 'It was the one time we always spoke. Then no answer to letters. But we couldn't make the trip till now. My husband's business commitments.'

'When did you last see Len?' asked the sergeant, sticking to the formalities, though more and more convinced.

'Oh, years ago. We left for Banff in 'seventy-two. He was going to come over, but he could never afford it. He's lived in Warfleet all his life, you'd think somebody would notice.'

The sergeant sighed. It was his experience that people noticed very little. He made an appointment to visit Marjory Alsopp and took some photos from a file. The body they had buried.

Marjory and Bob Alsopp were staying at the Holiday Inn in Stourbridge. They were in a patterned room which clashed noisily with the vibrant checks they were wearing. Marjory identified the photos. She began a tearful whine and Bob patted her padded shoulder. 'He was always a loner,' he said gruffly to the sergeant. 'Never married, y'know?'

'He had friends,' asserted Marjory as if in her brother's defence. 'He was always mentioning Mr and Mrs Radcliffe.'

Sergeant Plummer's eyebrows shot up. Not another intrigue involving them, surely. 'In what capacity?' he asked, poising his ballpoint.

Marjory thought through her sniffles. ''E worked with them. In London. 'E often went up to town with Mr Radcliffe.'

Sergeant Plummer pursed his lips. That might make a friend in Canada, where he'd heard there were no class distinctions. 'I'll look into it,' he said. 'I'm sorry t' bring you bad news.'

'But why?' broke out Marjory. 'Why did he do it?'

The sergeant left her to the consoling checked arms of her husband and got off back to Warfleet.

He drew into the drive at Four Trees as Delia was hostessing a picnic. She waved french bread and beckoned him over. Several young people were doing exercises on the lawn. One was standing on his head. The sergeant hoped he hadn't eaten.

Four Trees was a source of gossip and rumour in the town, but so far he'd had no trouble. As he sat uncomfortably cross-legged on the grass, he was charged at by Harry who clambered on to his lap. These days Sergeant Plummer was rather good with children.

When he could get Delia's attention, he said, 'Is Mr Radcliffe about? I need to check something with him.'

'He's in town,' said Delia, 'talking to a man about planting fruit trees.' She waved an arm at a tangle of bushes at the bottom of the garden. 'We're going to clear that patch.'

Sergeant Plummer looked hard at the greenery as she hoisted Alex into her arms and took a breast out of her bodice.

Seb came up the drive on an ancient bicycle. He dismounted and came over with punnets of strawberries. The assembly fell upon them making appreciative noises in a variety of languages.

Sergeant Plummer rose, gently dislodging Harry who was chewing his buttons, and drew Seb aside. 'Have you any recollection of this man, sir?' he said, showing Sebastian a photo he had been given by Marjory. The man in it was in his fifties, he had a plain face with a pleasant smile and his hair had been neatly brushed for the picture.

Seb frowned at the face for a moment and then shook his head. 'He does look a little familiar,' he said, 'but I couldn't put a name to him . . . Darling . . . ?' As ever when in doubt, Seb called upon Delia.

She came over with the placid Alex tucked beneath her arm. She shrugged at the photo and asked who it was. The sergeant, in a suitably low voice, told them. Delia took hold of the photo, showing more interest now. There was a curious expression on her face as she said, 'Poor man. He brought us together in a way. And we don't even know him.' She seemed moved as she gave the picture back and looked at Sebastian. The sergeant felt he was intruding on a private moment, and pocketing the photo he walked back to his car. It didn't matter, anyway. It was only for his own peace of mind. He hated loose ends dangling.

*　　*　　*

208

When Caro came down for her next weekend retreat – she was proofreading her novel – Delia told her the story. 'Len Butcher,' puzzled Caro, 'I know that name.'

Delia got out the copy of the *Warfleet Chronicle* which carried Len's picture and an obituary, 'Gone but not forgotten', from the Alsopps.

'That's Len the liftman,' said Caro immediately. 'Don't you remember, Seb? He travelled on the train with you. When you got out at the station he always said, "Welcome to sunny Warfleet."'

'Len,' said Seb, 'that's right! Cheerful little chap. The bastard company sacked him.'

Caro sat at the big table for some time after everyone else had gone to bed. She read the *Warfleet Chronicle* as she used to do, viewing it now as a distant and exotic manual. Even Charlie Barrett's ridiculous prose only provoked a giggle. At last she turned again to Len's picture. 'Gone but not forgotten'. How untrue, she thought, he'd been forgotten by everybody. His callous employers, his family, even the people who'd seen him every day, to whom he'd given a cheery farewell, 'Welcome to sunny Warfleet.' She went to the drawer where the kitchen scissors used to be kept and found to her pleasure that they were still there. Carefully she cut round the picture and its caption. She, at least, would not forget the man who had changed her life completely.

51

The dentist's instruments had held Sidney in a horrid thrall that morning. He wondered if he could get hold of some. He'd like to do unpleasant things to the dentist.

The faithful Dave was waiting at the corner. They set off to their meeting. The gang had taken over a disused shed at the end of what used to be allotments. The council had recently sold off the land to a property company and it waited forlornly for 'development'. The shed was hot in summer and cold in winter. The boys had assembled various things useful for their rituals. There were poster paints stolen from school, dead birds, barbecue bricks, garden shears, a Swiss army knife, a spade and a shovel. The usefulness of these objects was defined on an ad hoc basis by Sidney. 'That'll be good for tying things down,' he would say, eyeing a ball of binder twine and the tribe would nod obediently. One talisman might be singled out for particular praise and the finder would bask in it gratefully. The gang also had various trophies pinned to the wall, mostly the skins of small animals. There was a drawing of an Indian in full warpaint. It was pierced with several arrows.

'Now,' said Sidney, pinning his shivering troops, 'we've got to make a plan.' The gang looked at their leader, eyes rounded in anticipation. 'Iss nearly Halloween,' pronounced Sidney in apocalyptic tones. 'We've gotta make a sacrifice.' The boys looked at each other uneasily. Did he mean one of them? And what sort of sacrifice? 'It has to be blood,' said Sidney, causing a further frisson of alarm in his company. 'The blood of an innocent.' The boys breathed again in relief. None of them could be called innocent.

'Wha' about that old tramp?' said Dave. ''E should be glad to be out of his misery.'

'Yeah,' chorused the gang, 'no one'd miss 'im.'

Sidney shook his head. 'I said innocent,' he stressed, 'a human bein' without sin. Iss gotta be a baby.' The gang saw his logic. It was undeniable. They looked at each other, looks slippery with inadmissible excitement. 'So,' said Sidney, as if the decision was final, 'where can we get a baby?'

52

Rationalizing her in tray, preparatory to the Christmas break, Jade came across a letter from a literary agent, written on behalf of his client Sean McCaffety. '. . . Young Irish writer . . .', she read, 'recently published to success in America . . .' '. . . Your father was very interested . . .' She threw the letter down at this point with a discontented smirk. She received one of these on average once a fortnight. It was deeply undermining. Was she no one in her own right? With the letter had come a manuscript, a film by the look of it. She shovelled it into her Gucci handsack for glancing at later, the letter she tossed on to the 'answerable' pile, intending to write a polite but firm refusal.

Jade's rise in the company had been meteoric. In the eighteen months she had worked there she had become assistant producer on the show. Her success had not been without its sacrifices. A private life was one, as Briar would call at any hour of the night or day and seemed to regard Jade as everything from confidante to chiropodist. Soulmate was too sensitive a description. It was almost as though Jade were a hook for her to hang on. Nor could Jade count her brief sexual liaisons as relationships. They were more like attacks. Sudden frenzied couplings in corridors. Once the MD had grabbed her lapels and invited her to 'fuck like a rabbit'.

In a period laughingly known as her lunch hour, Jade drank black coffee and leafed through the pages of *Hello!* magazine. She stopped mid-breath, stunned by a picture of Warren. He looked wonderfully handsome. His hollow face had filled out, his lion's eyes twinkled, his hair was blonder and shiny. It was a while before Jade noticed there was a young woman on his arm. She too had a halo of wholesomeness. It was her birthright, as she was the daughter of the Marquis of Tolleymarsh. Apparently they were to be married. Jade took several deep breaths. She could see, stretching ahead, years of turning magazine pages and seeing pictures of the Peabodys – or would it be the Tolleymarshes – with their equally handsome, healthy, hazel-eyed children. An acute pain dug beneath her ribs, reminding her that she hadn't had her prescribed milk and biscuits. Bloody ulcer.

The buzzer on her desk rang and Briar's voice, slightly slurred as it was after lunch, demanded her attention. 'Get your ass in here, sweetheart. The MD wants this effing break-down *today*, not a week on Tuesday.'

On her waterbed that night after conferences, meetings, phone calls, faxes, the opera and two Christmas parties, Jade laid aside Sean's manuscript . . . not bad after all, perhaps it had possibilities . . . and composed herself for sleep. It was a long time coming as a review of her life took place beneath her eyelids. Fragmented scenes of triumph and social success, awards, riches, designer clothes, travelling. The pieces jumbled together and refused to be controlled, she wondered if this were like drowning. At last she fell into a twitchy slumber and dreamed busy dreams. She was in a house with many rooms and many, many people. She wandered among them constantly searching, but the faces were strange to her, not one of them recognizable. She woke with a terrible sense of loss. For what . . . ? What . . . ? She didn't know. She just knew something was missing.

Also available in Vista paperback

True to Form

YVONNE ANTROBUS

'I am only a spectator. It has always been my role just to stay watching while others take the risks.'

Sukie Buckley's now-deceased husband, Peter, taught her to love horses, and racing, yet left Sukie virtually penniless among friends who would never be seen dead in last year's fashions. But when she finds the body of one of the racing fraternity in compromising circumstances, she is forced to become a participant in the race to find a killer.

From the Newmarket gallops to Atalanta's Health Club: from Royal Ascot to the White Tie Escort Agency, the lives of those linked by a valuable horse, Triumvirate, come under Sukie's scrutiny. And as she investigates their preferences, social, financial and sexual, she uncovers disturbing truths about herself.

As the killer draws nearer to her, Sukie knows she has gambled with something more precious than money. But has she won – or has she lost?

ISBN 0 575 60369 0

VISTA

Land of My Dreams

KATE NORTH

Maisie should, by rights, be getting ready to die –
only she's just getting ready to live. After years
spent in the shadow of her domineering and
reclusive mother – now that her mother is dead –
Maisie finally has a chance at life.

The recently bereaved Clare and her teenage
son Gwyn – who will only answer to the name Joe
– don't know what to make of the shy old lady
next door. It is Joe who breaks down the barriers
around Maisie, and the unlikeliest of friendships
begins. At a time when he can't live easily with
his mother – or worse, her married lover Theo –
Maisie gives him the confidence and independence he needs to grow up.

Gradually the secret that kept Maisie and her
mother on the move and away from society is
revealed. Her extraordinary history, the life she
found for herself, and the friends she made,
despite her mother's hostility, give Maisie the
strength to make one last bid for happiness.

ISBN 0 575 60385 2

VISTA

A Kept Woman

FRANKIE McGOWAN

Serena Carmichael had knowledge. Knowledge of herself – who she was, what she had, where she was going. Her most precious possession was her family – Louise, Harry and Stephen, her husband.

The police thought she knew everything – a woman in so much control of her life must know her husband's whereabouts.

Her friends can't believe she didn't know. Which makes her a dangerous person to have around.

Her daughter only knows Serena doesn't understand her; her son isn't old enough to know much of anything yet.

Which leaves Serena very much alone. The only thing she knows for certain – can hold on to – is that Stephen loves her.

Doesn't he?

ISBN 0 575 60242 2

VISTA

Other Vista women's titles include

The Secret   Cynthia Victor   0 575 60391 7

What Matters Most   Cynthia Victor   0 575 60129 9

Land of My Dreams   Kate North   0 575 60385 2

A Kept Woman   Frankie McGowan   0 575 60242 2

True to Form   Yvonne Antrobus   0 575 60369 0

Dancing at the Harvest Moon   K. C. McKinnon
0 575 60390 9

Portraits in an Album   Jenny Glanfield   0 575 60225 2

The Shadowy Horses   Susanna Kearsley   0 575 60217 1

VISTA books are available from all good bookshops or from:
Cassell C.S.
Book Service By Post
PO Box 29, Douglas I-O-M
IM99 1BQ
telephone: 01624 675137, fax: 01624 670923